SO-FMH-452

The Sub
The Sub copied the latest in American submarine technology. Captain Chu wasn't certain how, exactly, it had been obtained, but the result was a boat beyond anything he had ever thought to command. He intended to use every scrap of her capabilities. And he would need to, once the Day of Fate was at hand. . . .

The Doctor
D.L. Childe had buried the memories of his Victoria Cross long ago. Memories of his skill as a killer, and memories of his capacity for love. Both would erupt as he drew near the Day of Fate. . . .

The Russian
Sholopov waited for the report. He was sure the missiles were there; he was sure he knew who had placed them. But no one would believe him. It would be too late soon. Very soon. On the Day of Fate. . . .

DAY OF FATE

THEODORE A. REES CHENEY

CP

POPHAM PRESS
An Imprint of Ace Books
A Division of Charter Communications Inc.
A GROSSET & DUNLAP COMPANY
51 Madison Avenue
New York, New York 10010

DAY OF FATE
Copyright © 1981 by Theodore A. Rees Cheney
All rights reserved. No part of this book may be reproduced in any form or by any means, except for the inclusion of brief quotations in a review, without permission in writing from the publisher.

All characters in this book are fictitious. Any resemblance to actual persons, living or dead, is purely coincidental.

A Popham Press Original.

First Charter Printing March 1981
Published simultaneously in Canada
Manufactured in the United States of America

2 4 6 8 0 9 7 5 3 1

With special thanks to John Cook

I

September 8
2155 hours

The two submarines floated like sharks on the surface of the night waters. The base at Luta was dark, patrolled by more than the usual number of taciturn soldiers in quilted coats. Occasionally, a flight of jets rumbled overhead, fighters from the Chou-Shui-Tzu Air Force Base under orders to report anything that moved from the Gulf of Liaotung to the southern tip of Korea.

Commander Chu Fa-tzu, captain of the submarine *Cheng Fu-Conquest* - was tense. *Cheng Fu* and *Sheng Li - Victory* - would be underway soon. It would be good to get to sea. It was almost impossible to keep a submarine secret in port.

Ta Liang, the executive officer, cleared his throat meaningfully. Chu wiped expression from his face before turning. It was not well to show emotion to the crew.

"Yes, Liang, I know. It is time. Stand by to answer maneuvering orders."

Liang keyed his headset. "Reactor and control rooms, stand by for maneuvering orders."

"Make rpm's for five knots." Chu didn't have to hear Liang relay the order. The submarine slid forward, the water rolling up to cover her rounded bow. Behind, the *Sheng Li* followed.

Radar and inertial navigation systems guided the two submarines down the unmarked channel out of the harbor. Sampans, night fishing with lanterns to attract the catch, were spread out beyond the harbor. Their absence would only have attracted attention, but none were allowed close enough to the channel to see what vessels had sailed.

In open water, Chu increased speed to twenty-six knots, the maximum on the surface. The bow wave covered the hull as far back as the sail in a mounded sheet of water. The vessels copied the latest in American submarine technology, the *Los Angeles*-class fast attack boats. Chu wasn't certain how, exactly, it had been obtained, but the result was a boat beyond anything he had ever thought to command. He intended to use every scrap of her capabilities.

He noticed Liang watching the sky, though what he thought to see in the blackness above the revolving radar was not clear. "Nervous, Liang?"

Liang's eyes jerked back forward. "No, sir. Of course not."

Chu sighed. "This is not a Party indoctrination, Liang. A submarine's officers must think, not simply obey. If you have doubts, let me know about them."

"Sir, my worry is—Well, sir, we will be well within the search radius of anti-submarine aircraft out of Korea before there is more than shallow diving depth beneath us." His voice stiffened, and he stared straight ahead. "I am sorry, sir. It is not my place to question a plan of the Naval Staff."

Liang would never make command, Chu thought, even though he was the best executive officer in the submarine service. He was a born second-in-command, politically qualified, well trained, but too inflexible.

"Yours is a proper tactical concern, Liang. Twelve

hours ago, and again eleven hours ago, torpedoes were fired at South Korean patrol vessels north of the Korean peninsula. All Korean and American anti-submarine patrols are now directed northward. And to the south—" He permitted a rare smile in spite of his dictum. "Our government has requested humanitarian aid in searching for an airliner which has supposedly gone down off the southern coast. The Americans' Seventh Fleet has concentrated its air-search capability in the southern Formosa Strait. We have practically a clear corridor to the Pacific."

The executive officer remained rigid. "I apologize, sir. I should have know better—" Suddenly he pressed the headset tighter to his ear. "Sir, control room reports one hundred thirty feet."

"Very good, Liang. Take us down to one hundred feet."

Chu slid down the ladder with his feet on the outside edges, a habit he had acquired in days of more open tension.

Liang climbed down more slowly.

In the control room everyone moved quickly and efficiently. Ta, the diving officer, watched the flooding of the tanks. The sonar and radar watches bent intently over their panels. The helmsmen, at their airplane-type wheels, guided the boat down.

"Make maximum rpm's, Liang," Chu said. "I'll be in my cabin."

The captain's cabin, directly behind the control room, would have seemed a box to anyone not of the submarine service. To Chu, after the small, coastal submarines, it was luxurious. It was as well he thought so, for he spent the next thirty-two hours, unsleeping, there or in the control room.

The weight of the mission bore on him heavily. He had followed the same route two years before in practice, and again last year in the first phase, but that would mean nothing should a misstep occur now. If there should be an equipment malfunction, or if an American anti-submarine craft—

"Sir," the sonarman announced, "I have a contact. High speed screws. Bearing two six five. Range twelve thousand yards."

"Sound signature comparison," Chu ordered.

Everyone tried to watch the young sonarman without seeming to as he recorded the prop noises and fed them into a computer with the IBM nameplate still on the front. Everyone except Chu.

He studied the chart, an imperturbable exterior covering the turmoil within. The day of fate was too close to be ruined now.

They were through the shallow waters north of Okinawa, out over the Ryuku Trench. He tapped the chart thoughtfully. A permanent thermal gradient, a layer of abrupt temperature change in the water that would reflect sonar transmissions, existed below them. Its depth varied from a safe one thousand feet to a five thousand feet they could not attain alive.

The computer printer chattered, the sonarman reading off the paper as it rolled out. "Sound signature comparison, sir. American *Spruance*-class anti-submarine warfare destroyer. Ninety-six percent probability vessel is the USS *Paul F. Foster*. Weapons capability readout—"

Chu silenced him with a gesture. "Take up deeper, Liang." He could only hope the captain of the *Sheng Li* would realize what he was doing, and follow. Liang turned from giving the orders. "Depth, sir?"

"Until we are below the thermal gradient." He ignored Liang's start. He had to consider reducing speed. Maximum rpm's also produced maximum noise. Reducing speed would reduce the noise that could attract the destroyer's attention, but it would also leave them exposed for a longer tme. Compounding the problem was the fact that *Spruance*-class vessels carried variable-depth sonar that could be streamed at a pre-set depth. Even below a thermal gradient. If the destroyer became aware of them before they reached the gradient's shelter—

"Sir," the sonarman said, "the Americans have begun long-pulse search sweeps." His voice was calm, but sweat ran down his face.

Chu merely nodded. Long-pulse sweeps meant random probes. The Americans might be suspicious, or they might be sweeping for any one of a hundred reasons that had nothing to do with the *Cheng Fu*. In any case, he could no longer consider slowing. They had to reach safety quickly.

"We are passing two thousand feet, sir," Liang announced.

Someone gasped, and Lieutenant Ta dropped his clipboard. Every eye watched as he picked it up, smiling nervously. Then they shifted to the depth gauge.

"Lieutenant Min," Chu said, "I want to know the instant water temperature shows we have passed the gradient."

The slender oceanographer merely nodded without looking up from his instruments. He was a scientist who had been commissioned because his expertise was needed, not a regular Naval officer.

As the submarine sank deeper, Chu began to find it difficult to keep his own eyes from the gauge. He had only been this deep once before himself, on the pressure tests. Twenty-two hundred feet. Twenty-three hundred. Twenty-four hundred.

They had just passed crush depth. The pressure of the water outside, the weight of it above, should be twisting the hull, tearing it open, forcing hammering jets of water through the smallest crack before ripping it wide. They should be plunging into the abyssal reaches of the Ryuku Trench in a ruin of crushed metal. Twenty-five hundred. Twenty-six hundred.

"Sir!" The sonarman's voice shook, and he had to begin again. "Sir, the pulses have cut off."

"A significant temperature change," Lieutenant Min said thoughtfully. "We must be below the temperature gradient." He stared around in surprise as a concerted sigh went up.

"The *Sheng Li?*" Chu asked.

"Her screw has just become audible, sir. She is through the gradient." Chu smiled openly.

The two submarines bored northward at thirty-eight knots toward *jih chien te t'ien ming.* The day of fate.

September 10
1140 hours

The green water in the last of the Panama Canal's Gatun Locks dropped slowly, lowering the grain ship *Pai Te Yün* to the Caribbean level. Hawsers bound the ship to electric locomotives on the banks, the motive force that had pulled it from lock to lock. A fetid smell drifted down from the slums outside Colón, and the air was heavy.

Captain Lo's broad face ran with sweat that had nothing to do with the heat. He simply wished that, like the *Hsin Te Yüeh,* ostensibly bound for the Norwegian island of Spitsbergen for a cargo of iron ore, he was out of the canal, with the accursed foreigners off his ship.

Two years before, during the practice run, and even last year, it had not been so bad. Now, with the American imperialists returning the canal to the Panamanians, parties from both governments were on board. And despite their protestations of solidarity with the Chinese people, the Panamanian Customs men seemed eager to find something amiss, anything, to show up the Americans. And this was no practice run.

His face creased in a worried frown, he walked out on the wing bridge and looked aft. Even knowing where they were, he could not see where the cuts had been made, the hatches and ramps and power lifts installed between the giant grain bins. But the men on deck were closer.

"We're almost finished, captain."

Lo whirled. For a moment he could only stare at the lanky American canal pilot who had conned his ship on its twelve-hour journey from the Pacific. "That is good, Mr. Andrews," he said at last. "I must maintain my schedule."

Andrews, keeping an eye on the lock operation, suddenly raised his walkie-talkie. "Team four! Adjust that line slack, please. Sorry, captain. You have a tight schedule? On your way to Canada, aren't you?"

Lo hesitated. But that much was open knowledge, and the man was obviously just making conversation. "Yes, Mr. Andrews. To the port of Churchill, on Hudson Bay. It is a major center for grain shipments. My country buys a great deal of grain from Canada."

"Maybe it won't be long before you're buying a lot from us as well. What with the improved relations, I mean."

"Of a certainty," Lo said blandly. With a sudden metallic groan, the massive, rust-covered lock gates began to swing open. "And now, Mr. Andrews, if you please. My schedule."

In moments the hawsers were cast loose, and the pilot and the rest of the foreigners were escorted over the side. As the grainer steamed toward the open sea, Lo breathed freely for the first time since entering the canal. The last real danger of discovery was past. Soon would come the day of fate.

September 11
0940 hours

In a conference room twenty-three miles west of Peking and one half mile below the surface, Admiral Yü

Chui Ta studied the polar projection map of the northern hemisphere that covered one wall. He knew every inch of the map by heart, but he studied it for the effect it caused, as he did many things. It was for effect that he shaved his head; the British Ambassador had once told him he resembled Genghis Khan. He looked very much like Genghis Khan at that moment.

He turned to face the other four members of Implementation Group One, seated at the long table that was the only significant furnishing in the room. There were, as always, no aides or staff present.

"It is begun," he said. "After the seventeenth day of October, the day of fate, China will stand astride the world."

II

D. L. Childe ignored the Manitoba muskeg slipping past outside the train at a bare thirty-five miles an hour. He'd seen the bogs and swamps a thousand times traveling to and from Churchill, and there was never anything new in the chill, green scrub.

His face was weathered, and the black at his temples was touched with gray. Exactly six feet tall, and well muscled, he moved like an outdoorsman. A nose that had once been broken heightened the image. A caribou hide parka and gray eyes with the look of open spaces made most of the people he passed in the swaying corridor take him for a northcountry guide. More than one woman gave him a second, interested, glance.

He braced against the lurching and crossed to the Newsy car. A long counter down one side of the car was covered with large glass jars of doughnuts and crackers. Coffee and tea urns stood at the far end, and the wall behind displayed cigars, cigarettes and tobacco. Three Indians slept huddled together on the bench running the other side of the car.

The runty little man behind the counter looked up from setting out the newspapers, and a smile made more

9

creases in his face. "Hi, Dr. Childe. Coming back late this year, ain't you? Want a cup of tea? Or coffee?"

D.L. wanted a table in the dining car and a steak, but he recognized the ceremonial nature of the offer. "Coffee, Billy. I took my vacation late this year, to avoid the fly season."

"That was smart." The Newsy set a thick, china mug of coffee in front of D.L. "Sometimes I figure they can bite right through a parka."

"Almost. How's Martha, Billy?"

"Oh, the wife's doing great, Doc. Good thing for us you was there. Who'd of thought of appendicitis coming on like that? I mean, she never complained about pain or nothing till she keeled over."

"It can happen fast. The important thing is, she's all right now."

"Yes, I guess so." The Indians were now awake and talking softly among themselves. Billy shook his head. "Poor buggers. They're heading up to look for work at the grain elevators in Churchill. Couldn't pay nothing, but I let them ride in here." His face twisted anxiously. "Doc, I know free rides are against regulations, but hell, they're just trying to get along like everybody else. And they ain't got much."

"Since when have I been a stickler for rules, Billy?"

"I guess I should've known better," the Newsy laughed. "Anyway, maybe they won't have to cadge rides much longer. I hear some Cree, or Eskimos, maybe, struck gold up on the Bay."

D.L. shot an amused glance at him. "Billy, I've heard ten thousand tales of gold strikes on the Bay, and they were all born in the bottom of a whiskey bottle."

"I don't know, Doc. Back down the line at Waboden, I heard two trappers, just down from the Bay, talking. They said some fellow, Eskimo or Indian, like I said, tried to charter a flight to Montreal with a bag of nuggets. Didn't sound like no whiskey tale to me."

D.L. frowned into his mug. Perhaps he'd better check it on his circuit around Hudson Bay.

He was about to ask questions about exactly what Billy had heard when the door from the front of the train opened and a Canadian Army captain came in. His parachute badge and regimental flashes held D.L.'s eyes against his will. The 21st Regiment. Princess Patricia's Light Infantry. Unwanted memories washed over him. The rush of air as he fell toward the ground a thousand feet below. The jerk of the harness at shoulders and crotch as the canopy opened overhead. Korea. Helen. He realized the captain was returning his gaze curiously.

"Fine outfit, Captain," he said at last.

"Thanks. You know the Princess Pat's?"

"A long time ago." Desperately he cast around for a path away from how he knew them. The feel of the parachute harness was still strong in his mind. "You enjoy jumping, captain?"

The captain shook his head ruefully. "When I can, but my current assignment doesn't allow much time for it. A desk at the Ministry of Defence in Ottawa. I'm up here on leave." He stuck out a hand. "Name's Donald Beauprie."

D.L. kept his face blank. He set down his mug and shook hands perfunctorily. "Nice to have met you," he said distantly. "Thanks for the coffee, Billy," Before they could speak, he hurried out toward the dining car.

Beauprie watched in surprise, his smile frozen on his face. Finally, he said, "Who is he, anyway?"

"Doctor Childe works for the government, flying around the Bay to the Indian and Eskimo villages." Billy paused, seeming to feel a need to explain D.L.'s abruptness. "He acts kind of strange, sometimes. Comes from too much time above the tree line. Why, I hear they want to promote him to a cushy desk job in Ottawa, but he won't leave the Bay."

"Childe," Beauprie said thoughtfully. "You wouldn't

know his full name, would you?"

"All I ever heard him use is D.L.— No, wait. I did see it wrote out, once. Daniel LeTellier Childe. That's it. Hey, what's the matter?"

The effect of the name on Beauprie was galvanic. He whirled to face the door as if he expected to see through it to D.L. "It was him," he muttered. "So he became a doctor."

"You know Dr. Childe?"

Beauprie shook his head slowly. "I never met him before." He saw the curiosity building in Billy's face, and tossed some coins on the counter. "A pack of Senior Service," he said in a tone that cut off all thought of conversation.

D.L. pressed the heels of his hands tighter against his eyelids, trying to press away the images. Especially Helen's. Doe-eyed Helen, the beautiful Korean girl who had married him when they were both only seventeen. And died because of him.

"Dr. Childe, are you all right? Can I get you something?"

With a start D.L. realized he was in the dining car, with Bristol, the white-haired maitre d', watching him worriedly.

"No. No, I'm all right, Bristol. I'd like a table," he added to forestall more questions.

He fellowed Bristol to a table halfway down the car, and ordered coffee, but after it came he let it grow cold.

It had been a shock after so long. He'd almost forgotten there was anyone who could connect D.L. Childe with Daniel LeTellier Childe. But if anyone could, it would be an officer of the Princess Pat's. He'd first gone to Hudson Bay because there were few people, and fewer soldiers, God, he couldn't wait to get back. Hard work would drive the memories away, and keep the dreams at bay.

* * *

Dogs barked endlessly outside the ramshackle trapper's cabins south of Churchill as the train pulled toward the station. Five miles up the track the giant grain elevators loomed, dwarfing the two-story whaling factory on the bank of the Churchill River. Three freight canoes, outboard motors hanging off the sterns, were tied to the factory, their Inuit owners seeing to the hauling of fifteen-foot Beluga whales up the chute.

As soon as the train slowed D.L. shouldered his duffle bag and jumped to the station platform. The mud-splattered Jeep that Jack Snyder had left for him was nosed into the platform. He tossed his duffle in the back and rummaged under the seat for the key. Suddenly he realized how foolish it was to hurry that way to avoid Beauprie. There were only two thousand people in Churchill, and fifty places they could run into each other. All he could do was fly out first thing in the morning.

The air already had a nip to it as he drove into town, though the first snows weren't due for more than a month. July and August were the warmest months in Churchill, and even they were more like early spring in lower Canada.

As he passed the outskirts of town, Jack Snyder, tall and balding, ran out of his warehouse, waving his arms. "It's come, Dr. Childe! That carving's here!"

D.L. made a sharp U-turn and swung in to the curb. He hadn't expected the gallery to make shipment so soon. "Is it all right, Jack? It didn't get damaged?"

"Not that I could tell, but see for yourself." Snyder led the way inside. "It just came this morning. I was going to send a boy down to leave a note on the Jeep when I saw you going by."

A wooden crate sat on Snyder's desk behind the counter, a crowbar beside it. D.L. quickly pried off the top and burrowed through the excelsior to lift out a crush-proof shipping container. In that, nestled in straw, was the buffalo. He set it on the desk. Finely detailed, feet braced, the head bearing the great horns lowered warily, it seemed softened by the light, and almost alive.

"Damn," Snyder breathed. "Doc, that's something else. Jade, isn't it?"

He nodded. "Ming dynasty. About five hundred years old."

"Must be worth a lot."

"More than I could afford on what I'm paid. Four rich Americans on a hunting trip weren't having any luck, so they decided to pass the time by teaching a poor benighted Canadian to play poker. They went home poorer, and I was able to add this to my collection."

"Good for you, Doc," Snyder laughed. "You know, it always catches me by surprise when I think about you collecting Oriental art. You just don't fit my idea of somebody who'd be interested in porcelain and stuff like that. But then, somebody did tell me you were born in China."

D.L.'s face tightened. Carefully, he returned the buffalo to its container. "Yes," he said finally. "My parents were Anglican missionaries. I was just a boy when we had to leave. The Communists didn't approve of missionaries."

"How about that?" Snyder leaned over the counter inquisitively. He was the biggest gossip in Churchill. "And that was the first time you'd been home to Canada?"

"We didn't come to Canada. They accepted a post in Korea." He stood up suddenly. "Keep this for me overnight, Jack. I'll pick it up in the morning, before I leave."

"The morning? You flying out tomorrow, Doc? You must be real eager to get back north of the tree line."

"That's the word, Jack. Eager."

He left before Snyder could take the conversation further. Too many paths were opening up, paths leading into the past. He had to lose himself in something. The gold would do.

There was only one man in Churchill he was certain he could ask and have it go no further. At the small airport, out toward old Fort Churchill, he stopped in front of a long building with Dawes Aviation Mechanics across the front in International Orange. The same sign was repeated, even larger, on the roof, where it could be seen from landing planes.

A man in greasy overalls looked up from a half-dis-assembled engine when he walked in. "Hi, Doc. Back late this year."

"So everyone says, Tom. Is Harry around?"

"Sure, Doc. He's in back. You might as well go on back if you want."

In back was hanger space the length of the building. Half a dozen engines on stands were scattered about, and two de Havilland's and a Cessna with inspection hatches open and cowlings off. A pair of mechanics worked on the de Havillands.

Harry Dawes was in the middle of it, feet up on a desk stuck in the center of the hanger floor. He frowned down a nose that seemed to make up half his face at a pilot's maintenance log.

"It's a bloody crime, is what it is. The damned idiots muck up their logs with phony entries, trying to stretch the bloody time till the next inspection's due, then raise hell because it costs more for repairs than if they'd brought the bastards in on time." He tossed the log on the desk and dropped his feet to the cement floor. "Hello, D.L. You're—"

"—back late this year. I know."

"Yes. Well." Dawes rubbed at his nose. "I had your Otter put back on Warkworth Lake. Overhaul's com-plete, but she's bloody old, D.L. The government should be able to afford to buy you better."

"I'm way down the list of priorities, Harry." He could

barely keep the bitterness from his voice. He was a one-man, one-plane program funded by the Ministry of National Health and Welfare and the Ministry of Indian Affairs and Northern Development. Neither was entirely convinced he was needed, and both spent most of their time complaining that the other wasn't paying a large enough share. After seventeen years, he was still funded year to year, and making do with a de Havilland that had been a year old when he started.

"So quit. Take that damned promotion they keep trying to force on you. Go down to Ottawa and fight the bastards who don't know a good program from their own asses."

"I'm a doctor, not a bureaucrat."

Dawes made a sound as if he wanted to spit. Every year he had the same argument with D. L., and every year D.L. dug in his heels on the same point. "Anyway, your gear's all ready, and the trailer's out. You have Snyder's Jeep again, don't you?"

"It's outside." D.L. hesitated, looking at the mechanics. Neither was close enough to hear. "Harry, I need some information. It may be important."

Dawes took his own glance at the mechanics. "If I have it, D.L., it's yours."

"Have you heard anything, anything at all, about gold being found on the Bay?"

"As a matter of fact, I have. It's just a story, you understand. But it seems an Eskimo, or maybe these days I should say an Inuit, tried to charter a flight down to Montreal. Seems he wanted to pay with a sack of gold nuggets. I've heard it maybe three times now. One said it happened in Saglouc, two said Inoucdjouac. But like I said, it's just a story."

The tale was spreading far, D.L. thought. Not that whiskey stories weren't spread the length of the Bay at times, but he was beginning to think there was a kernel of truth in this one. Saglouc and Inoucdjouac were both on his circuit, on the far side of the Bay. He could get first-hand information there.

"D.L., what's this all about? I can't think of five men I'd believe if they said there was gold on the Bay, but you're one of them. And I never heard you ask idle questions."

"Maybe it *is* just another whiskey tale, Harry. But what if some Inuit have made a strike? What if they're mining without licenses?"

"I'd say Ottawa would bloody well burn some Eskimos. What are you going to do, D.L.? And do you need any help?"

"I'll try to find out if it's true. After that, God knows."

III

Samantha Keenan grimaced and tied a green silk scarf around her auburn hair before getting out of the Land-Rover at Warkworth Lake. She hated early mornings, and the driver hadn't made it any more enjoyable. She'd put on high-heeled boots and an old pair of Calvin Klein jeans as suitable for Hudson Bay, but he'd taken tight pants for an invitation. He was still red-faced and rigid. She just hoped he hadn't brought her to the wrong dock to get even.

The lake was really only a widening of Warkworth Creek, but it held ten moored floatplanes, including two with the markings of the Royal Canadian Mounted Police. All of them, the last especially, looked better than the scruffy, high-winged plane moored at the end of the dock.

She studied the man loading the plane as she walked down the dock. Handsome enough, in a rugged sort of way. The doctor's pilot, she decided. Certainly not the doctor. And he probably played the macho bush pilot to the hilt. As if she hadn't had enough of that since coming to Hudson Bay.

He was bent over the last bundle on the dock when she stopped behind him. "You the pilot?"

D.L. jerked erect, and his eyes widened when he saw her. "Yes, I am. What can I do—?"

"Just fly the plane, sport." His jaw tightened, and she sighed. Another tender ego.

"Miss, who are you? What do you want?"

"I'm Samantha Keenan. Of *Newsworld* magazine." He kept on staring at her. Didn't he read? "We do an energy roundup every year. I'm doing the section on Canada this year. Right now I'm working on the dam that's being built on the La Grande River. I'll be making the circuit of Hudson Bay with Dr. Childe to find out what the people here think about that environmental monstrosity." She stopped suddenly. With a glance at her watch she took three quick steps down the dock and put her fists on her hips. "Where *is* that damned Childe?"

"I'm Dr. Childe," D.L. said. She whirled to face him, but before she could speak, he went on. "And I'm afraid I can't take you along, Miss Keenan, *Newsworld* magazine or not."

"Ms Keenan," she said automatically. She couldn't avoid the irrational thought that he looked the way he did just to make a fool of her. "And *I* am afraid I *will* be going with you. I—."

"Miss Keenan," he began tightly.

"*Ms* Keenan."

"—what you don't seem to understand is that the places I go don't have many comforts. In fact, some of them don't have any. I'm afraid a woman like you, used to the big city, would find it pretty bleak. Besides that, I work for the government. I can't just give rides, even to somebody as pretty as you. Now, if you'll—."

Her green eyes glinted dangerously. She rummaged in her shoulder bag and pushed two folded papers into his hands. "Letters from the Minister of National Health and Welfare, and the Minister of Indian Affairs and Northern Development. You *can* recognize your bosses' signatures, can't you?"

"I recognize them," he growled. His brow furrowed ominously as he read.

"Then you'll see you're instructed to give me transportation. If you don't like it, go argue with the Ministers."

He folded the letters with a grunt and handed them back. "You'd better understand something right now. You're just along for the ride. I won't make any side trips for your story. I won't leave one hour early or one hour late. And that's the way it's going to be."

She eyed him. She was going to have to spend two weeks in the company of this handsome dolt, and there was no need to make it any less pleasant than it had to be. She could bring up side trips later. "I quite understand, Dr. Childe. I'll try to be a model passenger."

Suddenly, he smiled. The corners of his eyes crinkled, and he looked warm and gentle. "We're off to a bad start, aren't we? We'll be spending the next few weeks together, so let's start over. Most people call me D.L."

She returned his smile almost hesitantly. She felt uncertain about the abrupt attraction she felt for him. He wasn't her type at all. "I'm Samantha, D.L."

"Samantha. How long do you need to get your bags here? I want to take off as soon as possible."

"Just two minutes. They're in the LandRover."

The driver was still hunched over the wheel. She smiled at him icily as she leaned in to get her suitcases. His ears reddened, and he pulled his head deeper into his collar. Before she'd taken two steps back toward the dock, he roared away in a spray of dust.

On the way to the Otter, she considered D.L.'s effect on her. That sudden smile, those disturbing gray eyes. There must be something wrong with him.

He was kneeling in the long cabin of the plane, checking the fastenings on the cargo stowed where the canvas seats on one side had been removed. He raised an eye-

brow at her designer luggage before strapping it down.
    An irresistible impulse came over her. She bent to put
her lips to his ear. "Are there any more at home like
you, cutie?"

His eyes widened in shocked surprise at the put-down,
and his mouth fell open. She began to giggle, and that
became a full-throated laugh. She fell back on a seat,
overcome. He looked so stunned, so disbelieving. She
took another look at him, and found herself staring at
icy gray eyes that cut her laughter off short.

Silently, he climbed out and loosened the moorings.
Pushing the plane away from the dock, he jumped back
aboard and stalked to the pilot's seat in the front of the
cabin.

"Fasten your seat belt," he growled without looking
at her.

She straightened irritably, and complied with a glare
at his back. For a moment she had almost been afraid.
She ran an eye over the cargo, taking in the two pairs of
scuba tanks sticking out from under the tarp, and the
cased rifle behind the pilot's seat. He was playing the
macho bush pilot to the hilt. Definitely a phony. She
dug a paperback book out of her shoulder bag and settled back to read, ignoring the roar as the engine came
to life.

* * *

The prop swung, slowly at first, then spinning into a
blur. D.L. watched the tach as the runup began, a hand
on the throttle to keep the rpm's low until the engine
was warmed up. When the oil pressure stabilized, he
glanced back at Samantha. She was bent, frowning, over
a book. He grimaced and returned to the gauges. Normally, he might have enjoyed having a pretty woman for
company, and this one was certainly pretty, but she had
the personality of a rasp, even after he'd tried to be
pleasant. And she was a reporter, probably one of those
opinionated Americans who'd bend the facts to fit the

story she wanted to write. If there *was* gold, and she got hold of it, God only knew what she'd do with it. Well, he'd have none of her games. Cutie!

He cleared a north-south takeoff with Churchill Control as he taxied out into the lake. As soon as the floats left the water he climbed to five thousand feet and headed out over the Bay. Land disappeared behind the Otter, and for over an hour there was nothing to be seen but blue sky and blue-gray water. Then, ahead, low, rocky, treeless fingers of land appeared, stretching into the Bay. On one about eighty unpainted, frame houses stood, most with tin roofs. At least one boat for every house lay drawn up at the water's edge. He banked and began to lose altitude.

"Are we landing?" Samantha braced herself on his shoulder to peer through the front windscreen. "Where is this, anyway?"

"Eskimo Point," he said shortly. "Sit down and fasten your seatbelt."

She gave an exasperated sigh and made her way back to her seat. Briefly he wondered why she seemed to get under his skin without even trying.

The Otter slid onto the green water between two fingers of land, and taxied to within a hundred yards of shore. D.L. cut the engine. In the shelter of the point the Otter floated without drifting while he climbed out on a float to drop the anchor.

An open launch piloted by a short, dark Inuit in jeans and a plaid work shirt nosed in to the plane. "Hello, Dr. Childe," the boatman called. He eyed Samantha with frank curiosity.

"Hello, Lucassie. This is Samantha Keenan, an American reporter. Samantha, Lucassie Owlyoot, the best fishing guide around here."

Lucassie helped D.L. load his chests into the boat, and as soon as Samantha was aboard they headed for shore.

A crowd, largely smiling children, had gathered to meet them. When D.L. stepped out on the rock-strewn beach they began to call out greetings. The children crowded around, some of the smaller ones tugging at his clothes for notice. Laughing, he swung one into the air, then another, and another. He always enjoyed the children. Except, occasionally, when he saw one who looked like Helen must have as a little girl.

"Enough," he said at last. "Enough. Everybody up to the schoolhouse. I'll begin the examinations when everybody's there."

Laughing and shouting, the children raced away toward a building only slightly larger than the houses. Their parents followed more slowly.

"Quite the great white father," Samantha said.

D.L. kept a rein on his temper. "Nothing much happens in a village this size. Even the doctor coming is a big event." He shook his head. "Peter, will you help me carry the chests up to the school?"

Ignoring her, he shouldered one of the chests and started up the beach. Peter followed with the other.

The National Health Service Nurse was already taking names in the schoolhouse, arranging his examinations. A resident of the village, she could handle any routine medical matter. It was the out-of-the-ordinary he was there to find, and to take care of. But everyone wanted their problems looked at by the real doctor, routine or not.

An endless stream passed through the examining room he set up in the teacher's office. Broken bones and gashed hands. Expectant mothers and nursing mothers. Children with colic and children with croup. He ran two electrocardiograms and arranged for one of the men to go to the Churchill Hospital. He performed three tonsillectomies. He treated vitamin deficiency, carbuncles, and gonorrhea. By the time he ushered out the last patient, an old woman with osteoarthritis, the day was gone.

He stopped on the schoolhouse steps and wearily rubbed his eyes. The shadows of the houses stretched toward the water.

"I'll wager," Samantha said as she stepped out of the shadows, "that you didn't even stop to eat."

He looked at her in surprise. Why had she waited for him? "You're right. I didn't. There was always another patient waiting. Can you believe I pulled eighteen teeth today?"

"And dentistry doesn't appeal to you," she laughed.

"They should have good, healthy teeth. When I first came here, there were men who, if a nut was too hard to turn by hand, would use their teeth to turn it. Now they have cavities because their diet is full of sugar and starch that we introduced."

"So you feel that the white man has damaged the Eskimo's health?"

He suppressed a smile at her careful phrasing. So that was why she'd waited. "No, *Ms* Keenan. I won't let you set me up for a quote in your article. If they used to have stronger teeth, they also died from diseases that could have been cured with a few doses of antibiotic. No, that's just one of the hobby horses I get on now and again. You mustn't pay too much attention. Now, I'd better see about a place for you to spend the night."

She shook her head. "I already have a place. A woman I met, Mary Pikkok, asked me to stay at her house."

"I know Mary and her father. They're good people. May I walk you to their house?"

"I haven't heard a question like that since I was fourteen," she laughed.

He shifted his medical bag to the other hand and offered his arm. She shot him a derisive look, pointedly thrusting her hands into her hip pockets. Without a word, he turned and started up the village's dirt main street. She strolled along beside him, her shoulder casually brushing his arm from time to time. He decided to make one last attempt to be pleasant.

"And how was your day, Samantha? Did you get your story?"

"No. I didn't get anything. Some of them walked away as soon as I asked my first question. And those who did answer just didn't seem to care whether the dam is built or not."

"It *is* on the other side of the Bay, Samantha. Are people in New York concerned with all the same things as people in, say, Chicago?"

"But this is important. Important to them. Important to—." She hesitated, and went on in a lower voice. "Well, it's important, that's all."

"Important to you, perhaps?" When she didn't answer, he went on. "I don't understand them walking away. Many Inuit don't like to be asked a direct question. It's bad manners under the old ways. But not many are rude, and most understand if a white makes an honest mistake. What did you ask them?"

"The same thing first, every time. I'd introduce myself, then ask what they thought of the damage that would be done to the Eskimo way of life by the dam."

He sighed. "Samantha, you just ran head on into growing ethnic awareness. Eskimo comes from an Abnaki Indian word, esquimantsic, 'eaters of raw flesh.' Most of them prefer Inuit, 'the true people.' It's their own name for themselves."

She stopped and pulled him around to face her. "Damn it, D.L., do you mean I've been throwing ethnic slurs at everybody I've talked to? Oh, hell!"

"Not quite that bad," he laughed. "Not everyone insists on it. It's generally better to use Inuit, but—"

Two houses down a door banged open, spilling light into the street. A woman ran out into the darkness, long skirts held high. "Help! Somebody! Oh, thank God, Dr. Childe!" She fell against D.L.'s chest, sobbing.

"Mary, what's the matter?" he asked.

"It's father! He's dying! He's choking, and I can't help him!"

"Was he eating? Quickly, now."

"No! Dinner was over an hour ago."

Before she finished he was running. He took the steps in one leap and dashed into the house. On the floor by an over-turned kitchen chair, Henry Pikkok gasped futilely for breath, his hands and feet scrabbling weakly on the linoleum. His lips already had the bluish tint of cyanosis, a lack of oxygen in the blood. There was no time to make a diagnosis. He had to act while there was still a chance. He pulled a scalpel from his case as Samantha came in with her arm around a still-weeping Mary.

"Hold him," he ordered.

"What—?"

"Hold him! Damn it, woman, move! Grab his arms. Hold his shoulders down, hard. Now!"

Before they had time to more than kneel beside the old man, he caught Henry's head in the crook of his arm. He forced it back, stretching the neck taut. In the same move he made a vertical incision down the center of the throat. Blood welled up. Samantha gagged and shut her eyes, but he noted in the corner of his mind that she didn't loosen her hold.

He didn't worry about the bleeding. It was capillary blood, from tiny vessels in the skin. Rapidly he deepened the incision, separating the two sternohyoid muscles that ran the length of the neck. Shifting the large, pulsing vein that led to the thyroid, he exposed the segmented, blue-gray cartilage of the windpipe. The old man's hands suddenly went still.

"Oh, God, he's dead," Mary wailed.

The tough cartilage resisted the scalpel, but D.L.

forced it through, his practiced hand making a clean cut less than half an inch long. Thrusting the scalpel handle into the incision, he pried it open. A rasping whistle brought a sigh of relief from him. The old man was breathing.

A smile bloomed on Mary's face through the tears still streaming down her cheeks. Samantha touched her shoulder comfortingly.

D.L. took out a sterile-pack and ripped it open with his teeth. The cartilage closed around the tracheotomy tube firmly as he withdrew the scalpel. A strap went around Henry's neck to hold the tube in place. He took his stethoscope from the case and checked the old man's heartbeat. It was weak, but regular.

"Mary," he said, "this swelling in his throat looks as if it might be an allergic reaction. Has he eaten anything today that he hasn't eaten before?"

"No, Dr. Childe," she replied slowly, "nothing. Of course, he hasn't eaten like this in fifteen or twenty years. He bet Billy Tilak this morning that he could still find food the old way, without any of the white man's food. All he had for dinner was tern eggs and shellfish."

D.L. nodded and sighed. "That could do it. An allergy can develop in less time than that, and eggs and shellfish are both common causes of this kind of reaction. He'll be all right now, though, Mary. Samantha, would you go get Miss Keller, the National Health Service nurse? Hers is the fourth house down from the school. Samantha?"

She started, and got to her feet looking at him. At the door she paused. "You know, D.L., you're not so bad after all." And she was gone.

He stared at the empty doorway before returning to Henry with a snort. She must be trying a new game.

September 15
2100 hours

Chu made his way forward slowly, trailed by Liang,

beginning in the engine room. It was his habit to make such a walk-through periodically, to allow the crew to see him. It increased efficiency.

The control room crew performed their duties briskly, not looking up as he walked through. The Duty Officer turned toward him, but he motioned the officer to carry on.

"They appear very alert, sir," Liang said.

"Yes, they do," Chu said dryly. Almost as if they had been told when he would be coming. "I will continue to the crew's quarters."

"Sir?" The walk-through was always confined to the duty sections. He hurried after the captain.

Chu continued down the passage, but he stopped short of the crew's quarters. He motioned Liang to silence as the executive officer came up behind him. Through the hatch he could see a crewman on a top bunk, flying a tiny kite in the flow from a ventilation duct. At the far end of the compartment men huddled in a circle on their knees. He didn't need to see to know what they were doing. Cockroach races. It had been the same on the diesel boats.

"I'll put them on report, sir," Liang said.

"No," Chu said. "We will walk the lower deck." He would not interfere with the ways submarine crews had always found to combat boredom when submerged. There would be much boredom now that they were under the ice cap. He *hoped* there would be much boredom.

IV

An emergency appendectomy had made them late
taking off from Coral Harbor, but D.L. had no worries
about making Saglouc before dark. He *had* thought
Samantha might be nervous about arriving so close to
nightfall. A night landing on water was something he
didn't relish himself, even if Saglouc had the flare-path
set out properly. Instead of being on edge, Samantha
was curled up in the copilot's seat, listening to her taped
interviews on a button earphone.

He realized he should have expected that. He'd come,
reluctantly, to respect her. She wasn't the pampered
flower he'd expected. She'd shown grit while holding
Henry Pikkok. And she'd changed since then. She was
still tart, her remarks could still bite, but the intentional
acid had disappeared.

She shifted to change cassettes. He glanced at her and
looked away before she noticed. Somewhere along the
way, at Whale Cove, or Rankin Inlet, he'd stopped
thinking of her as a reporter and a nuisance, and begun
to think of her as a woman. It was something he
couldn't explain. She was as far from the sort of woman
he liked as was possible. She was brassy and pushy, and

31

she had a mouth like a trapper. But he was aware of the scent of her, and he could sense the feel of her whenever she was close to him. It was stupid. He wanted no part of it. And he hoped she wasn't aware of the effect she was having. He couldn't even be sure of that. At Chesterfield Inlet, when he'd asked her if she wanted to sit up front, she'd smiled knowlingly, with a touch of the old acid in it, before accepting. Still—.

The engine coughing cut into his thoughts. Even as he scanned the instrument panel, the prop slowed to a stop. No warning lights were on. Every gauge except for the slowly unwinding altimeter read in the green. The port fuel tank read half full, and the starboard tank read full. With a muttered prayer he switched tanks and tried to restart. The starter motor whirred. The prop swung through half a turn. And stopped. The slipstream rushed by hollowly.

Samantha slowly took the earphone from her ear. "Is it—Is it serious?"

"I hope not. A float Otter has a glide angle like a brick, but we have a few thousand feet to play with yet." Once more he attempted to restart. Once more the prop spun, and stopped without completing a turn. "Damn," he muttered. He scanned the blue-gray Bay in every direction, hoping for a ship, or even a small boat. A smudge on the horizon to the east was the only break in the emptiness. He put the plane into a flat bank toward the smudge. "Samantha," he said levelly, "will you get on the radio? Keep it simple. Mayday, m'aidez, aircraft down at Nottingham Island. Keep repeating that. I just hope it does some good," he added half to himself. He measured the distance to the island, and adjusted the flaps slightly. They should just about make it. With luck.

"D.L.?" Samantha asked faintly. "D.L., why *shouldn't* it do some good?"

"Sometimes there are magnetic disturbances in this

area. Radio traffic can be shut down for days at a time."

"Oh, Christ!"

A touch of desperation in her voice caught his attention for the first time, but he realized it had been there for some time now. He glanced at her, and could barely hide the shock. Her face was drawn, her eyes wide and on the brink of panic. Both hands were clenched in white-knuckled fists pressed against her thighs. "Samantha, it's going to be all right. We'll make it." His words didn't make a dent. "Samantha, get on the radio. Samantha! The radio!"

As if in a trance she unhooked the microphone from the instrument panel. She stared at it a moment before keying it. "Mayday! M'aidez! Aircraft down at Nottingham Island. Mayday! M'aidez! Aircraft down—."

She went on in a dull monotone, and he returned to flying the plane. He couldn't believe the complete collapse of her confidence, but there was nothing he could do about it now. Getting the Otter down required all his attention.

The tops of the cold gray swells below were being whipped white by a wind out of the west. He was counting on that wind to stretch their glide. The barren, rock-strewn beach was clearly visible, and the boulders jutting out of the water in algae-covered masses. He had to take a straight-in approach and hope there were none just below the surface as well. He couldn't afford the luxury of maneuvering. He aimed straight for the navigation light on the southwest point of the island.

A part of his mind could hear Samantha, still repeating her litany, but all of his awareness was concentrated on the onrushing beach and the rapidly dwindling numbers on the altimeter. Two hundred feet. One hundred. Fifty. And altitude ran out, far short of the land.

Even as the floats kissed the water he knew the Otter's momentum wasn't enough to carry it to shore. Before the plane stopped moving he had the door open. He dropped into icy, chestdeep water and fumbled the mooring rope free. Clutching it, he began to slog ashore. There was no current in the water. He'd caught it at dead high tide. For that he was grateful. An incoming tide would have helped, but he could never have towed eight thousand pounds of airplane to shore against an outgoing tide.

The mooring rope went taut before he was out of the water. He put it over his shoulder, and bent his weight into it. Rocks turned under his boots, and the dead weight of the plane made progress a matter of inches at a time. If the plane hadn't been on floats, he could never have moved it at all. At last the floats grated on stone in shallow water. Panting from exertion, he tied the rope around a boulder and hurried back to the plane.

Samantha still sat staring blankly ahead, clutching the mike desperately. "Mayday! M'aidez! Aircraft down at Nottingham Island! Mayday!"

"Samantha," he said gently, "we're down. You can stop for a while."

She fell silent without looking at him, fumbling the mike back onto its hook. A shudder ran through her, and she slumped with a heavy sigh.

"Are you all right, Samantha?"

"I'm all right." The words were barely audible. "Just leave me alone. Please."

With a last, troubled look, he backed away. He knew her for a strong woman, and guessed she didn't like having a witness to her fear.

The sun was dropping in the west. Little more than an hour of light was left, he estimated. They'd be spending the night there. He hoped it was only one. He began to unload what they'd need.

Once he had two tents up, in hollows that would shelter them from the wind off the Bay, and coffee making on the camp stove, he looked around. Samantha had moved to the beach. She sat pensively on a flat rock near the water, staring at the small waves lapping at the shore. He touched her shoulder. "Coffee's hot, Samantha."

She shrugged his hand off, and turned away from him. "Go away." She bit off the words. "Leave me alone. Do you hear?" Angrily, he stalked back to the Otter and dug out his tool chest. He knew she'd been afraid, but there was no time for prima donnas. And he was damned if he was going to be a target for her bile. Muttering to himself, he began loosening the zeus-fasteners on the cowling.

* * *

Samantha lay awake in the darkness of her tent, shaking despite her blankets. Partly it was because it was cold, and she was naked beneath the cover. She had still been in a daze when she came to the tent. When she realized she'd taken off all of her clothes, she'd just crawled into her blankets, unable to muster the energy to put on anything against the cold. It had been all she could do not to burst into tears.

And that all went back to the second part. Fear, and the memory of fear. On the plane, gliding without power, she had known with deathly certainty that she was going to die. No hope of survival, no chance of life. Just a choice between drowning and being ripped apart in a twisted ball of flame and wreckage. And it didn't matter what D.L. did.

That, she managed to admit, was why she'd snapped at him, why she'd avoided even looking at him since they'd gotten ashore. He had calmly and competently done what was necessary to save their lives, and that had made her own collapse all the more bitter. She'd behaved like the stereotype of a hysterical woman, while he'd acted like a movie hero.

No, he didn't deserve that. It was the kind of remark the men she was used to, the businessmen who cornered her at cocktail parties in New York, would make with a sneer. But D.L. didn't deserve sneers. He was real. He was solid. Those account executives became pale shadows in comparison.

She couldn't help thinking of him, of his strong hands on the plane's controls, of the crinkles at the corners of his eyes when he smiled, and the way his blue eyes lit up. He was so alive. So alive. Abruptly she came to a decision. With a muttered "Damn" she surged to her feet, blankets wrapped around her shoulders, and hurried out of the tent, unmindful of the rocks bruising her bare feet.

The moon, still climbing, cast a pale light across the beach. The air had the crystal sharpness that came only with near freezing temperature. She was shivering uncontrollably by the time she ducked into D.L.'s tent. He was only a shadowed mound of blankets in the dark.

"D.L.?" There was a quaver to her voice she couldn't disguise.

"What—?" The mound heaved, and he rose on one elbow. "Samantha?" he asked sleepily. "Is something wrong?"

"D.L.—" Suddenly she was fighting to keep back tears, and everything poured out. "I'm cold, and I'm afraid, and I can't stop shaking, and, and—I want to be held. I just want— " She stopped, hating the plaintive quality in her voice.

D.L. hesitated, then turned back the blankets. "If you want, Samantha," he said quietly.

She dropped her cover and darted in beside him, not even hearing his gasp as the whiteness of her skin flashed in the dark. She pressed herself tight against him, feeling the roughness of his woolen shirt against her cheek, and the hard muscle beneath. His chest was strong and durable. He was a rock to cling to. At last she could let the tears begin to leak out.

He shifted awkwardly against her nakedness, and gingerly put an arm around her. "Samantha, I—"

"I knew I was going to die." Her words were muffled against his chest.

"You're safe now," he said gently.

Violently, she shook her head. "You don't understand. I was going to die. I *was*. And it would've been almost fitting. I'm thirty years old, and I'm finished. The only way my career is going is down."

"That's stupid." His voice was sharp. "You're—"

"I'm a failure. I wrote my first articles in college. Real articles, not school newspaper crap. Hard hitting. They called me a *wunderkind*. All the newsmagazines wanted me. When I was hired by *Newsworld*, the managing editor wrote a special editorial to welcome me. Everybody expected great things. Everybody. Me included." She laughed bitterly through her tears. "At first, for a year, it was what I expected. Then it all started going wrong. I went to cover an election in Bolivia, and spent a week in the hospital with flu while a coup, and a counter-coup, took place. I did a terrific piece on corruption in the multinational corporations, only to have a week of massive terrorism, followed by major political upsets in the French and German elections, followed by—Oh, hell! By the time it was over, my piece was lost in the shuffle. That's the way it's been. When the big story happened, I was somewhere else. Or if I was there, a bigger story happened somewhere else. After a while, my name wasn't mentioned when they talked about who to send to cover the big stories. New wonderchildren came along. Bit by bit I was relegated to garbage like this, a God-damned part of a God-damned energy roundup without even a God-damned byline." She made an effort to get hold of herself, a futile attempt to still the panic in her voice. "When I first realized what was happening, I called *Time* and *Newsweek*. They weren't interested anymore. I—I'm washed up. A has-been going nowhere."

"You're a fraud, is what you are," he said quietly.

"Samantha Keenen is a phony."

She gasped. "Damn you! Damn you!"

"You just put up a front. Able to take care of yourself. Able to stand the gaff. Bull! You can't take it at all. Things don't go exactly the way you want, and you crawl off to cry about it. You aren't up to the real world, are you?"

She was pounding on his chest, and shouting, "Stop it! Stop it!" But he wouldn't stop. Suddenly it seemed a natural way to shut him up to pull his head down and cover his mouth with hers. Her hands tightened in his hair, and she was kissing him eagerly. Gently he turned her onto her back and moved over her. With a sob, she welcomed him.

After, she lay in the crook of his arm, breathing contentedly. She ran her hand in where she'd ripped the buttons off his shirt, and traced the teeth-marks on his chest. "You, doctor, are full of surprises."

"I—I apologize for taking advantage," he said awkwardly. "I mean—"

"Advantage?"

He sounded uncomfortable. "You came to me wanting to be comforted, and I—I know it's not much, but I'm sorry, Samantha."

She smiled to herself. He was a very old-fashioned man. "You didn't take advantage, D.L. If anything, *I* did." She twisted around to rest her chin on his chest.

"You did?" he chuckled. "Somehow, I don't remember you wrestling me to the ground."

"Just the same, if I hadn't wanted it to happen, you'd have known about it, and fast."

"I suppose. It's just—Well, I'm not much for one-night stands. I'm old-fashioned, I guess. I like there to be more to it than that."

"Don't put too much on it, D.L. No ties. No commitments. I'm not the kind to wait in a cabin somewhere, keeping your pipe and slippers warm till you get back.

And you. You may know how to take care of yourself with wolves and polar bears, but the cocktail party barracudas in New York would strip you to the bone in ten minutes."

"Are you proposing marriage, Samantha?" He sounded amused. "I'd hate to give up the widow Hilton in Moosonee, or Janet in—"

She fisted him in the ribs hard enough to bring a grunt. "Watch it, buster," she growled.

His tone became more serious. "All right. But if this is more than a one nighter, but it's still not serious-. Well, what are we?"

She kissed his chest, right over his heart. "But it's very simple. We're lovers." She sensed his shock at the word. "Yes, my old-fashioned friend, lovers. Lovers until you kick me out of your bed, or I kick you out of mine. Lovers." She threw one leg across his thighs. "And now, since you have to get up early to finish fixing the plane, isn't there anything you'd like to do before going to sleep?"

He laughed and pulled her on top of him. His hands ran down to cup her behind. "Yes, there certainly is."

September 21
1130 hours
Samantha sat curled up in the copilot's seat, watching D.L. and letting her thoughts drift with the rhythmic roar of the engine. She was surprised at how much enjoyment she got from watching him. She hated anything to do with grease or mechanics, but she'd spent two hours watching him clear a clogged fuel line, all the while muttering under his breath about people who sold contaminated fuel.

"Saglouc," D.L. said.

She looked up and gasped. They were flying into the mouth of a fjord, with thousand-foot cliffs along the eastern side. She felt a flow of adrenaline watching the rock face slip past outside the airplane window, and worse, above them. They swung around a high neck of land - Black Point, D.L. said - and dropped into the inlet, surrounded by brown, stony hills.

A dock stretched into the inlet, with dozens of small, open boats and a white-hulled trawler about fifty feet long moored to it. The village of Saglouc rose from the water's edge up the side of the hills, fifty small, neat frame buildings, with here and there one of rough field-stone.

D.L. taxied to the dock astern of the trawler, the *Baie du Nord* by the name across its stern. Even as the engine died, a tall, dark man with a bushy mustache ran to take their mooring line and drop it over a bollard.

"Hello, D.L.," he called in a thick, Qúebecois accent. "You are just in time. Jacques halted in surprise as D.L. handed Samantha out of the plane.

"Samantha," D.L. said, "this is Martial Faschereau, captain of the *Baie du Nord*. Martial, this is Samantha Keenan, a reporter for *Newsworld* magazine."

Faschereau's dark eyes lit up. "A reporter? I am pleased to meet you, Miss Keenan, You come to do story on Quebec independence, *non*?"

"I'm afraid not," Samantha laughed. He was everything she expected a French-Canadian trawler captain to be, from his high fisherman's boots to his red-and-black checked woolen shirt, to his black stocking-cap. "I'm doing a piece on the dam down on the La Grande River."

The trawler captain's face twisted. "Dams. Rivers. Bah! I don't get no further from salt water than I got to. I don't care about no dams or rivers. Aye! You come with D.L. and me. I give you some bouillabaisse like no bouillabaisse you never had before." He put his arms around their shoulders and began to guide them toward the *Baie du Nord*. "Good fish here in the Bay. No pollution, like in Mediterranean."

She exchanged amused glances with D.L. and let herself be guided.

The main cabin of the *Baie du Nord* was plain and clean, the wood well scrubbed and the brass fittings burnished. Samantha and Faschereau slid onto the bench around the table built into the corner, and D.L. was about to join them when a man with a lantern jaw and a two-day beard put his head through the companionway from below.

"Doctor Childe," he said in surprise. "That one good thing you here. Eduard, he got him one by damn pain in his middle. You take a look at him, non?"

D.L. sighed. "All right, Auguste, Excuse me, Samantha, Martial. This shouldn't take long. If I know Eduard, he's eaten something he shouldn't have."

After D.L. left there was a moment's awkward silence, as between people who don't really know each other well enough to converse, and yet must make the effort. Finally, Faschereau reached behind him and took a bottle and two glasses from a cabinet.

"Some cognac, Miss Keenan?"

"Yes, thank you." She took a glass from him and sipped. "But please call me Samantha."

"If you will call me Martial, Samantha."

"Martial. Tell me, Martial, you've know D.L. a long time?"

"For twelve, maybe thirteen years, we are good friends. Who knows if that is a long time or not?"

"It's longer than I've know him. I only met him little more than a week ago."

"Ah," he said sagely, "but I think maybe you do more for him in that week than I do in thirteen years."

Samantha arched one eyebrow. "Oh?" She was pleased to see him color.

"Please don't take no offense. Sometimes, what I say don't sound like what I mean. What I want to say is, there used to be this wall behind D.L.'s eyes, and behind that wall was one dangerous man. Now, I see him look at you, and that wall not there any more."

"Dangerous!" Samantha hooted. "D.L.? Martial, he's one of the gentlest men I've ever known." Her mirth faded as she realized Faschereau was unsmiling and troubled.

"That is true. It is just there was that wall." He shook his head. "You got to understand, only one time I know him to lose his temper, one time somebody break through that wall. He don't go around acting like no dangerous man, but somebody who can sense such things, he know you don't push D.L. too far."

"I don't believe it. You're joking, aren't you?" But suddenly she remembered the first day she'd met D.L., blue eyes blazing at her like fire behind ice.

"I tell you about that one time. There is this man, Jean Berthier, he used to trap the Ungava, this Upper Quebec. A big man, six feet six inches, two hundred eighty pounds, and he don't have no speck of fat on him. Berthier hate everybody, Indian, Inuit, Anglais, even other Québecois. He bully anybody he can, and if they fight, he put the boot to them. He love to fight, anybody, everybody."

"I don't understand. What does this Berthier have to do with D.L.?"

"One day, two year ago, Berthier was in the Hudson Bay Company Store at Ivujivik. He was cursing some Inuit, and they scared to leave because they got to pass him to get to the door. Everybody hesitate, because nobody want to fight Berthier. Then, before anybody can say "enough," D.L. come in. He don't say nothing. He just take those Inuit, and he lead them to the door."

Samantha wanted to applaud. "Good for him. That sounds just like D.L. And not at all like your 'dangerous man.'"

Faschereau frowned into his cognac and went on as she hadn't spoken. "Berthier start to curse something terrible. He know D.L. is too much respected for him to beat up, but he say all kind of horrible things. At first, it don't have no effect. D.L. go on like he don't hear no word at all. Then Berthier, he say, you love them God-damned gooks. You got some damned gook woman shacked up some place?" He shivered, as if at an unpleasant memory. "D.L., he stop, and turn around real slow. Only, he wasn't D.L. no more. Face like iron, eyes like ice. Berthier, I don't think he never been scared of nothing, but he back up, and he pull his knife. We all jump up to save D.L., but before anybody can take one step, it is done. D.L. take away the knife, and he break Berthier's arm, and his jaw, and six ribs. He do it quicker than it take to say. And for minute I think he is going to kill Berthier. He stand there, his hand raised like an axe blade, and I know Berthier is going to die. And then he is D.L. again. All that cold anger drain away. He call for his bag, and he patch Berthier up."

Samantha realized she'd been holding her breath. "I just can't picture D.L. like that, Martial."

"Just that one time, when somebody smash through that wall. I just tell you because you have pull down that wall. I know you are the one when I see him look at you. I still sense the danger, but it is much less, and I think every day with you it will grow even smaller."

"But— " Samantha began, and stopped as D.L. clambered up the companionway from below. She wasn't certain what she'd been going to say, but she didn't want D.L. to know she'd been talking about him behind his back.

"Martial," D.L. said as he slid onto the bench beside her, "where on earth did Eduard get two pounds of chili peppers up here? He ate nearly a pound of the things. He has the granddaddy of all bellyaches."

"You know Eduard. He will eat anything." Faschereau glanced at her uneasily, as if he thought she might bring up D.L.'s fight again. When she caught his eye, he turned away quickly. "Jacques! Jacques, where is that bouillabaisse?"

D.L. laughed and said something about Jacques' cooking, and she took the opportunity to study him without being noticed. He looked as he had since she'd known him, strong, yet gentle. When he looked at her and smiled, the crinkles in the corners of his eyes made them look warm. There certainly weren't any walls. She realized they had changed subjects, and the topic caught her interest.

"Gold?" Fashereau said. "All I hear is what I always hear. In this village I can find you ten trappers who each found the biggest damn gold mine in the world, and can't find their way back again. But I never heard about no Indians or Inuit with no bottle mine."

"Bottle mine?" Samantha said.

Faschereau laughed. "That the kind of mine that only exist in a bottle. And that the only kind of gold mine we got around here. Jacques, where are you? When he get here, you hear a story from a bottle better than any gold mine."

"That story not from no bottle!" The man who came frowning into the cabin was short and skinny, with a pointed nose and chin. He wore a long, bib apron that flapped below his knees, and carried a tureen in front of him. He put it on the table and glared at Faschereau. "I see what I see."

"Then tell them what you see," Faschereau said.

Jacques looked at D.L. and Samantha uncertainly. "I see a submarine." Faschereau doubled in laughter, and the cook straightened angrily. "It was last year, in October. We was heading toward Ivujivik, but the wind she was high, like often that time of year, and we can't go behind Isles Digges on the *détroit* - how you say it - the strait side. I was on deck with my pipe, because they all say it smell like a dead seal, when I see it. It was night, but the sheet lightning, she make everything bright every time she crash. Then, one time, I see it. First I think it the biggest bowhead whale in the world. Then I realize it a submarine. I start to yell for the rest of the crew, but the next flash come and all I can see is that tower thing sticking out of the water. And when she flash again, it all gone. So I don't say nothing to nobody."

"Until he get a case of beer in his belly," Faschereau roared. "Then he make up this story."

"I don't make up nothing. You believe me, don't you, Dr. Childe?"

"I believe you, Jacques," D.L. said.

Faschereau stared at him incredulously. "You believe that story? A submarine?"

"It happened before," D.L. said insistently. "When the Mid-Canada Line was being built, some Navy ships in the Bay picked up an unidentified submarine. They tracked it until it made it out through the Hudson Strait into the Atlantic. Everybody figured it was a Russian trying to check up on the construction. If it could happen once, it could happen again."

"Certainly," Samantha said. "After all, Hudson Bay is just about as big as a sea. There could easily be a submarine in it."

"About as big?" Faschereau said. "The Bay is over three hundred thousand square miles. That is a sea. Why, we got storms make a typhoon look like a spring breeze. One time, in October, before the ice close in, we sail out of Inoucdjouac. The wind, she begin to rise, and the waves go straight up and down."

Samantha settled back, and lost herself in listening to Faschereau's tales, and even a few of D.L.'s, each one topping the one before. She didn't even think of the story of D.L.'s fight until after the goodbyes had been said, and they were on the dock again. He had just turned from directing which of their things were to be taken to Mrs. Tyler's boarding house, when a pretty, little Indian girl went running by.

He froze, staring after her, his face twisting painfully. "Helen," he murmured, almost too low to be heard.

"Who's Helen?" Samantha asked.

D.L. flinched. "She was my wife." He looked at her bleakly. "She died, a long time ago."

She knew what Faschereau had meant by a wall, now. It was back.

V

D.L. was seated at the dining table reading a two-day-old Montreal newspaper when Mrs. Tyler, the landlady, bustled in like a ruffled hen. She was a short, stout woman, with a moderate mustache and a permanently pursed mouth. She planted herself across from him, hands clasped in front of her.

"Dr. Childe," she said to a spot somewhere over his head, "I realize that you are a man." She made it sound a dubious "I would never think to censure you for what you might do elsewhere. Under this roof is a different matter. Last night there were lascivious goings on."

"Were there?" Samantha asked in a shocked voice. She darted into the room to sit next to D.L., an innocent look on her face. "Why, whatever can you mean?"

The landlady swelled up like a frog, and scurried out without giving him a chance to speak. He turned his head to look Samantha in the eye. "Samantha, I realize she's a little old-fashioned, but—"

"She's very old-fashioned. And we're paying customers, not guests."

"But propriety—"

"Propriety can go to hell," she grated. For the first

47

time he realized that she was really angry. Before he could say anything, she went on. "*I* am not ashamed to have you in my bed, D.L. I'm not going to hide it. If you want somebody to sneak around corners with, find somebody else. I don't care who knows we're lovers. In fact—" She threw back her head and shouted, "D.L. Childe sleeps with Samantha Keenan!"

She whirled away from him, her back rigid. He got up and put his arms around her. "Samantha, I'm sorry. I didn't mean to make you angry."

"Well, you did. And I am." She kept her face turned away. "All this about taking separate rooms, and sneaking over in the night. You make me feel like a whore."

He felt as if he'd been hit in the pit of his stomach. "No," he managed at last. "Samantha, you have a reputation to protect—"

"Screw my reputation!" Her green eyes glittered at him. "It's mine, not yours. You let me worry about it. Damn you, D.L. Childe, you—"

"All right. All right. I'll have your things put in my room. I'll carry a big sign that says, 'Samantha Keenan is good in bed.'"

"Only good?" she laughed.

"Great. Terrific. Magnificent."

"I'm glad you realize it. I don't like being taken for granted."

"I realize that more every hour. Now, how would you like coffee aboard a Coast Guard icebreaker?"

"You mean the one that came in this morning? I saw it drop anchor. I'd love to, but how are you going to arrange it?"

He smiled. "It's already arranged. Jim Milne, the captain, is a friend of mine. He sent an invitation an hour ago. Get your coat, and I'll arrange a boat."

The Officer-of-the-Deck of the frigate-sized icebreaker CCGS *N.B. McLean* assigned a bosun to guide

D.L. and Samantha to the captain's cabin. He knocked on the door, announced, "Your visitors, sir," and departed with a nod for D.L. and an appreciative glance for Samantha.

Milne opened the door with a hearty, "Hello, D.L. It's good to—" He cut off short when he caught sight of Samantha.

He was a portly man of medium height, with a round nose and a fringe of graying hair. His whites had knife-edge creases. He blinked at Samantha several times as if he wasn't sure she was actually there. D.L. quickly made introductions.

"A reporter," Milne said blankly when he was done. He started suddenly, as if he'd just realized he was still standing in the door, and moved aside. "Come in. Come in."

D.L. had seen the cabin many times before, but Samantha studied the furnishings, spartan except for a leather chair and sofa, as if searching for a clue to the man.

"You don't seem to like having a reporter aboard, Captain Milne," she said.

"Not at all, Miss Keenan. I don't *dis*like reporters." She smiled. "But you have reservations."

"Some, Miss Keenan," he chuckled. "Some." His voice took on a patronizing tone. "You see, I've found that reporters often see things from a prepared position, and that position is seldom mine. Of course, I'm sure a lovely lady like yourself would never distort facts, but—"

D.L. spotted a dangerous light in Samantha's eyes, and stepped in as she opened her mouth. "Jim, you mentioned something to drink in that invitation."

"Of course, D.L. I have some good scotch. Haig and Haig. And of course there's coffee for the lady, or perhaps sherry."

"The lady," Samantha said sweetly, "will have scotch. A triple, on the rocks, no water."

Milne stared at her, then quietly took a bottle and three glasses from his liquor cabinet. In his world, ladies did *not* drink scotch. He handed Samantha her glass with the air of man close to a wild animal of uncertain temperament.

D.L. watched her warily, but she only smiled.

"What exactly does the Coast Guard do up here?" she asked. She seemed to be expressing real interest, D.L. thought with relief.

"Actually," Milne answered, "a touch of everything. We provide rescue service for marine accidents, prevent smuggling though there's not much of that up here, enforce the fisheries regulations, keep an eye on the native whale catches—only Inuit and Indians are allowed to hunt whales, and they under a quota—and run safety inspections on ships in this jurisdiction." His mouth tightened. "Those we're allowed to. Of course, a big part of our job is escorting ships, especially late in the season."

"The season?" she said.

"The ice season." He began to smile, appearing to enjoy displaying his knowledge to a woman. He almost seemed to have forgotten D.L. "You see, Hudson Bay ices heavily every winter. Lloyds of London, who cover most marine traffic into the Bay, set the season during which they will insure. It's quite short, really. It doesn't begin until July 23, when the last ice is clear in the northern approaches. The closing date varies according to port of departure. For instance, it's October 10 for the grain ships out of Churchill. Outside of those dates, the premiums skyrocket. Nobody is willing to pay them, even if they were willing to risk having a hull stove in." He scowled into his scotch. "Except for those damned Chinese, of course."

"You don't like the Chinese, captain?"

"No, ma'am, I do not. At least, not the communist kind. I had my first service in Korea against their sort, and I don't expect they've changed just because they're trading with us now."

"I didn't know any Chinese vessels came into the Bay," D.L. said. Milne blinked at him as if just remembering he was there.

"Actually, it's just one grainer. The *Pai Te Yün*, out of Canton."

"The *White Cloud*," D.L. murmured. Quickly, to cover, he added, "But what's so special about this grainer?"

"She comes in late, every year, and doesn't sail until after the season closes, not until every skipper with sense has his ship out of the Bay. And why do they come here at all?" His scowl returned, deeper, "Why not go to Vancouver? That's where all the other Chinese grain shipments are from. She has to come halfway around the world to get here. It's ridiculous."

"So you think they're up to something?"

"D.L., I'm positive of it. But I don't know what."

Samantha shrugged. "I don't see the problem. Why don't you board them to make one of those inspections you talked about? If they're carrying heroin instead of wheat, you should find out fast enough."

Milne hesitated, not looking at either of them. "No one," he said carefully, "boards the Chinese ships, here or in Vancouver, and that includes the *Pai Te Yün*. Not even the marine assayers get aboard her. She sails without insurance, ice or no."

"That *is* odd." D.L. frowned. "And you haven't found out anything about her? I mean, is there anything unusual you can connect to her? Drug traffic, like Samantha said. Have you heard anything about drug traffic through Churchill?"

"Not a whisper. The crew never leaves the ship in port. They handle the onboard part of loading themselves, so not even the longshoremen get on board. And—"

"Just a minute," Samantha broke in. "You keep talking as if you can't *get* on board the ship. Are you exaggerating, or is that the way it is?"

"Miss Keenan, I—," Milne cleared his throat. "I hope you haven't jumped to any conclusions because of anything I said. It-. It could be very prejudicial to my career if anything I said ended up in your magazine."

"I'm sure that wouldn't happen," D.L. said. "Would it, Samantha?" He looked at her in surprise when she didn't answer. She was frowning at the carpet, one toe tapping furiously. "Samantha? This *is* a friendly conversation. You wouldn't use anything you heard in a story, would you?" She kept on tapping. After a moment, her foot stopped. She sighed, and shook her head wordlessly. He looked at her doubtfully, then turned back to Milne. "You see, Jim, whatever you say is off the record. And I'm interested myself, now."

"I don't think—," Milne began stiffly. "Oh, hell," He took a stiff swallow of scotch. "There's a directive in my safe that came straight from Ottawa. It's classified. Confidential. You understand, I wouldn't tell anyone about this except you, D.L." He studiously avoided looking at Samantha. "It begins by stating that the People's Republic of China is a prime trading partner of Canada, and that nothing must be done to offend the Chinese or endanger the trade agreements. Then there's a list of things not to do. D.L., I can't board that grainer. That directive forbids boarding *any* Chinese ship for *any* reason without the express permission of the captain, approved by the Embassy in Ottawa. They could be growing opium poppies on deck, and I couldn't do a thing."

"Why," Samantha began excitedly, "that'd blow the lid off—." D.L. caught her eye, and she cut off. For a moment they battled silently, and then she slumped. "Damn you, D.L. Childe," she said quietly. "Listen, captain, couldn't you fake something? A distress signal, or something? If you got on board and found out they were smuggling heroin, or whatever, then Ottawa'd have to—."

"Miss Keenan! I don't make my country's policy, and I'm not required to like it. But I am required to obey the orders that implement it. In thirty years, I've never yet disobeyed an order, and I don't intend to start now."

Samantha's voice was beginning to heat. "But if you're sure they're up to something-."

"Hold it," D.L. broke in. "Let's don't let this get out of hand. It's all supposition, and it can't go any further than an argument, so I propose we drop it right here. No more Chinese. No more grainers. No more directives."

"That suits me," Milne muttered. "Let's get the chess board set up. We have time for a game or two before your evening clinic."

"Fine," D.L. agreed. "We can— Samantha, are you all right?"

She had shut her eyes. Now she opened them, and he was shocked to realize she was angrier with him than she had been that morning. "D.L.," she breathed, "you play chess."

"Yes. Samantha, I don't understand."

"You wouldn't. Even now, you wouldn't. I play chess, too, D.L. We've flown half way around Hudson Bay, and you never thought to ask if I played. I'll bet you've had a game at every stop we've made."

He put up his hands defensively. "From now on, Samantha, I'll play chess with you. And I'm sure that Jim will agree to let you play the winner of our game. Won't you, Jim?"

Milne seemed startled. "What? Oh, of course. Of course." He smiled tolerantly. "And I'm certain that Miss Keenan plays a very nice game, indeed. I'll get the board."

Samantha scowled at the captain's back as he went into the next compartment. "Nice game indeed," she mimicked. "I'd like to shove the queen up his—"

"Samantha," D.L. said quickly, "he's not a bad sort.

You just seem to get on each other's nerves."

"Oh, he doesn't matter. I don't give a damn about him one way or the other. But you, now. By the time I'm finished, you might be almost civilized. But-." Her voice turned serious, and she fixed him with a level gaze. "I'm just going to tell you this once, D.L. I have never, never in my life, turned aside from a story just because someone asked me to. And I don't care if they *were* sharing my bed. You have just seen the one and only. It'll never happen again, so don't expect it. If you're smuggling cocaine in that plane of yours, be prepared to see it on the cover of *Newsworld. Capisce*?"

"I understand," he said. And he resolved to ask his questions about gold where she couldn't hear, in the future.

September 22
2130 hours

In the *Sheng Li*'s control room there was no hint of the night that covered the polar ice above. Three hundred feet beneath the jagged bottom of the ice cap - four hundred beneath the surface - there was never any change. All hours were the same.

That unceasing sameness had infected some of the crew with boredom, but not the captain. Chu watched the mission plot with a feeling of pride. The tracks of the two submarines were diverging, *Cheng Fu* toward Spitsbergen, and *Sheng Li* beginning the curve that would take her down and around Greenland. They had come halfway across the world, halfway through the mission, and still they had not been detected, not in the slightest. It was a thing to be proud of. No one knew.

And no one would know, until it was too late.

September 27
0945 hours

D.L. taxied the Otter toward the concrete pier at In-

oucdjouac, cutting the motor to let it close the last distance on momentum. Two men on the pier, employees
of the Hudson Bay Company, rushed to fend off the
floats and tie off the mooring line. The small settlement,
with its tall red-and-white radio masts, lay slightly back
toward the river mouth.

"We're there," D.L. said. "Inoucdjouac." He pulled
their bags out of the cargo bundles and slid open the
door.

Samantha didn't look up from the magnetic chess set,
open on her knee. "I'm going to beat you yet, D.L. It
just takes practice."

He climbed out and carefully reached back in for the
crate containing the jade buffalo. "You almost did already. Remember? In Povungnituk?"

She scowled at him. "Almost, hell. I'm going to do it.
Why didn't you tell me we were down?"

"You did, I know, and I did."

Hastily she put away the board and got out her camera and tape recorder. "I'll bet I get some good interviews here. This *has* to be close enough for people to
have opinions about the dam. God, I'm tired of people
saying, 'I don't know. I just wish they'd build one here.'
It's frustrating as hell."

"Well, don't get your hopes up. Look, can you put off
the interviews for a while? There's somebody I want you
to meet." He hefted the crate under his arm. "And
something I want you to see."

"All right, D.L. An hour or so won't make any differ-
ence."

The frame house he took her to was small and unpainted. An empty dog run stood to one side of the
house. A canoe, upside down on a rack and covered
with canvas, lay on the other.

An old Inuit, his face deeply seamed and weathered,
but his black eyes bright, answered D.L.'s knock. When
he saw who it was, he smiled broadly. "Doctor Childe.

It is good to see you. And you bring a friend."

"It's good to see you also, Kopekoolik. My friend is Samantha Keenan, an American. And I also brought something to show you."

"Another strange animal?" Kopekoolik said eagerly. "Come in, please."

The front room of the house was sparsely furnished; a single electric light hung on a wire from the ceiling.

D.L. put the crate on the table and pried off the top. Samantha watched curiously, the old Inuit with anticipation. When he set the buffalo in the center of the table, she gasped.

"Oh, D.L., it's beautiful. It's Oriental, isn't it?"

"Chinese," he said simply, and was relieved when she let it go at that.

Kopekoolik was running his fingers over the jade carving, murmuring to himself and nodding. "It lives. It lives. The man who carved this talked to the stone. I do not know this animal, like many of the animals you bring, Dr. Childe, but it is what the stone wanted to be."

Samantha cocked her head. "He talked to the stone, Kopekoolik? What do you mean?"

"Everything has life in it. Bone, wood, stone, everything. Before carving, you must talk to it, ask it what it wants to be. Sometimes it says, I want to be a stone, and you must put it away. It cannot be carved. But sometimes it will say, I want to be a fox. Then you work with it, and it becomes a fox, because it wants to be a fox."

"Do you carve?" she asked.

The old Inuit smiled. "I carve a little."

"Would you show her some of your carving?" D.L. asked.

Kopekoolik nodded, and knelt by a cabinet.

Samantha eyed D.L. curiously. She'd bought half a dozen pieces at the Eskimo Sculpture Cooperative.

The Inuit brought a box, covered with a scrap of caribou hide, to the table. He took out a piece wrapped in sealskin. Slowly he let the sealskin slip away to reveal a walrus. Samantha gasped, and D.L. smiled at the way her eyes lit up. The soapstone figure's head was tilted at just the angle of a wary old walrus listening for something suspicious on the pack ice. The blubbery folds of its skin, with the scars of a hundred battles, seemed ready to ripple with movement.

He removed another wrapped carving. The walrus was joined by a whalebone weasel, sleek and serpentine, poised on the brink of darting across the table. An otter came out, and a wolverine, and a fox. There were others, until the table was covered by a dozen pieces. The style was very different from the Ming buffalo, but in some fashion they seemed to go together very well.

"So lovely," Samantha breathed. "So lovely. I must have one. Kopekoolik, please say you'll let me."

D.L. had his wallet out before she finished speaking. He folded some bills and passed them to Kopekoolik. "Let me buy it for her. A gift."

"D.L.," Samantha said warningly.

The old man looked from Samantha to D.L. "She is your woman?"

D.L. paused, and looked at Samantha. Her green eyes regarded him expressionlessly. "She is my woman," he said slowly.

"Then this is too much." Kopekoolik handed back half the money. "Part of the price was in her face when she saw the walrus. Miss Keenan, you will choose the piece you want?"

She didn't hesitate. She picked up the walrus and cradled it. "This," she said, and gave D.L. a look he couldn't read.

They stayed to have tea and talk with the old man, but throughout the conversation he was aware of her, sitting with the walrus on her lap, stroking it idly with her fingers and watching him with inscrutable eyes.

As they walked toward the village afterwards, he decided to find out what she was thinking. "I hope I didn't make you mad by paying for the walrus. I know how you feel about being your own woman, but I did want to give you a present."

"You did." Her enigmatic smile was back. "Pretty soon you'll say, this is Samantha Keenan, my lover, without even flinching."

He laughed, but he had the feeling that that was just what she expected. "Why did you choose the walrus? I was sure you'd pick something sleek. The fox, or the weasel."

She gave him that inscrutable look again. "It reminds me of you. Strong and stubborn, wearing its scars with dignity. And a little bit blind. Whenever I look at it, even years from now, I'll think of you."

Samantha went off into the village to tape her interviews, and D.L. went to the National Health Service nurse's house to hold his clinic. After, he walked to the airfield, to the Arctic Wings, and got into conversation with the charter pilots over coffee. Bit by bit he steered the circle of men around the pot-bellied stove toward the rumour of an Inuit with gold.

"Sure, I remember that," Sy Frank said. With his handlebar mustache, his leather jacket, and his white silk scarf, he played the part of a bush pilot to the hilt. Actually, he was a cautious pilot who'd quit the pressure cooker of a large commercial airline to get rid of ulcers. "In fact, I was the one he came to."

"You mean he really had gold?" D.L. asked intently.

"Look, doc, it was like this. Maybe six, eight months ago, this Inuit comes in here wanting to charter a plane down to Montreal. He had this leather pouch he said was full of gold. Hell, D.L., you know there isn't any gold on the Bay. It had to be fool's gold."

"Did you look at it, Sy?"

"What was the point? Anyway, I told him it was probably just fool's gold, and I asked him, if it really was gold, where did he get it. He just stuffed the pouch back under his parka, mumbled something, and left. I hear he tried the same thing that afternoon at Austin Airways. Got the same result, too."

"I wish you'd checked that pouch," D.L. sighed. "Or at least found out his name."

"Hell, I did *that*. You know him. Simon Maktaq, from out on the Belcher Islands. That's one reason I'm sure it wasn't gold. The Belchers are the last place to find gold."

"Sure," D.L. said. His face was calm, but he was thinking furiously. There was iron pyrites, fool's gold, in the Belchers. Like almost everyone on the Bay, where every second man dreamed of a mineral strike of some kind, D.L. knew some geology. He knew, for instance, that sometimes gold *was* found with iron pyrites. And he didn't think Simon Maktaq was fool enough to mistake one for the other, or to try paying for a charter with pyrites.

He started as a hand rested on his shoulder. "Gentlemen," Samantha said, "do you mind if I borrow D.L. for a while?"

The pilots all stared at her, open-mouthed. Women who looked like her were rare above the tree line. Before they could say anything, though, she had D.L. out of his chair and walking out of the hangar. Outside, the sun was low, and the evening wind off the bay carried a chill that cut through cloth.

D.L. followed her brisk pace down the unpaved street. "What is it? Does somebody need a doctor?" He caught her arm and swung her around. "Samantha, what is this? You—"

"Tell me about the gold, D.L."

He managed to keep from pausing more than a second. "What gold?"

"Don't hand me that. I was there for five minutes before you knew it. I heard."

"Oh, that. Just a story about an Inuit with some fool's gold, Samantha. That's all." His voice trailed off as she shook her head.

"You asked Faschereau about it. You talked to Milne about it when you thought I wasn't listening." She smiled suddenly. "D.L., the man who taught me to play chess. Harry Andress, who interviewed some of the most influential men of the last thirty years. He said if he could play ten games of chess with a man, he'd know more about the way his mind worked than with ten years of personality profiles. I know you, now. You're cool and analytical. You only defend until you can get on the attack. You won't accept feints, and you can smell a bluff at a mile. D.L., there is no way you'd put that much energy into something as insubstantial as a rumour. There's something to it, or you believe there is. Now talk."

He took a deep breath. Her face had a determined set, and he couldn't let her start stirring things up. "If you promise that it won't get into your magazine—."

"No! You used that one already, D.L. Remember? I won't turn aside from a story just because we share a bed." He kept a level gaze on her. She returned it, almost fiercely. After a minute, she looked away. "Damn you. All right, D.L. I'll hold off. But that's all! I'll hold off, but if there's a story in this, it goes in. That's the deal, or I start digging on my own."

It looked like that was the best he was going to get. "All right," he said. And he told her about Simon Maktaq, and what an unlicensed gold mine could mean.

"But you still don't know if there's anything more than fool's gold," she said. "How do you intend to find out?"

"The Belcher Islands are our next stop. I'll ask Simon about it." He frowned. "Samantha, don't do anything to hurt these people." He wasn't sure what he could do, but he wasn't going to let her bring trouble to Simon or the Belcher Islands' Inuit.

VI

As the Otter swung to make its landing at Flaherty Island, the only one of the Belcher group with a protected anchorage, Samantha kept an eye out for anything that remotely resembled a mine. There wasn't anything. The island was largely barren, and the only thing to be seen was the small settlement on a harbor that was almost a lake. A long, narrow arm of land hooked around to enclose it, leaving only a small gap that provided passage for the large canvas canoes scattered about on the surface and drawn up on the shore.

Once down, D.L. taxied to a mooring buoy. Almost immediately a twenty-four foot long canoe appeared, the boatman making fast their line. "That's Simon," D.L. said as he began unstrapping their gear.

Samantha pressed her face to the window to study the man. He was almost six feet, extremely tall for an Inuit, she now knew. His face was weathered, but unlined. He could have been any age from twenty-five to fifty. When he saw her at the window, he flashed a smile.

D.L. slid open the door. "Hello, Simon. How've things been?"

"Fine, Dr. Childe." He shook D.L.'s hand warmly.

"No one is hurt, or even sick. But I think they will all want to see you anyway."

"I expect so, Simon. Samantha, this is Simon Maktaq. I've told you about him. Simon, this is Samantha Keenan, an American reporter."

"I am pleased to meet you," Simon said. "I hope you have a pleasant stay here."

"Thank you, Simon," she said with a smile. "I hope so, too."

As Simon began stowing the bundles that D.L. passed to him in the front of the boat, her smile disappeared. D.L. *had* told her a great deal about Simon during the flight. That he was a spokesman for the Belcher Islands' Inuit, but refused every year to accept election as headman of the village. That he was the best guide on the Bay, honest and dependable. That they had been friends for over fifteen years.

What he refused to believe was that he was too close to Simon to know how to question him about the gold. She decided to try one more time to convince him. "D.L., could we talk a minute?"

He barely glanced at her before shaking his head. "We've already talked about it, and I made my decision. Besides, there's no time." He climbed down into the boat and held out a hand for her.

She sighed angrily and took her place on the wooden seat without his aid. Simon twisted the throttle on the outboard motor, and the canoe curved away from the plane.

"Has anything new happened?" D.L. asked.

Simon shrugged. "There is never anything new here. Some men look for iron ore, and I hope they find it, but there is nothing new."

Samantha decided to step in before D.L. came out with a blunt question about gold. She was sure that was where he was headed. "Simon, do you mean you want them to find iron? Don't you realize mines will rip up your island, scar the land for generations?"

"It will mean jobs," he said quietly.

"But your way of life will be destroyed."

"We will keep what we wish to keep. Some things *will* go. Poverty will go. The shame of taking handouts from the government will go. What you call our way of life is halfway between our old way of life and the white man's way of life. The old way was hard. People often starved. There was even murder done for food. We do not want to go back, and we cannot stay as we are. We must keep the best of our ways and make a new life."

"I hope they find the ore, too," D.L. said. "But tell me. I've heard of some Inuit out here making a gold strike. That's even better than iron. Have you heard anything about it?"

Samantha suppressed an urge to kill him. Simon's face became a mask. "I do not know of any Inuit who have found gold," he said in a flat voice.

From then on, all the way to shore, he spoke only in monosyllables. Samantha kept getting glares from D.L. because she tried to get Simon to talk about the iron mine, but she could tell he was ready to ask flat out if Simon knew anything about gold himself. And if he did, Simon would close up for good.

The boat grounded on the pebbly shore, and Simon helped D.L. manhandle it above the highwater mark. He wouldn't look at either of them.

"Simon—" D.L. began.

"I am sorry, Doctor Childe," Simon said. "I must go now." He bobbed his head in her direction and hurried off down the beach, towering a head above the other Inuit gathering to meet D.L.

Samantha shook her head. "Damn it, D.L.—"

"Simon knows something," he said without looking at her. He began unloading their gear onto the beach. "I could have found out what if you hadn't kept breaking in."

"You could-! D.L., you need help to find out the time. I hope you realize you've probably scared him off for good."

"I know," he sighed. He leaned on his hands on the boat, and looked at her miserably. "There's no more doubt about a mine. He could go to jail, Samantha, and everybody else who's involved."

His concern touched something inside her. She tried to remind herself that this was to be treated as just another story, but she couldn't quite succeed. "You go ahead with your clinic. I'll find him. It won't be easy, now, but I'll lay you eight to five that whatever he knows, I'll find it out. You can name the stakes."

He gave her a grin that was almost his normal one. "I'll think of something."

"I just bet you will." She winked, and set off down the beach with her cassette recorder slung over her shoulder.

She walked the village's dirt streets between frame houses, indistinguishable from the streets and houses of any of the other villages she had visited, asking the Inuit villagers what they thought of the La Grande River dam. Most of them were more interested in whether iron would be found in the Belchers, and if the promised jobs would actually come. Normally that would have been enough to send her digging deeper. Now she asked her standard questions, and went on, always watching for Simon. His height should have made him stand out. Bit by bit, though, she realized that he was no longer in the village. He must have left as soon as he parted from them.

September 29
1000 hours
It was a gray, blustery morning, but D.L. thought neither about the chill nor Samantha's comforting hand on his shoulder as he trudged down to the beach. She'd taken back her earlier comments, said he hadn't really

been clumsy with his questions, but he knew differently. She'd been right the first time. He'd frightened Simon into leaving the village, something he'd never done during one of D.L.'s visits. It underscored the urgency. He had to find a way to help. But how? How?

Samantha's hand pressed his shoulder, and he looked up to find her smiling. Then he saw why. Simon was among the Inuit loading the freight canoe to take them out to the Otter. The tall guide looked at him, then climbed into the boat without speaking.

As soon as D.L. and Samantha were aboard, the other Inuit pushed the canoe far enough out to allow the outboard to be lowered. Simon opened the throttle, and the nose of the boat raised. His face was blank, but he kept tightening his lips as if something were troubling him.

D.L. remembered Samantha's words about tact. "Simon—"

Simon twisted the throttle. The canoe slowed to barely move through the chill gray water. "I—I did not tell you the truth, Dr. Childe."

D.L. felt Samantha stir on the seat next to him, but his attention was all on the guide. "Simon, I think you need help. And you know you can trust me."

"I do, Dr. Childe. I did not have to leave you yesterday. I was afraid to talk to you. I do know about gold." He reached under his parka and pulled out a leather pouch. "I have some."

D.L. opened the drawstring and poured nuggets out in his hand. The first sight of the dully gleaming chunks confirmed that it was real gold, soft, not hard like the fool's kind. But there was something wrong. It took a moment for him to realize what. The nuggets were pure gold, with no rock, as if they'd been panned rather than mined, but they were too rough. They had none of the smoothness that water wore onto gold.

"Where did you get these?" he asked.

"On Kidney Island, in the Sleepers. It was in Harding's Fjord. You remember, Dr. Childe? You were with Captain Faschereau when I guided the scientists he carried to the island into the fjord. They wanted to study the ancient Inuit graves."

"I remember. But the water's a hundred feet deep there, or near enough, and there's no beach in the fjord. Did you find a vein in the fjord wall?"

"No, Dr. Childe. No, it was not me. The gold was found by the other men, the men who look like Inuit, but are not."

"Men who look like Inuit?" D.L. shook his head and poured the nuggets back into the pouch. "Simon, *what* men?"

Samantha leaned close to him. "Let him tell it his own way," she said quietly.

Simon gave no sign that he'd heard her, but he began to speak. "Last winter, when the pack ice had formed, I went hunting. I went to the Sleeper Islands on my snowmobile. When I passed Kidney Island, I saw something moving. It turned around and around above the wall of Harding's Fjord. That was very strange. This thing had to be tall. The side of the fjord from which I looked is fifty feet high. From the south, from where I could see nothing, they are taller, but fifty feet is very high. I went across the island to see what could move that way fifty feet above the water. When I was closer, I could see it was a radar antenna, like on Captain Faschereau's boat. But this was on a submarine."

"A submarine!"

"Yes, Dr. Childe. A submarine. I saw a picture of one in a magazine one time." He heaved a sigh. "It was very strange, Dr. Childe. There were mounds and strips of white, like plastic, all over it. A man who did not look closely could think it was a rock ridge with snow on it."

"But you're certain it *was* a submarine," D.L. said insistently.

"I am. And there was a machine to make bubbles in the water, so no ice could form. Many men dove beneath the water with tanks of air, as you do. I did not know what they did, but I wanted to leave before they saw me. I turned, and there were men with guns behind me. They did not hurt me, but they took me to the submarine. The captain asked me many questions. Who was I? Where did I come from? What was I doing? When was I expected back at the village? Did anyone know where I had gone? Many questions. Then he talked with the other men in a strange language I never heard before. He told me they were mining gold on the bottom of the fjord, and they did not want anyone to know they were there because they did not want to be bothered. If I did not tell anyone, they would pay me gold to bring them fresh meat until they left. But only me. If I told anyone else, they would give nothing to anyone." He slumped, shamefaced. "I hunted for them, Dr. Childe. I took the gold. It was wrong. I know it was wrong. They mined the gold without papers from the government. But we have little, here. The iron mine, the jobs, are far away. And my people could have no claim on gold so far from our village. I thought to have money, to see a city, perhaps. I have seen pictures of them, pictures of buildings that could hold my entire village a hundred times. I would like to see such a thing. But everywhere I took the gold, people asked where I got it. Always they asked questions. In the end, I returned to my house. I did wrong, and to no purpose. I have been right all these years not to let my people make me headman."

"That's foolish," D.L. said sharply. "Even headmen make mistakes. And if these people are mining illegally, you may get a reward for turning them in. But we have to make sure it *is* illegal."

"Simon," Samantha said, "you said these men looked like Inuit. How like Inuit?"

"Very much like," Simon replied. "Their skin was

brown like mine. Their hair was black, and straight, and they had no eyebrows. Their eyes were black, too, and shaped like Inuit eyes. Their language was not Inuit, though. It sounded like birds, like this." He broke into a sing-song chant.

D.L. felt his hackles rise. Looking at the epicanthic folds that gave Simon's eyes their almond shape, he was certain what the language was. It couldn't be, but it was Chinese. He would have sworn to it.

"Orientals," Samantha said flatly.

D.L. nodded slowly, "Yes. I suppose—Simon, don't tell anybody else about this until—until I can find out more." Samantha looked at him strangely, but he wouldn't meet her eyes.

"I will do as you ask," Simon said.

The canoe scraped against one of the Otter's floats, and Simon cut the motor. D.L. helped Samantha into the plane without noticing the intent way she was studying him. His mind was in turmoil. They couldn't be Chinese. They couldn't be. The entire idea of a submarine full of Chinese in Hudson Bay was ludicrous. But there *had* been a submarine. And the crew had probably been Oriental. He didn't think Simon would lie about what he'd seen. And if they *were* Chinese? After so many years of trying to forget, how would he react if he came face to face with a Chinese again?

He bent to take a chest from Simon, and his hands trembled.

The Otter swept low over the breaker line marking the sand bar that kept ships of any size out of the Grande Baleine River and continued up the broad river valley past Poste-de-la-Baleine. After the villages she'd seen, Samantha was ready to call it a town, even if the largest building was an old RCAF hanger, now declared by a huge sign to be Nordic High School.

D.L. set the plane into the water, and began to taxi toward a dock. She looked at him and heaved an exasperated sigh. Since takeoff he'd answered her every attempt at conversation, about the submarine or anything else, with grunts, when he'd even noticed she was talking. Something was troubling him, something he'd put together that she hadn't. She intended to find out what.

D.L. chopped the throttle, and the plane coasted in to the dock. An Indian in the ubiquitous checked shirt, dungarees, and logger's boots, darted in to fend them off and grab the mooring line.

"Hello, doc," he called. "Welcome home. I got everything ready at the house."

"Fine, Willy." D.L. climbed out of his seat and went back to slide open the door. "Samantha, this is Willy Adan, guide, trapper, and general handyman. He takes care of my place while I'm gone. Willy, this is Samantha Keenan, an American journalist."

"Miss Keenan," the stocky Cree acknowledged. He began taking the bundles D.L. passed out to him, stacking them on the dock. "I brought the Jeep, doc. Should get everything in one trip."

"You go ahead and start carrying things to the Jeep, Willy. I'll finish unloading."

"Okay, doc. Say, you feeling okay? You sure don't look too good. Maybe I'll get my grandmother to whip up something." Without waiting for a reply, Willy started up the dock with a suitcase in each hand and a bundle under his arm. "His grandmother knows all the herbs around here," D.L. explained. "Sometimes I don't believe she thinks I know enough medicine to take care of myself."

"He likes you," she said. "And I think you like him."

"We've been friends a long time."

"How long?"

Instantly, she knew it was the wrong question at the wrong time. His eyes turned icy and bleak. "A long time," he said hollowly. "Since the army. Since Korea."

Shouldering a chest he walked away up the dock, his back rigid.

"Damn," she muttered to herself. He was erecting the wall again. Sooner or later, she knew, she was going to have to find out what was behind it.

When the Jeep swung to a halt on the gravel drive in front of D.L.'s house, Samantha gasped. Whatever she'd been expecting for a bush doctor's home, this wasn't it. The house sat on a hill overlooking the river, surrounded by a stand of spruce trees, a white, two-story Victorian house complete with porches and bay windows and turrets. Inside, she clapped her hands delightedly. It was the sort of place she should have known D.L. would have. The furniture was substantial, in dark wood and leather. Every room had a Persian rug and a large, stone fireplace.

It was his study, though, that came closest to what she'd thought his home would be like. And also gave her the biggest surprise. On either side of the fireplace was a gunrack. There were game heads on the walls - moose, mountain sheep, deer - and a bearskin on the floor. Chess sets were displayed in spaces on the bookshelves that stood on every wall. Another sat on a table before the fireplace, the pieces arranged in a problem. It was carved in animals of the Bay, and in the almost living pieces she was certain she could recognize Kopekoolik's touch.

Two glass-fronted cabinets caught her eye, and held it. The items there were very different from the other things in the room, but they seemed to fit, in some way. A seated bronze Buddha. A delicate, green porcelain bowl. Vases of the same material. Carvings of jade and ivory. They took her breath.

"D.L., I didn't realize," she breathed. "Even after I saw that buffalo, it never occurred to me that you collected Oriental art. This is beautiful. Did you start in Korea?"

"No." His voice was so sharp that she looked at him in surprise. "It was later."

Willy scuffed his feet in the door. "I brought in the bags, doc. You want me to put Miss Keenan's things in the front spare bedroom?"

"Yes, Willy. That'll be—"

She had stiffened, and knew that was the reason he'd stopped. Deliberately, she began to study the Buddha. It was time he made up his mind about their relationship, and he was going to have to do it on his own.

After a moment, D.L. said, "Put Ms Keenan's luggage in my room."

A whistle of indrawn breath through Willy's teeth cut off as abruptly as it began. His black eyes darted from D.L. to her. "Sure, doc. Sure." He started to say something else, then ducked his head and left instead.

She went to D.L. and kissed him lightly on the mouth. She couldn't hide her amusement at the look on his face, as if he were disconcerted by his own actions. "You're learning."

"I guess. It's not easy, changing years of habit." His forehead creased suddenly. "Oh, hell, Samantha. *You* know what's important here. If that really is a Chinese sub—"

She pounced on the word. "Chinese?"

"I—I thought I recognized Simon's imitation."

She recognized that as an opening to his past, but now that he was talking about the sub, she didn't want to let him get away from it. "The question, D.L., is, how reliable is Simon? I mean, could he be making this whole thing up for some reason?"

D.L. shook his head. "You saw how he felt about what you'd probably consider a white lie and a little evasion. And that's the closest I've ever known him to come to lying."

"But it's a crazy story. You do realize that, don't you?"

"I tell you, Simon couldn't make up a story like that if he wanted to. Where would the idea of a Chinese crew come from? If he did manage that, how could he find out what the language sounds like? Samantha, he knows everything there is to know about the Bay, but he's never left it in his life. As for the sub itself, remember Jacques Rideau, on the *Baie du Nord*, said he saw one last year, too. Crazy or not, I believe it."

She nodded, and gave a satisfied sigh. "Good, then. And for the record, I believe it, too."

"Then why-?"

"I needed a devil's advocate, and I had to be it, myself. If you came up with the same arguments in favor of it that I did—This may not be a cover story, but it should be worth a byline. Of course. I'll have to tape an interview with Simon." Her mouth tightened as he frowned and shook his head. "I warned you about this, D.L. I won't kill the story. God, this has everything. I just wish I could get pictures. Mysterious Chinese using a submarine to mine gold illegally in Hudson Bay."

"If it *is* illegal."

She laughed humorlessly. "Bad joke, D.L." His face didn't change its grim set. "My God, you're *not* joking. Be serious. Canada wouldn't allow another country to mine secretly in Canadian waters."

"I don't know what Ottawa would allow. Samantha, we have a strange situation in this country. There are people in our government whose main preoccupation is the fear that Canada will somehow become an appendage of the United States."

"You mean the idea that Canada may break up and become states if Quebec goes independent?"

"It certainly hasn't helped. Anyway, these people sometimes go to ridiculous lengths to get separation between our countries, especially regarding trade. You heard what Jim Milne said about not being allowed to board Chinese ships."

"But letting them start a mine-?"

"That's a bit much, all right. But if you were used to our government, you'd know it's *only* a bit."

She threw up her hands. "Christ, D.L. This thing doesn't make sense any way I look at it. Are you sure Simon's telling the truth?"

"That I'm sure of. As for the rest—" He shrugged. "The first thing to do is get in touch with Ottawa. Either they know about it and are trying to keep it secret, or else it'll come as a huge shock. Either way, they should get back to us in just a few days."

"And I'll bet you know who to contact, too."

"The Commissioner of Mines. Name is Spence, I believe. I can give the letter to the pilot on tomorrow morning's Nordair flight and have him drop it in the intra-government mail slot. It can be on the Commissioner's desk by tomorrow afternoon."

"Then write." She took him by the shoulders and turned him, pushing him toward the desk. "Write."

"All right," he laughed. "I just hope it turns out there's something you can use for a story."

She frowned behind his back, not answering. She was going to file a story. One way or another, she'd file a story.

VII

October 3
0440 hours

The engine room repeater rang bells for all stop, and the *Pai Te Yün*'s four propellers stilled. The grainer floated, motionless and all but invisible in the early morning dark, beneath a moonless sky three hundred eighty seven miles southwest of Coats and Mansel Islands. She was seventeen hours late reporting her presence in Hudson Bay to the Ice Information Office in Churchill.

Sonar, its presence unsuspected by anyone other than the builders and crew, listened to the waters of the Bay. Radar watched the sky and the surface, aided by twenty lookouts, half with powerful binoculars, half with Starlight Scopes, the night vision device developed by the United States Army. For the last, the Bay seemed bathed in misty green daylight.

Caption Lo's broad face wore a frown that was fast becoming permanent as he paced the bridge. Occasionally he raised his own binoculars to scan the darkness. He didn't like being late with the report. It could only create suspicion. The necessity had been created by the captain of the icebreaker *McLean*. The previous two years, when Captain Lo sent the report, the icebreaker had appeared within hours and shadowed the grainer halfway across the Bay. It had been decided that lodging a protest would only draw unwanted attention. This year, though, no chance could be taken of anyone seeing what was to be done.

"Captain." Lieutenant Teng, the wiry executive officer, paused defferentially. "Sir, sonar, radar, and visual watches report no contacts. The drop crews stand ready."

Lo nodded. "Very well, Teng. Commence the drop."

Teng saluted and turned to the intercom. "Commence drop."

Almost immediately, from aft, came the soft whine of hydraulic machinery. Lo stepped out on the wing bridge to watch. He could see little, but he knew the procedure by heart.

In the spaces between the grain holds, what appeared to be ordinary deck plates opened in hatches, eight of them, each stretching two-thirds the beam of the ship, alternating to port and starboard. Even as the hatches opened, lifts rose, locking into place with a muted clatter.

On each lift rested a cylinder, fifty-one feet long and ten feet in diameter. The cylinders appeared to be made of bundles of smaller, inflated tubes of some plastic material colored exactly like the murky waters below one hundred feet. On the entire ship only Captain Lo knew what was inside the cylinders. The crew were all naval regulars, though, none below petty officer, and they asked no questions.

The whine of hydraulics began again, and the lifts slid outward until their bases were level with the sides of the ship, then rose to near vertical. Releases clicked open. The eight cylinders dropped, raising thunderous geysers, and sank trailing phosphoresence. Before the splashes had completely subsided, the lifts were dropping again. In eighteen minutes the deck was once more unbroken except for the hatches of the grain holds.

Beneath the water, the cylinders sank rapidly, the buoyancy of the inflated tubes overcome by automatic flooding of chambers in the cylinder bases. At a depth of one hundred eighty feet a weight on a cable dropped from each cylinder. As each weight touched bottom, a simple sensor system locked the cable reel, stopped the flooding, and exploded a small charge in the weight, sending an anchor pin four feet into the bay floor. Eight cylinders danced slightly on short tethers in the murky current.

Eight red lights glowed on a panel on the bridge. Lo grunted with relief as the last came on. The cylinders had deployed as designed. "All ahead full, Teng."

Powerful diesels roared to life. The grainer resumed her course through the black water, throwing off a silver bow wave.

Lo himself picked up the phone to the radio room. "This is the Captain. Send the message."

```
TO:    ICE INFORMATION OFFICE
       CHURCHILL, ONTARIO
       COMMONWEALTH OF CANADA
FROM:  PAI TE YÜN
       CANTON
       PEOPLE'S REPUBLIC OF CHINA

       REPORTING ARRIVAL HUDSON BAY.
       DESTINATION: CHURCHILL GRAIN LOADING DOCKS.
       ESTIMATED TIME TO ARRIVAL: THIRTY-ONE HOURS.
       ESTIMATED DATE OF DEPARTURE: TWELVE OCTOBER.
```

One final sentence was sent in Chinese.

```
       WE TOAST THE FRIENDSHIP AND BROTHERHOOD OF
       OUR PEOPLES ON THIS PROPITIOUS DAY OF FATE.

                                       WHITE CLOUD
```

* * *

In the Churchill Ice Information Office, Sam Gerard, holding down the graveyard shift alone, yawned and took the yellow radiogram from the messenger. He read it and snorted. Thirty-one hours. Regulations said the report had to be made by forty-eight hours out. Somebody ought to fire a rocket at this captain.

Then the last line penetrated. Whatever it meant, it looked like Chinese. The way Ottawa was about the China trade, *he* wasn't about to be the one to fire rockets. Let somebody on the dayshift handle it.

He tossed the radiogram in the Pending Processing tray, put his feet up on the desk, and picked up his paperback book. In ten minutes he had forgotten all about the grainer *Pai Te Yün*.

Precisely one thousand miles north-northeast of the Denmark Strait, a float bearing an antenna disappeared beneath the surface. A cable drew it down two hundred feet until it mated with a niche in the hull of the *Cheng Fu*. The submarine dove deeper.

Commander Chu looked up from his chart of Hudson Bay as the executive officer tapped respectfully on the doorjamb. "What is it, Liang?"

"Message received, sir. Day of fate, White Cloud."

"Very good, Liang. Carry on." After the executive officer had gone, Chu permitted himself a smile before returning to the chart. All proceeded on schedule.

In the underground complex twenty-three miles west of Peking. the grainer's transmission was monitored. Ten minutes later a copy lay on Admiral Yü's desk. The Admiral merely glanced at it. It was expected. He opened the right-hand drawer of his desk and took out a phone.

"Notify all members of Implementation Group One. There will be a meeting immediately in the level twenty-seven conference room."

As Yü expected, he was the first member of the Implementation Group to arrive. Even so, he barely had time to lay down his cap before Chang, the slender Air Force General, walked in. The Admiral refrained from the slightest acknowledgement of his presence. He frowned at the polar projection map as if the study were of life and death importance. After a moment, Chang grunted and sat down at the conference table. The Admiral continued his study.

One by one the others arrived. General Lien, of the Army, stocky, with a flat nose and a scar acquired against the Americans in Korea. Yin, the personal representative of Premier Hua, unable to hide the slight pudginess that good living had given him since Mao's death. Kan, from the Central Committee of the Party Congress, with the shadowy, retiring air and cold eyes of the professional revolutionary.

Yü waited until their murmured conversations died. When feet began to shift and throats were cleared uncomfortably in the silence, he turned.

"The following message has now been received from the grain ship *White Cloud* and the ore carrier *New Moon*. Day of fate." The military men settled back with smiles and satisfied murmurs. The civilians remained rigidly erect in their chairs. "You do not seem pleased, Comrades."

Yin pursed his lips angrily. "You know my reasons. Despite the approval of your—operation, there are still questions, still doubts." Kan merely listened, his bland face, as usual, giving no sign of where he stood.

The Generals swiveled bullet eyes toward the civilians.

"Doubts?" Lien growled. "So late?"

"That is not good," Chang said.

Yin returned their gaze levelly. "Perhaps the thought of military adventure blinds you. I must see beyond such things. Failure in this will mean disaster for China."

"There will be no failure!" Yü snapped.

"All eventualities must be—"

"I said, no failure, Yin. Every detail has been planned, every eventuality considered." Yin opened his mouth, but Yü hurried on before he could speak. "There are now eight missiles in Hudson Bay, and another eight off Spitsbergen Island. In a few more days they will be in place on their launchers. On the day of fate, one will rise from the Canadian emplacement, and a one megaton warhead will destroy the Ballistic Missile Early Warning System base at Thule, Greenland. There will be no warning, as that base, and those at Clear, Alaska, and Fylindales Moor, England, look north across the polar cap. When the other seven missiles launch from Hudson Bay, there will be no way for the Americans to tell where they have actually come from. One of those will strike Cheyenne Mountain, beneath which is the headquarters of the North American Air Defense Command. It is too deep to be destroyed, but they cannot but be convinced that such was intended. Two warheads will be outside of Washington, D.C. The American government will be left largely intact, and aware that it is under nuclear attack. To drive home the point, the remaining missiles will destroy the cities of New York, Boston, Chicago, and Pittsburgh. Simultaneously, missiles will rise in the same manner from the waters of Novaya Zemlya. The Advanced Warning Station at Mys Zhelaniya will be destroyed. The Dalnova Deistviya Aviatsiya Command Center beneath Narodnaya Mountain will be struck. Warheads will strike outside of Moscow. Leningrad, Severodvinsk, Gorkiy, and Kazan will cease to exist. Both the Russians and the Americans will be in shock. Each will be able to conceive of only one origin for the attack it has suffered. Each will launch the entire weight of its nuclear arsenal —at the other. And China will resume her rightful place astride the world."

"Very impressive," Yin said. "However, Admiral, we have heard every word before. It is the success of the plan that is in question here."

General Chang shifted in his chair. "I, for one, have no doubts of the plan's success. But I *could* wish it were certain we would not have to deal with Europe when it is finished."

Yü smiled. "Believe me, General, we will not. Once the exchange of intercontinental ballistic missiles begins, American and Russian tactical nuclear weapons in Europe will quickly be used. Inevitably and inexorably the nuclear capabilities of the NATO nations will become engaged. No, in the world we face after the day of fate, the major nations confronting us will be Japan and Australia, and perhaps Brazil and South Africa. Hardly giants."

Chang nodded, but Yin leaped in angrily. "You are still presupposing success, Admiral. What if they do not retaliate immediately? What if they pause long enough to question why only eight warheads have struck?"

"Can you really believe they would, Yin? A Russian Premier who waited would be removed from power by a bullet. Even the Americans, with their strange rituals of leadership, would destroy a President who hesitated while his country was being struck by nuclear missiles. They will not stop to count the number. The Russians, certainly not. As for the Americans, what can they do once Russia has launched its strike except retaliate before they are destroyed?"

"But you still depend on them acting as you say they will."

"And you still question. This plan has been approved at the highest levels. Approved! The time for questioning is past."

"We are not your junior officers," Kan said quietly. After he had sat quietly for so long, the other men at the table jerked as they had forgotten he was there. "We are your equals on this council. We have the right of questioning, the duty of it if we feel there is need."

"Chairman Mao," Yü said in a deceptively mild voice, "said, 'Let ten thousand voices be heard. Let ten thousand blossoms grow.' " His voice hardened. "He also said, 'When decisions are made, let all men act as one.' The decisions have been made. The plan is underway. China is on her way to world dominance. There is no more time for questions."

"We do not seek hegemony," Yin said piously. "We seek only to spread the Marxist-Leninist revolution across the world."

Chang snorted, and Lien openly chuckled. Yü's ears drew back. He had never looked more like Genghis Khan. "But which revolution, Comrade Yin? I think I may ask that of a man who seems to build obstacles at every turn. Is it our revolution you wish furthered, or that of the Moscow revisionists?"

The room was suddenly charged with tension. The days of the Cultural Revolution and the hasty trials for ideological impurity were not so far in the past as to be forgotten. And being connected even slightly with the Moscow line was still a sentence to a reeducation camp, at best.

Yin wet his lips. "That is—that is ridiculous. My loyalty is not to be questioned."

"Neither is the plan. Not any longer." Before Yin could regain his balance, Yü added, "The purpose of this meeting was to inform the members of the Implementation Group of the completion of the first phase. That has been done. Therefore, the meeting is at an end." He picked up his cap and headed for the door.

"Admiral?" Kan pushed back his chair and rose. "Admiral!"

Yü sighed, and stopped without turning around. "What is it, comrade?"

"The recall signals, Admiral. The signals to terminate

the mission. You are the only one who knows them."
Kan hesitated. "In the unlikely event of some accident
befalling you—"

"As you say, an unlikely event. As for sharing the
signals with the group—" He turned enough to brush
Yin with his glance. "The more who know them, the
greater the chance of security being compromised. Or of
the signals being misused. That is the reason it was
agreed that I alone should have that knowledge. Do you
know of a reason to change that decision?"

He surpressed a smile. Kan's face was expressionless,
but his hands gripped the back of his chair. Yin licked
his lips anxiously. "Comrades," Yü said, and left the
conference room.

Lieutenant Kou, his aide, was waiting in the hall. "It
went well, sir?"

"It went well," he said shortly. He started toward the
nearest elevator, his aide at his heels. The corners of his
mouth lifted in a bare smile. It *had* gone well. The doub-
ters had failed. Now they had no time left to succeed.
There were only fourteen days left to the day of fate.

VIII

D.L.'s breath frosted in front of his face as he trotted through the Korean night toward the waiting DC-3. His parachute dug its straps into his shoulders and groin. The Thompson submachinegun swung heavily at his side. The boots of the rest of the squad slapped the tarmac loudly.

He was back in the nightmare. He knew it, but there was nothing he could do about it. He was a rider in the mind of the teenaged D.L. Childe. Sometimes it began after the wedding, when he told Helen he'd enlisted in the Canadian Army. Sometimes it began just before graduation from jump school in Canada, when his knowledge of Korean and Chinese got him assigned as an interpreter with Regimental Intelligence, 21st Light Infantry Regiment. This time he was past being called into Colonel Gatineau's office, past being told that Helen had volunteered to return to the village where she was born, outside Kaesong. In North Korea.

He used the single metal step to boost himself into the plane. Its olive-drab paint was chipped and peeling. The canvas benches running the length of the cabin were dirty and stained.

87

"Settle the men in, Sergeant Childe," Captain Gordon said. He fingered his close-clipped mustache and headed forward to talk to Lieutenant Kim, the compact Korean who was second-in-command, by the cannisters that carried most of their supplies.

Lance Corporal Willy Adan grinned as he made his way past. "A piece cake, Sergeant."

D.L. nodded, but checked the men to their seats without talking. Four Candians and four Koreans. Counting the officers and him, eleven men. The entire mission should never have been mounted.

He'd been stunned when Colonel Gatineau had told him about Helen. He stood in front of the Colonel's desk, trying to find words. Captain Gordon and Lieutenant Kim stood against the wall, watching him like cats.

"Sir," he managed at last, "why? Why Helen?"

"You have a right to ask," Gatineau said. "Your wife, and all that. But I can't tell you, of course, unless you're going along. There's a need for someone who speaks Chinese." He put his fingertips together and studied D.L. over them.

D.L. stiffened to attention. "Then I volunteer, sir."

"Of course, of course. Stand easy, Sergeant." He carefully shifted the paperweight on his desk two inches to the left. "There is a radar station somewhere in the vicinity of the village your wife was born in. It's causing us some very heavy losses. Photo-recon can't find it, so we can't bomb it. Your wife was recruited by Korean Military Intelligence because it was felt she could return home without exciting comment. She will be the team's contact in the village. There may be Chinese technicians there, hence you. I felt you should be given the chance to volunteer since your wife is involved." He glanced toward Gordon and Kim. "Some felt that relationship should disqualify you. Emotion instead of logic, you see."

"We're to find the radar station, then, sir?"

"No, Sergeant," the Colonel had said. "To destroy it."

Suddenly he realized the plane was in the air, but he didn't remember sitting down, or the takeoff, or-. The plane rattled like rocks in a can, and let in air at every seam. It was a chilling wind that turned the metal tube of the cabin into a freezer, but the air in the cabin still stank with a mixture of stale sweat, aviation gas, and fear.

The amber READY light over the door went on.

"Stand up," the Captain ordered.

Boots clattered on the floorplates as men stood. Some coughed, or cleared their throats, but no one spoke. D.L. held his static line in his hand.

"Hook up," Gordon said. He swung the cabin door open and latched it out of the way. The opening added a hollow roar to the noise of the plane.

D.L. followed the orders in a daze. He hooked his static line over the cable running overhead, gripping it till it left an imprint on his hand. There was a cold knot in his stomach.

"Check the man in front."

"Check the man behind."

Willy Adan gave him a thumbs up and a grin.

"Stand in the door."

Lieutenant Kim took his place in the opening, gripping the sides. D.L. moved up behind him. Captain Gordon, who would be the last man in the stick, stood beside the jump master, by the door.

Kim looked over his shoulder at him. "I understand," he shouted above the roar, "that you have Black Belts in Karate. Both Korean style and Chinese."

He tore his eyes away from the night rushing past. "Yes, sir."

"We must have a session some time."

The green light flashed on.

"Go," the jump master shouted.

Kim dove out the door, dropping from sight. D.L. took one step forward to take his place, and the next step into the dark. For an instant he was falling, then came the tug of the static line. Almost immediately the harness jerked hard into his armpits and groin, and he was swaying below the black canopy. Low cloud cover hid the moon and stars. He descended through total dark.

The drop had been from low altitude to avoid detection, little more than six hundred feet. Before he had warning or a chance to get ready, the ground came out of nowhere. The shock knocked the breath out of him, but he rolled from remembered training. Quickly he spilled the air from his chute and bundled it up. He knew he was on a hillside, in brush, more from the angle of the ground beneath his feet and what he felt than from the little he could see. He wondered if any of the others were close by. He wondered if that was even the right place. The clouds parted briefly, giving him a glimpse of thick brush, a few stunted trees, and a village in the valley below.

A rustle brought the Thompson into his hands.

"Sergeant?" came a hiss. Willy Adan scrambled out of the bushes. Mud streaked his face. He stared at D.L. and heaved a sigh of relief. "You don't know how good you look, Sergeant. The Captain's dead."

"Dead!"

"He broke his neck."

"But *I* am still alive." Lieutenant Kim appeared from the dark. The rest of the team followed him. "We will continue with the mission. Lance Corporal Adan will take the bazooka. Private Park, take the point."

They filed out of the hills toward the village, two dozen unlit, wooden huts beside a broad dirt road. By the bridge, a hundred yards beyond the village, was a barracks for the bridge guards. A lone sentry leaned against an abutment.

Not even the village dogs stirred as they made their way into the cluster of huts. Somewhere a door banged in the wind.

The point man stopped and knelt, his Thompson at the ready. Lieutenant Kim studied the house ahead and motioned D.L. forward. With its rough, weathered planks, the tiles missing from its roof, it was indistinguishable from any of the others.

"This is the house of her grandmother," Kim said. "You will go in first so she will know for certain who we are."

D.L. nodded, but a sense of forboding flooded him. The hut had an air of emptiness. He stopped short of the door. The feel was wrong. In a crouch, he went around the side of the house, through the chicken yard. There were no chickens. His hackles began to rise. He gripped the submachinegun tighter and carefully edged around the corner to the back of the house.

Helen was there. Shadows dappled her naked body, spread-eagled between pegs in the ground. The chopping block had been forced beneath the small of her back.

The Thompson fell from his hands. He stumbled forward, panting hoarsely. Suddenly he wanted to scream, but nothing would come out. Her beautiful face was a mask of dried blood from the gash that almost severed her head. Her long, black hair was matted with it. The ground below her head was black with it. He managed to turn away before he fell to his knees and vomited. The retching went on, and on, wracking him even after there was nothing left to come up. He rubbed at his mouth with a shaking hand.

Dimly he heard Lieutenant Kim. "At least she did not betray us. Otherwise they would have been waiting. It appears she was raped. Their usual way is to go by rank. Some women last thirty or forty men. Perhaps from that barracks-."

D.L. listened with mounting horror. She was dead, and Kim could look at her and talk of the mission, talk of what was done to her as if it were nothing. He surged to his feet, a scream of denial ripping from him. "Noooooo!"

Kim seemed to move in slow motion. The toe of D.L.'s jump boot drifted under his attempted block to bury itself in his middle. He stepped in as the Korean doubled. As precisely as in a dojo one hand gripped Kim's arm, the other his shoulder. The Lieutenant rose into the air, pivoted, and slammed against the side of the house. He fell in a crumpled heap at the base of the wall.

The others stared disbelievingly. Willy kept repeating, "Jesus, Jesus. Jesus." He darted to Kim's side. "Jesus, Sergeant. I think his arm's broke. He's alive, but— Jesus."

D.L. heard only vaguely. He picked up the Thompson and carefully wiped off the dust. He realized he was humming, and stopped abruptly. It was the song that had been on the radio when he proposed to Helen. He walked to the road and turned toward the bridge.

Willy followed him to the chicken yard fence. "Sergeant Childe?" he hissed. "Sergeant. Where you going? Oh, Jesus."

The sentry didn't hear him until he started across the bridge. The soldier straightened, peering at him uncertainly, but he kept his steady pace. "Who are you?" the sentry called. "What are you doing here? No one is allowed—"

"I have come to kill you," D.L. said in Korean.

The sentry froze for an instant, then tried frantically to raise his rifle. D.L. fired from the waist. Three .45 slugs smashed the soldier down. A light went on in the barracks, and a gabble of voices broke out.

D.L. took a grenade from his belt as he walked toward the barracks. He let the handle fly off as the door opened, and lofted the grenade through the opening. The explosion shattered most of the windows, and turned the voices to screams. He tossed in another, and followed the explosion through the door.

The long room was badly lit by flames licking at the wall by an overturned kerosene stove. The floor was a jumble of bunks and bleeding men. Some were on their feet, though. At his entrance they whirled from the rifle racks, guns in hand.

He pulled the trigger almost caressingly, and the group disintegrated, men being slammed into the wall or spun to the floor under a hail of bullets. He continued to fire short bursts at anything that moved until the bolt slammed forward on an empty chamber.

The fire had taken hold on the wall. its flickering light dimmed by thickening smoke. Somewhere a man groaned, but nothing moved. He replaced the empty magazine and stalked out. Behind him, the groaning man fell silent.

Willy led the rest of the men across the bridge as D.L. reached the front of the barracks. Two of the Koreans carried Kim on a makeshift litter. He was still unconscious. D.L. didn't even look at him. A pair of headlights was bouncing down a side road from the hills across from the barracks. He slung the Thompson and took the bazooka from Willy.

"Sergeant, we got to get out of here."

There was a rocket in the bazooka. He slipped the ignition wire over the stub and walked into the road. The headlights bounced closer.

Willy shook his head. "Oh, damn! Oh, damn!" He motioned furiously to the others. "Spread out! Spread out!"

D.L. watched the headlights coolly. He could hear excited shouting above the grating roar of the truck motor.

He shouldered the bozooka and waited. Closer. Closer.

The rocket lanced out on a tail of flame to explode between the headlights. Flame engulfed the cab, and the truck swerved off the road. Before it stopped moving, men were spilling out of the back. Before the first of them touched the ground, he was firing, and then the rest of the squad. The enemy soldiers fell like marionettes without strings, even as they leaped from the truck. And then there were no more. The fire reached the gas tank, and with a whomp, the truck became a beacon fire.

D.L. glanced at the dead as he started the way the truck had come. A part of his mind noted that two of them were Chinese, and remembered that that should be important, but he couldn't remember why. What he did know was that at the end of that road would be more like those in the truck, more like those who'd—He pushed away the thought of what had been done before he could begin screaming, and trudged on. The small corner of his mind that still had some pretense to reason realized that the squad was following. Why, he wondered. To order them back would have taken too much of his thoughts from the eager contemplation of what was ahead, so he let it pass.

At first it seemed like just a farm, though it had more buildings than any Korean farm he'd ever seen. The others spread out in a rush. He continued up the center of the road.

Suddenly a machine gun began to chatter from one of the outbuildings, chopping the road around him to dust. He turned, firing back, and heard his bullets ricochet off concrete beneath the wood. A rocket from Willy's bazooka whooshed past and exploded against the pillbox slit. The gun fell silent. Somewhere a bell whirred insistently.

D.L. ran toward what seemed to be the main farmhouse. More Korean soldiers came spilling out of other buildings, but the members of the squad put down a murderous fire that took them as soon as they appeared. Willy methodically sent bazooka shells into the buildings. Flames crackled in two of them.

As D.L. reached the main building, one of the rockets hit a corner of the barn. Slowly the wall and half the roof folded down to reveal a web of machinery topped by a large disc. He kicked open the door and went in firing. Two men running out of a tunnel at the back of the room went down, and he hurtled them without stopping.

In the back of his mind he knew this was the radar station, that the tunnel had to lead back into the hill behind the farm house to the control rooms. All he could think of was that he had found more of them.

He hunted through the passages, from chamber to chamber with Thompson and grenades. Men who opposed him died. Only those who fled survived to reach the surface and the rest of the raiding party.

And then he was in the control room, with its radar screens and banks of radios to vector planes in on targets. Two of the men who remained there lay dead. The third, a lanky Chinese with blood running down his face, laughed on the bitter edge of hysteria. "American?" he said in accented English. "I should have known she would not be alone. I should—"

"You," D.L. whispered. The man's eyes widened as he slowly raised the Thompson. He smiled as he pulled the trigger. The man was smashed back into the corner, turned into a bundle of bloody rags, jumping, jerking, twisting under the impacts.

D.L. sat up in bed screaming. "Helen!"

Samantha woke with a jerk. She looked at him, and wondered what kind of dream could affect him so. He was hunched over, breathing hard, slick with sweat. She touched him, and he jumped and stared at her wildly. "Are you all right, now?"

"Just a nightmare," he mumbled. Slowly his breathing calmed, and his voice firmed. "It happens sometimes, when I worry too much. Like about Spence." He tossed back the covers and stood up. "I might as well get up. I won't get to sleep again."

She piled pillows against the headboard and sat up, watching him towel and dress. "You'll get an answer, D.L. It hasn't been that long. Not for government."

"I'm not requisitioning paperclips. I'm asking whether or not they're letting Chinese submarines mine in Canadian waters. Either way—" He sat down to put on his logger's boots, then stopped to look at her. "Are you staying there? By the time we get to the airfield, the morning Nordair flight should be down. Maybe I can talk Bill Pepp into checking the mail bag."

She scrambled naked from the bed. "I'll be ready to go in a minute."

Gray dawn was just beginning to show, and the lights were still needed at the airfield. They created yellow pools around the Nordair 737 and the single, brick building that served as passenger terminal, freight terminal, and control tower all in one. The landing ramp still stood to the plane, but the few passengers had already disembarked. A squat electric cart stood under the plane while two men unloaded baggage onto it.

She bounced out of the Jeep before it came to a complete halt. Her boots beat an impatient tattoo into the terminal ahead of D.L.

Bill Pepp, a tall young man with protruding teeth, threw up his hands as soon as he saw her. "I know, I know. Is there any mail for Dr. Childe, especially from Ottawa?" He reached down behind the counter and held up a long envelope. "Just so happens there is. From Ottawa." She reached for it, and he twitched it back out of reach with a half-leer. "For Dr. Childe."

D.L.'s hand reached past her to snatch the letter.

"Then I'll take it," he growled. He took her arm in the
other hand and started to turn away, then stopped.
"And if she asks for my mail again, just give it to
her."

She had to suppress a laugh as Pepp's mouth fell
open.

D.L. led her to the wall and ripped open the envelope.
She could tell from his face it wasn't good news. He
grunted angrily and crumpled the letter. She took it
before he could toss it away, and smoothed it out.

Dear Dr. Childe;

Commissioner Spence has instructed me to reply to your letter of September 29. This department has no knowledge of any gold mining opera-
tions in Hudson Bay, nor of any such operation in
all of Canada that uses submarines.

There are, I understand, many rumors which
circulate on Hudson Bay. I fear that you have
fallen prey to such a rumour. When one has lived
in 'the Northcountry,' as it is termed, for some
time, one learns not to believe anything for which
one does not have positive proof.

I hope that we have been able to be of some aid
to you, and urge you to call on us again should
you require further information.

Sincerely,
Justin MacLean
Assistant to the Director
Public Information Office
Department of Mines and Tech-
nical Services

She folded it with a sigh. "He sounds like you're a
tourist reporting the Loch Ness Monster."

"It's just about as fantastic, isn't it?" He took the letter back and scanned it again. "Proof, is it? I'll give him
proof."

"What are you going to do?"

"I'll fly to the Belchers and pick up Simon. He can show me exactly where this was all going on. There ought to be something I can use for proof. If necessary, I'll dive for it."

"Diving alone isn't safe," she said. "I dive. I took my Coast Guard Recertification Test this past summer, and I've been to one hundred fifty feet in open water."

"Then you'll be my partner." He measured her with his eye. "I think I can borrow a wetsuit to fit you."

She had to smile. A few weeks before, he'd likely have refused to take her along because it was too dangerous for her. "A wetsuit is only one of our problems, D.L. The best proof we can bring back is pictures. Do you have an underwater camera?"

"It's being repaired. And there isn't one I can borrow, either."

He hesitated, and she said, "But-?"

"I might be able to rig your camera in a watertight box. It'll be safe enough, but I can't guarantee how good the pictures will be."

That camera had been a present from a very dear man, and had been with her a long time. She managed a smile. "Then rig away, and let me worry about the pictures. Now, how soon can we leave?"

He put an arm around her shoulders and started back to the Jeep. "I won't risk taking off from the river at night, but we can be ready by daylight. You'd better pack for a day or two, just in case."

His words barely impinged on her. This *was* going to be a big story. The pictures alone would be enough to make it. And the letter—she unobtrusively pushed it down in her coat pocket. It would make a nice touch that D.L. had tried to get through to the government and been rebuffed. It certainly couldn't do him any harm. He might even get a promotion out of it. In any case, she thought it was about time D.L. got a little public notice.

IX

Simon's canoe came out to meet D.L.'s Otter before he had a chance to moor, as usual. D.L. slid back the window and stuck out his head. "Tie us both to the buoy, Simon, and come aboard."

The Inuit hesitated before complying. When he did climb through the door, he stared at D.L. and Samantha, then sighed. "It is about the gold. You have come about the gold."

"Yes, Simon," D.L. said. "I want you to show me exactly where the submarine was. I want to dive and look at what they were doing."

"I will do it, Dr. Childe, but it may be dangerous to go there if the men have come back as they said."

"Back!" Samantha said. "They said they'd come back?"

"Yes, Miss Keenan. They said if I told no one, and returned in October of this year, they would give me twice as much gold to hunt for them. I will not go. I will not do wrong a second time."

"D.L.," Samantha said excitedly, "don't you see how much better this is? A picture of a submarine actually in the fjord is something everybody will *have* to accept."

"If they've come back yet," he cautioned. "Or if they ever mean to come back. They could just have been trying to keep Simon quiet longer. Simon, how soon can you be ready to go?"

"I am ready now, Dr. Childe."

"Then loosen the Otter's mooring. We'll take off immediately."

As soon as they were airborne, Samantha unfastened her seatbelt and went back to Simon. He was wary of talking into her tape recorder, but she soon had him chattering away about the sub while she took everything down on paper.

D.L. had another worry. Right after takeoff he climbed, and began scanning the water. He thought it was probably useless—submarines traveled under the water, not on top of it—but the thought of being caught in the fjord by the sub's arrival wouldn't leave.

Less than thirty minutes after leaving the Belchers, he began to descend toward the Sleepers, a barren string of rock poking above the surface. He made his first pass over the fjord at a thousand feet. On the second he came lower, and banked into a tight turn. The fjord was empty.

It was no more than seventy feet across for most of its length, and ran a thousand feet into the rough, ribbed rock of the island. The walls overhung at places, but everywhere they ran straight down to the water without so much as a ledge or the smallest beach. In every direction from the fjord the island spread in a plateau of sharp ridges.

"D.L.," Samantha said suddenly, "I can see something. There, above halfway up the fjord."

He made another pass, below a hundred feet and just above stall speed. There *was* something, but it was more an impression of something too angular to be natural than actually seeing anything. "We'll go down," he said.

He swept around and made a landing on the Bay, then

taxied in to the mouth of the fjord and dropped anchor. Immediately he and Samantha peeled off their outer clothing to reveal orange wetsuits. Pushing aside a tarp in the back of the plane he pulled out flippers, masks, weight belts and scuba tanks. Samantha began getting into hers.

"Simon," he said, "you'll have to keep a watch up here. For the sub, I mean." He was aware of Samantha looking at him, but he went on. "If you see anything that looks even like a sub, take the boathook and pound as hard as you can on one of the pontoons. We should be able to hear that under water."

"I will do it, Dr. Childe."

Hurriedly, D.L. finished getting into his gear. Samantha was already climbing out on the float with the plexiglass box that held her camera. He joined her, and they lowered themselves into the gray-green water. The cold ate into him right away. Even with the wetsuits they'd have a very limited time below. He rubbed spit inside his mask to prevent fogging and snugged it in place.

Samantha grinned impishly at him from below her mask. "If you really think that sub could come, we'd better hurry. Last one to the bottom is a rotten egg." She inserted her mouthpiece and flipped backwards to disappear beneath the water.

He followed at a slower pace, slightly irritated at her for taking the lead. She didn't have any idea what she was rushing into. But then, neither did he.

The clarity the water had shown from above disappeared beneath the surface. The water was relatively free of suspended mud, but the deeper they went, the less light there was. He could see her bubbles ahead, and barely make out the orange of her suit. She was treading water, working with the camera box. And then he saw what she was taking pictures of.

A spidery metal structure, open on one side like a U,

rose fifty feet from the bottom of the fjord. Beyond, he could make out a shape that might be another. He kicked closer to examine the first.

The girders had been drilled for lightness, but the structure seemed to have been stressed for great force. The base of it was a plain concrete slab with a low metal stand in the middle. Heavy cables ran from the stand to a large, featureless box beside the slab. At the slab the cables, ending in quick-fasteners, were bolted to a rack as if waiting to be attached to something. But there was nothing. No hoists, no lifts, no signs of how it could be used in mining at all.

He swam to the second tower, and when he saw another beyond that, continued down a row of them. Eight open towers built on concrete slabs, each with its heavy cables connected to nothing, each devoid of any sign of what they were meant for. One thing he was certain of. It was no mine.

He turned in the water as Samantha grabbed his shoulder. She pointed emphatically up, repeating the gesture. Without waiting for a reaction, she started rapidly for the surface and the plane. He stared after her wonderingly. Then it hit him. There must be something wrong with her gear. He swam frantically after her, but he couldn't close the distance.

When he reached the surface, she had already lifted her tanks into the plane and was scrambling in after them. "Simon, any sign of that sub?"

"No, Miss Keenan, the sea is—"

"D.L., get out of the water and get this thing in the air. Hurry!"

He pulled himself into the plane. "Samantha, what's going on? You scared the hell out of me. I thought—"

"*Please*, D.L. I realized what those things are. Missile launchers. Christ, you're the one who was worried about that sub showing up. Now will you get us out of here?"

Without another word he shed tanks and flippers and

went to the controls. He knew she wasn't the sort to shy at shadows, but she was afraid now. All during the takeoff she kept watch at the window, scanning the horizon, repeatedly tapping her fist against the cabin wall. Only when the Otter was in the air and headed away from the fjord did she slump in her seat and expel a long breath.

Simon looked at her curiously. "There is no gold mine?"

"There is not," she said. "There *are* missile launchers. Christ. I was thinking I had the story of the year, when all of a sudden I remembered D.L. talking about the sub coming back. I couldn't get it out of my head." She shivered. "Then I started thinking about it popping up while we were still down there."

"Are you sure, Samantha?" D.L. said. "I know that's no mine, but missile launchers?"

"I'm sure. When the US Navy began testing the Polaris missile, the submarine to carry it wasn't ready yet. They built underwater launch stands for their tests until the first sub was delivered. I've seen pictures of those stands, D.L. These are almost line-for-line copies. It just took me awhile to realize why they looked familiar."

D.L. was silent, pondering the implications. Chinese missile launchers in Canadian waters. The only possible reason was too horrifying to contemplate. And since the Chinese couldn't count on them remaining undiscovered for long, they must be meant for use soon. Abruptly he realized Samantha was still talking. "What?"

"I said, do you realize what this means? Nobody builds something like that for the fun of it. God. You talk about nuclear war, but you never really think it could happen." Suddenly she gave a short, mirthless laugh and patted the plexiglass camera box. "If this cockamamie jury-rig of yours works the way it's supposed to, the pictures in here are worth the cover story of the century, but by the time they get to press, there may not be a *Newsworld* to print them, or anyone to read it."

"Those pictures will stop it. They have to." He caught the edge in his own voice, and took a deep breath. "Simon, if you don't mind, I'm flying straight back to Poste-de-la-Baleine. You can stay at my house if you need a place."

"I have friends among the Inuit there," Simon said.

"Samantha, you and I are catching the afternoon Nordair flight out."

"I need time to develop these. I don't want to trust anyone else with them."

"You'll have to hurry, then. If we miss this flight, there's not another until the day after tomorrow, and by that time I want to be in Ottawa, ready to knock on doors. We'll stop it."

"D.L., promise me something."

He looked over his shoulder at her. Her green eyes were intent on him. "It depends. What is it?"

"If I know governments, they'll form a study committee and try to sit on this until they decide what to do. D.L., every minute is a minute somebody else could be getting a leak and filing my story. I want you to promise you'll help me get it out even if your government wants to stop it. What are you looking at me like that for?"

He tried to compose his face. To her, getting that story was as important as stopping a war. It didn't really surprise him. He'd known how much her work meant to her, how much getting back on top meant to her. If it hadn't, maybe she wouldn't be the person she was. And day by day he liked that person more.

"I promise," he said. "I'll help however I can."

She leaned forward to put a hand on his shoulder. "Thank you."

He put his hand on top of hers, and held it as he flew.

October 6
1650 hours

Thomas Eldon, a second assistant to the Deputy Minister of Justice, thumbed through the photographs again with pursed lips. "Yes," he said at last. "Yes, I suppose this *could* be what you say it is. Of course, it could be almost anything. It's rather blurry, you know."

Samantha saw D.L.'s brows drawing down, and stepped in before he could explode. "They were taken under very difficult conditions, Mr. Eldon. I've explained how we had to jury-rig the camera."

Eldon flashed her a quick, Civil Service smile. "Yes, of course. What I don't understand is why you and Dr. Childe should bring them to me. The Ministry of Justice is hardly the place for, for missile launchers."

"Because," D.L. growled before she could speak, "we've been to every Ministry we could think of, already."

"Yes, I heard," Eldon mused. "Oh, not about you, precisely. But I had heard that some, somebody had been making the rounds with some story about the Chinese."

"Story! Damn it, I'm talking about missile launchers. I've seen them. She's seen them. The pictures are on your desk."

"What Dr. Childe means," Samantha stepped in smoothly, is that we feel we've given you enough for you to take steps to verify it. Perhaps aerial photographs of Harding's Fjord."

"Miss Keenan, the Ministry of Defence is the proper place for that sort of thing." He took another folder from a desk drawer. "Now, Dr. Childe. When you made this appointment to talk about Chinese submarines," the professional smile flickered again, "I took the liberty, on discovering that you are a government employee, of requesting your personnel file. I see that you have refused five offers of promotion in the last six years."

"That file is supposed to be confidential. And what in hell does it have to do with this, anyway?"

"Well, Dr. Childe, it *is* rather odd. You've spent over fifteen years, ah, north of the treeline, as it's called."

She realized what Eldon was getting at before D.L. did, and felt her face flush with anger. She found herself on her feet. "I saw it, too, Eldon. Or are you suggesting *I've* been north of the treeline too long?"

The beaurocrat squared the folders on his desk fussily. "Not at all, Miss Keenan. But you *are* a reporter."

D.L. was on his feet before she could speak. He loomed over Eldon's desk. "I think you owe Miss Keenan an apology," he said coldly.

Eldon stared at him with his mouth open. "Why, ah, why, I didn't mean to suggest anything, of course." He edged back his cuff and darted a glance at his watch. "It's, ah, it's time for me to go. My wife will be waiting cocktails. I'll, ah, I'll take this under advisement. My secretary will show you out." He stuffed the folders under his arm and hurried out as if he thought D.L. was about to attack him.

Samantha leaned her hands on the desk. Frustration pressed in on her. Two days of this was more than anybody should have to put up with. And she didn't know what had gotten into her, blowing up like that when that fool attacked D.L.

"D.L.," she said, turning. He was gone.

Suddenly she realized that he was capable of going after Eldon physically. He'd been mad enough. She had to stop him.

The secretary was already gone, her typewriter covered. In the hall she saw him, striding rapidly, back rigid. She started to run. He disappeared through the glass front door before she could reach him. She ran through, ready to find him accosting Eldon on the broad steps that led to the street. He stood instead to one side with his shoulders hunched and his back to her. The evening sun silhouetted him.

"D.L.—."

"I messed that one up good, didn't I?" He barked a laugh. "Funny, when he suggested I was cabin-crazy, it hardly affected me. But when he as much as called you a liar—. I was ready to go over the desk at him."

"Don't you know yet I'm big enough to fight my own battles?" she said, but her tone took all the sting out of it. "Thank you, D.L."

He turned, and his face was bleak. "Three others took copies of the photographs. Maybe one of them will—."

"No, D.L. You might as well face it. They might have been polite, but they'll do the same as Eldon with the pictures. The trash basket or the nut-case file."

"Damn it, can't they see? The launchers are plain as day in those pictures."

"They're plain if you've seen the launchers. If not—those pictures could be a kid's erector set in a bath tub. That camera just wasn't made for underwater work." She took a deep breath and plunged ahead. "D.L., we're going to have to give up on your government."

"But—."

"If I get in touch with my magazine, this story could be in next Monday's issue. I have enough credence with the editor that he'll buy it, with you, and Simon, and the pictures."

He shook his head slowly. "Monday. Five days. It could be too long, Samantha. There's one more thing I can try, tomorrow morning at the Ministry of Defence."

"That was the first place we went. That Colonel wouldn't even keep copies of the pictures, remember?"

"There's somebody I met once." His eyes were sad and painful. "And maybe I can resurrect a dead man."

X

The *Sheng Li*'s propellor stopped, then reversed briefly. The submarine floated silent beneath the still water of a narrow bay behind Poluostrov Admiralteystva, a peninsula halfway up the island of Novaya Zemlya. Fore and aft her sleekness was marred by the cylinders she had retrieved south of Spitsberbergen, lashed two-by-two atop her hull.

Because of the Norwegian and Russian fishing fleets operating in the Barents Sea, the Soviets maintained an active fisheries patrol with Beriev flying boats out of Murmansk. And because of the flying boats, the *Sheng Li* could not risk surfacing. The missiles would be transferred by frogmen working underwater.

Lieutenant Shan and Lieutenant Hua led the black-suited frogmen out through the forward escape hatch. Each man carried a sea-scooter, both to shorten swimming time and to aid in towing the missiles to the launchers. Not even the officers had hydrophones, though. There was too much danger of the underwater transmissions being picked up.

Shan moved to the first cylinder, and ten of the divers left the group to join him. They swarmed around the cylinder, laboriously unbolting the straps that held it against the hull. The flotation chambers had been deflated to minimize problems for the submarine. Now a hose from a fitting in the hull was connected to each tube in turn. When just enough buoyancy had been attained to lift the cylinder clear of the hull, Hua led his first squad forward. Each man attached a strap from his sea-scooter to the cylinder. Twelve electric motors whirred to life, and the cylinder slowly moved off toward the northwest corner of the bay and the launchers, a shark surrounded by pilot fish.

Shan quickly led his men to the second missile. It was towed away, and then the last squad took the third. Speed had been drilled into all of them. The missiles had to be implanted and the submarine out of the bay as quickly as possible. Shan hurried his squad on to the fourth missile. It would be ready when the first squad of frogmen returned.

The bolts were removed, the straps unfastened, and the flotation tubes inflated. The missile-bearing cylinder lifted off the deck of the sub.

Shan looked around for the first squad. In the limited range of his vision, his own men were the only things moving. Still, if Hua was adhering to the schedule, his first team should be returning at that moment. Shan frowned. If there were delays, they would not be laid at his feet.

He assembled his men with hand signals and directed them in moving the cylinder twenty feet from the sub. It hung motionless where they left it. Shan studied it for a moment. There was no current to speak of in the bay. The container would remain there until the men came to take it to the launcher. All they would have to do would be tow it away. Any impediment to the schedule would be Hua's. He signaled his men to begin on the next cylinder.

Unseen by the working men, a stream of bubbles began to run along the groove between the two bottom-most tubes, and rise behind the cylinder. At first, the impulse was not enough to stir the massive container. Then, slowly, it began to move. Silently, picking up speed, it glided away, disappearing into the gloom toward the launchers.

The fifth cylinder was almost ready when Shan looked up to see if the first squad had come yet. His eyes almost started from his head. There was nothing but empty water before him. The other frogmen wouldn't have taken the container without reporting to him. In his mind was only one possibility. The missile had sunk.

For a moment he was torn over reporting to the captain. Sooner or later the facts would have to come out, but if he made recovery before that, it might serve as mitigation. Hastily he gathered his men and started down. He would search the bottom first.

At the launchers, the first missile was finally in place. Lieutenant Hua watched impatiently as his men rolled and strapped the deflated flotation tubes. The operation had taken longer than planned, even though a safety margin had been added to the time developed in practice.

The men were almost ready. He turned toward the submarine, and stopped in consternation. Something was moving out there in the grayness. At first he thought it was a whale. It came slowly closer, growing clearer. With mounting horror he recognized one of the missile cylinders.

He floated in frozen disbelief. How? How could it have gotten free? And then he realized it was heading straight for the launchers. Even at its slow speed, no more than seven or eight knots, it was massive enough to do damage. A launcher, or more than one, could be put out of action. Fuel tanks could rupture and explode, destroying all the missiles, drawing the Soviets down on the *Sheng Li.*

There was no time for him to communicate with the men. He turned his sea-scooter and raced for the huge cylinder, nudging the nose of the scooter against the side of it. The tiny electric motor strained to change the momentum of tons of missile.

Hua kept an eye on the launchers, and the men working there. They were just beginning to notice what was happening. They milled around uncertainly, then half a dozen peeled off toward him. He knew they wouldn't get there in time. There were only seconds left. But he was shifting the course. The launchers might be spared.

He measured the distance carefully. The nose of the cylinder was now pointed beyond the first launcher, and it was too close now to think it could change back. He cut the throttle and drifted back.

Freed of the sea-scooter's impetus, the cylinder swung back. He had just time to scream before it smashed him against the launcher. His body acted as a buffer between the cylinder and the quivering launch tower as the container slid on past and continued on its way. The missile glided toward the open sea, and Hua's body drifted slowly to the bottom trailing a red cloud.

A petty officer forced the men back to their work, and raced to report the disaster as fast as his sea-scooter would tow him.

Shan had given up the search of the bottom by the time the petty officer reached him. He watched the NCO's with a sense of frustration. There was no putting a good light on it now.

He swam to the escape hatch and reached inside for the special underwater phone. The mike fit against his throat, and the speaker went against the bone behind his ear. On both ends voices sounded hollow and unreal. He made his report tersely, omitting any mention of who should have been in control of the missile when it escaped. There was a long moment's silence on the other end.

"This is the captain," a new voice said. Shan didn't need the identification. Even with the distortion he recognized the captain's voice, and the cold anger it now carried. "I do not care, for the moment, how this happened. That is for later. For now, I will send out Lieutenant Pei to assume your duties. You will take one of Lieutenant Hua's squads and find the missile. Is that understood?"

"Yes, sir. Perfectly, sir."

"Then do it. Now."

At the first launcher, Shan formed the men he was taking in a line abreast, with himself in the center. He avoided looking as Hua's body was taken away, back to the *Sheng Li*. The thought did cross his mind that it might perhaps be easier to assign responsibility now. He swung his arm forward, and the line started on the trail of the missile.

Once out of the bay, Shan found more to worry about. The open-water currents depleted the sea-scooters' batteries faster than had the still water at the sub. And there was still the matter of towing the missile back. If it could be found. Those currents could have changed its course, carried it anywhere. It could be washing ashore on the island at that very moment. He became immersed in the terrified contemplation of the consequences of such a thing.

A clanging drew his attention. The man on the far left end of the line beat his knife against his sea-scooter casing and pointed. Shan followed the man's outflung hand, and momentary joy turned to near panic. It was the missile, two of the flotation tubes deflated, drifting. Above them.

The others followed him up, but he motioned them to

stay back while he cautiously poked his head out. There was not so much as a bird in sight, but otherwise, it could hardly have been worse. To the east lay gray dawn, already beginning to streak with red. And the cylinder was no more than five feet below the surface. He didn't know how it had happened. Perhaps a salinity layer or temperature inversion changing the water's buoyancy. Whatever the reason, with the arrival of daylight, it would be visible to any aircraft that flew over.

Hurriedly, he swam back down and opened the access hatch in the base that hid the flooding controls. The valve didn't want to turn. Suddenly, it spun, and the inrush of water began with a hollow gurgle. The base began to sink, pulling the cylinder to an upright position, but taking it to a safer depth. He motioned the others to attach their tethers to the cylinder. They began towing while it was still sinking.

In the bay, the other missiles were all in place. The other divers schooled around the cylinder as soon as Shan got it back. In a matter of minutes the last missile had slid from the cylinder to its launch tower, the flotation tubes were bundled, and the frogmen were swimming back to the sub.

Shan didn't like the way the others surrounded him. It made them seem too much like guards. As he took his turn cycling through the escape trunk, he decided it didn't matter if they were. After all, he *had* retrieved the errant missile. The captain couldn't be too hard on the man who had saved the plan.

At dead slow, the *Sheng Li* crept out of the bay and turned for deeper water.

Twenty minutes after the submarine left, a polar bear came to the southern edge of the bay and waded in. It had always taken the long way around the sea's short intrusion before, but this time it fled in a straight line from a helicopter of the Krestovaya Guba Institute of

Marine Biology. The helicopter, taking infrared photographs for a study of how the polar bear conserved body heat, followed closely enough for its prop blast to ruffle the water around the bar. The bear altered course, trying to get away. Just before it reached the shore, it swam directly over the missile launchers. Ashore, it lumbered into the hills without slackening its pace. The sun was getting high enough to interfere with infrared photography. The helicopter pilot shut off the automatic cameras and turned south for Smidovich and refueling.

October 7
1055 hours

D.L. paused outside. the unmarked, frosted-glass door, and touched the folder of photographs under his arm. He and Samantha had begun trying to locate that office before eight o'clock, but he was still reluctant to go in. Taking a deep breath, he held the door for her.

The large reception area held nine desks in a precise grid, with an army enlisted man behind each. A young corporal at the desk nearest the door looked up as they came in. "May I help you, sir? Ma'am?"

D.L. couldn't help noticing his flashes. The Princess Pat's. "I'd like to see Captain Beauprie, please."

"Do you have an appointment, sir? You see, the Captain's due at a meeting in just a few minutes."

"Can I borrow pen and paper?" He hesitated over the note, then wrote in bold strokes, 'May I see you as soon as possible? Daniel LeTellier Childe.' He handed it to the corporal. "Please take that in to him."

He watched the corporal on his way back to the offices in the rear. Trying to be unobtrusive, he thumbed open the note. Suddenly he whirled in his tracks. His voice rose to a squeak "*Lieutenant* Daniel LeTellier Childe? VC?" His eyes held a touch of awe.

D.L. sighed. "Yes. Would you take that on in, please?"

"Yes, sir. Of course, sir. Right away, sir." He disappeared through a door in the rear of the room.

The other enlisted men stared at them curiously, but none were from the 21st Regiment. They didn't recognize the name. The corporal popped in again, and headed for the coffee urn.

"He'll see you in a moment, sir."

As if the trip to the urn were a signal, the others joined him in a cluster. A low murmuring rose, and there were frequent curious glances at D.L. and Samantha.

"VC," Samantha said quietly. "That stands for Victoria Cross, doesn't it? Like the Congressional Medal of Honor."

"Yes."

"And that boy—. It was like he'd met a statue come down off a pedestal."

Suddenly, he was telling her all of it, in short, choppy sentences that seemed to roll out of their own volition. After so long, it was a relief to be *able* to talk about it. Helen. The mission. And the years of nightmares, remembering. He couldn't look at her while he told it.

She gently touched the side of his face when he was done. "D.L., I'm so sorry."

He shook his head. "There's more. And maybe worse. They gave me a battlefield commission, and I started volunteering for every mission or raid across the truce lines. It didn't matter what, as long as it put me close to them. They're what the VC was for. The war only lasted a few more months, and then they sent me to England, to receive my medal from the Queen. Before I left, I saw an intelligence report on the radar station raid. I found out why Helen was killed. The other side discovered she was married to a Canadian in Military Intelligence, and that made her a spy. She died because she was married to me."

"Oh, no."

"So I had to take part of the blame. Not all. They

killed her. I still don't know if I could come face to face
with a Chinese without wanting to kill him. But part of
the blame was mine."

She leaned against his shoulder. "Oh, D.L."

"Dr. Childe?" Captain Beauprie said. He crossed to
them with an outstretched hand and a smile. "Perhaps
you don't remember me, but I met you briefly on the
train to Churchill last month."

D.L. grasped the hand firmly. "I remember, Captain.
In fact, I'm here to impose on that meeting."

"Anything I can do is yours." Beauprie had been
looking curiously at Samantha. He smiled and said,
"I'm Donald Beauprie. Miss—?"

"Samantha Keenan," she smiled. "Ms."

"Ms Keenan. Dr. Childe, do you mind if we talk on
the way to the elevator? I'm due at a meeting in fifteen
minutes, and I want to give you every minute possible."

Thinking of the listening enlisted men, D.L. nodded.
"That may be best, Captain." He waited until they were
in the hall, with the door shut, before he handed the
folder of pictures to the Captain. Samantha gave him an
encouraging smile. "Go ahead and look at those.
They're the only *hard* evidence I have for something that
half a dozen Ministries, including this one, think is a
pipe dream."

Beauprie frowned and began flipping through the
folder. "What are they?"

"Missile launchers."

The captain missed a step. "Missile—? Dr. Childe, is
this some sort of joke?"

"Last year, an Inuit hunter was paid in gold to hunt
for some Orientals who had a submarine in Harding's
Fjord, in the Sleepers. He told me about it. I thought it
was an illegal gold mine. Ms Keenan and I flew out
there to get evidence, and took those pictures. She's the
one who recognized what they are."

Samantha nodded. "I've seen pictures of the first

Polaris missile test launchers, and these are the same."

They stopped at the elevators, and Beauprie pushed the UP button. He was still frowning over the pictures. "They really don't look like much of anything, you know. Ms Keenan, I'm afraid it's very easy to make mistakes on things like this. You see something that looks vaguely like something you think you remember seeing somewhere else, and—."

She opened her mouth, but D.L. jumped in first. "I was in Intelligence. I'm not likely to jump to wild conclusions."

"Um. Yes. Maybe—."

"I'm not asking you to take this on faith. Get someone to check it. One photo-recon plane is all it would take."

Beauprie tapped the folder against his palm. "I suppose I can show these to some men after the meeting." The elevator door hissed open, and he stepped in. "I can't promise anything, but I'll call you this afternoon. Where are you staying?"

"The Beaulieu."

Beauprie nodded and the elevator door slid shut.

D.L. lay on his back on the bed, studying the smooth plaster of the ceiling. Samantha stood at the window, staring at the park across the street. It had been three hours since they'd left the Ministry of Defence.

"You shouldn't have talked me out of calling New York," she said suddenly. "I shouldn't have let you talk me out of it."

"I just want you to wait. Give Beauprie a chance to start some government reaction before we spread it all over the American press."

"There isn't that much time left, D.L. I'll have to clear this through the senior editor, but after five o'clock there won't be anybody there but the cleaning women."

"One more hour, Samantha. Please?" Suddenly the

phone rang. He rolled over to snatch the receiver. "Yes?" She watched him intently, arms folded tightly beneath her breasts.

"Dr. Childe? This is Donald Beauprie."

"Yes, Captain Beauprie." He looked at Samantha, and she held up both hands with her fingers crossed. "What did they say?"

There was a pause at the other end. "I'm afraid they thought the whole idea was, ah, rather fantastic."

"Can't you even get them to check it? One recon plane. A training flight. Anything."

"I'm afraid not. You have to admit, it *does* sound fantastic."

"Beauprie, I know what's out there. I saw it."

"I'm sure you think you know what you saw, Dr. Childe, but it's just too incredible to be believed. Perhaps it *was* a mine of some sort."

"Damn it, it wasn't a mine, I tell you."

"Um, yes. Well. I'm sorry I couldn't help you more."

"Not as sorry as I am," D.L. murmured. He replaced the receiver and sighed. "Samantha, maybe you'd better make your call now."

She gave him a look he couldn't read and darted to the phone. "This is room 1240. I want to make a long distance call to New York City. Yes, I'll hold." She put her hand over the mouthpiece. "D.L., they aren't going to do *anything*?"

"Nothing."

"You almost had me believing Beauprie could— Hello? Yes. I want to place a call to Sal Campana, at *Newsworld* magazine, area code—."

He got up and walked to the window. People were walking in the park across the street, men and women holding hands, children playing with dogs and climbing on the iron fence. What would it look like if one of those missiles was aimed at Ottawa? Wherever they were aimed, there was nothing close to Poste-de-la-Baleine that could be a target, not for them, or for the others that would come. Once the missiles started, there *would* be others.

Samantha slammed down the phone. "He's not there. He left early for his Thursday night poker. His secretary says he's at a meeting, but Janie always did lie like a trooper for Sal."

"Then you can't get your story through until tomorrow?"

"Not a chance. I have to tell him myself. Somebody else might make a hash of it."

He began pulling their suitcases out of the closet. "Then you can call him from Poste-de-la-Baleine. We're leaving." Before it's too late, he added to himself.

XI

October 7
2200 hours

The ZIL limousine bearing Gregori Sholopov, Deputy First Secretary, motored through the gates of the dacha thirty-one kilometers west of Moscow and up the drive without slowing. The lone guard swung the gate shut behind it and picked up his telephone to report the car's arrival.

At the villa, the car pulled into the last garage on the end, and the door whirred down. As the door locked shut, the floor began to descend toward Defense Command Headquarters East, two kilometers below ground.

An Army captain was waiting as a guide for Sholopov when he got out of the car. The short, round politician frowned at the meagerness of the reception, but he kept his peace through the gray, concrete corridors until he reached the Watch Room. Two other civilians were already there, looking through the glass wall at the cavernous heart of the command center. Below them, military personnel wearing headsets took reports from all over the Soviet Union and registered the information on the huge, electronic map that covered the far wall.

Sholopov took a wide stance in the doorway. "Can one of you tell me why I must drive here in the night?"

Aleksandr Kuibyshev looked over his shoulder. A black patch covered the left eye lost at Stalingrad, in the Great Patriotic War. "So, you are here, too, Gregori Mikhailovitch. No, all I know is that the Premier himself instructed me to attend."

Nikolai Malinov, the gaunt Deputy Minister of Defense, tapped a long, bony finger on the glass wall. "*Something* is happening." Flashing symbols began to appear on the huge map, indicating aircraft crisscrossing coastal waters in the Baltic and the Black Sea, the Pacific, and even the Arctic regions from the Barents Sea to the Chukchi Sea. "The Ministry should have been notified before so many aircraft were committed to anything."

The door to the conference room behind them opened at that moment. "Only a handful are military aircraft," said Marshal Fëdor Archipenko. He was tall and stern, with close-cropped, iron-gray hair. "Most are fisheries aircraft, or from various research institutes, with their search patterns computer directed to avoid the appearance of any pattern. It would not be possible to so disguise a search by military aircraft alone. If you will come in, Comrades, I will tell you why we must search our own waters in so secretive a fashion."

A long table ran the length of the conference room. The far side was occupied by military men, their staffs seated behind them. Sholopov took his seat without looking at them. Kuibyshev and Malinov slowed as they entered, and frowned thoughtfully as they sat.

"If this meeting is important enough for staff presence," Sholopov said, "why were we not informed?"

Archipenko moved to the head of the table before answering. A rear-projection screen covered the wall behind him. "The Premier and the First Secretary have been apprised of the situation within the last half hour. It has only been in that time that we have been certain exactly what we face."

"And that is?"

"This was taken early this morning, just north of Poluostrov Admiralteystva on Novaya Zemlya, by a helicopter of the Krestovaya Guba Institute of Marine Biology." A strange pattern appeared on the screen behind him, like a picture where objects were only haloed patches of light and dark. "The central shape is the bear they were studying. The brighter circle above the bear is what we are interested in."

For a moment, no one spoke. Sholopov felt a chill he hadn't felt since facing German tanks as a boy. "You'd better tell us what it is," he said slowly.

"Better," Archipenko said, "I will show you, so you will be convinced quickly. These were taken this afternoon by a Naval Underwater Reconnaissance Platoon." Pictures began to flash across the screen, each remaining only seconds before being replaced by the next, wide-angled shots and close-ups of spidery towers, each containing a clearly recognizable missile. "There are eight of these missiles there. I should not have to say that they are not ours."

"*Sookin sin*," Kuibyshev breathed.

"Son of a bitch indeed," Sholopov echoed.

The pictures still changed behind the Marshal. "We must assume that there are other, similar installations along the coast. The Premier and the First Secretary agree that, for the moment, we cannot do anything that will draw attention to our discovery of these launchers. The Praesidum is being called into session tonight, and those military units which can be brought to alert status unobtrusively are now receiving their orders. The purpose of this meeting is make suggestions for further action."

"But whose are they" Malinov asked.

Air Force General Andrenin, his blocky body giving no hint that he had once been a fighter pilot, answered by reading from a clipboard. "The missiles are nine point five meters long and one point three meters in diameter. They weigh approximately fifteen thousand kilograms. Those are very close to the specifications for the American Polaris A-3. The external appearance is also very close."

"The Americans, then," Archipenko said. There was a ring of satisfaction to his voice.

"There is positive identification?" Sholopov asked.

The Marshal looked at him in surprise. "Who else could it be?"

Admiral Koltsov, directly across from Sholopov, rumbled a bass laugh and shook his massive head. "This operation would require nuclear submarines, comrade. Other than the Americans, only the French and British possess such, and they are more for national prestige than anything else. By sheer logic it must be the Americans."

"Perhaps," Sholopov said. Archipenko's jaw tightened. "Do not let your personal dislikes cloud your judgment, Marshal. I remember a report some years back that the Chinese had built two nuclear submarines." A ripple of laughter ran through the military men, from the most senior down. "You cannot say that they would not rejoice to have a nuclear pistol to our heads."

"If they could, comrade," Koltsov replied. "But technology cannot be conquered by throwing another million peasants at it, or by making your physicists plant rice. Those two submarines sit in harbor, and may sit there forever. They have continuous problems with the reactors. As for submarine-launched ballistic missiles—. They are ten years away, at least."

"I would like confirmation that these submarines could not have been used," Sholopov insisted. "It should be of little difficulty," he added as Archipenko opened his mouth.

"Small difficulty," the Marshal said sourly. "We have

a few deep-plant agents inside China, comrade, but for this—small difficulty—such a sleeper must be activated to penetrate the Naval Base at Lüta. It is probable his cover will be destroyed even if he is successful. No matter. Your confirmation will be obtained."

Kuibyshev's hand slammed down on the table like a gunshot. "You talk so calmly, as if this were one of your military exercises. You, too, Gregori. We stand in the shadow of destruction. It is time to stop talking, and act."

"Good," Archipenko said. "At last we get to the point. I have had this prepared to show what we face, and from just the one set of launchers we know of." A map of the Soviet Union appeared on the screen behind him. "The range was based on the American Polaris." He gave a slightly mocking look to Sholopov. "It seemed a good model at the time."

On the map, spreading south from Novaya Zemlya, a red blotch grew. And grew. Sholopov felt that old chill return as city after city was engulfed. Leningrad. Korov. Moscow itself. And still the blot spread, reaching the border in the south, creeping east till only a thin strip on the Pacific remained clear.

"*Bog*!" It was the first time Malinov had spoken. "We must do something. Something."

Sholopov looked at his old friend in surprise. It wasn't like him to call on the diety. He realized suddenly that the other man was thinner than he'd ever seen him before, and his hand was unsteady. He ought to see a doctor. "What would you suggest, Nikolai?" he asked gently.

"Bomb them! Blow them up before they can be launched against us!"

"No! No!" Koltsov looked shocked. "If the trigger of one were to be exploded accidentally—." He seemed to restrain himself from a ponderous shudder. "The other warheads might even detonate sympathetically. From the first information I have, they can be anything from one to ten megatons each. Eighty megatons would send a tidal wave through the Barents Sea. Worse, the prevailing winds would carry the fallout cloud through the heart of Russia."

"Nikolai is quite right, though," Sholopov said. "I presume there is *some* provision for neutralizing them."

Archipenko nodded. "Of course. General Andrenin?"

"This plan," the Air Force General said, "was largely developed by one of my staff." A colonel behind him shifted as if to rise, then sank back as he went on. "There are Mi-12 helicopters available on Novaya Zemlya. Their vertical lift capacity is twenty-five thousand kilograms, more than enough to lift a missile out of the water once its connections to the launch tower are broken. The missiles will be deposited on the deck of a freighter that has already been diverted to the region. Naval personnel have been flown to the freighter to direct building temporary platforms for the missiles. The ship should be in place, with the platforms ready, by tomorrow morning."

"Of course," Sholopov said, "there will be study of the missiles, to confirm their origin."

"Only on board the freighter," Andrenin replied. "It would not be wise to bring them ashore if, say, they could be command detonated. The plan calls for disposing of them as quickly as possible. A pair of Mi-12's will land on the deck of a second freighter, and the two ships will steam into the Norwegian Sea. The missiles will be dropped in two thousand meters of water."

Sholopov shook his head. "No. Not in the water."

Everyone turned to look at him. "Then where would you suggest?" Archipenko asked.

"We will, of course, go to the United Nations with this." Instinct made him suddenly study the uniformed men across the table. "At least, I trust none of you is contemplating war. Not at this point."

An ominous silence met him. "Not," the Marshal said quietly, "if we find all of the missiles. If we can ever be sure that we have found all of the missiles."

Sholopov managed a calm smile. "The Americans have always swayed before world opinion. Perhaps this time we can use that to force them to *tell* us where the other missiles are."

"How?"

"Instead of dropping the missiles in the sea, put them where we can show them to representatives of the UN Security Council. The ice pack. Put them on the polar ice pack. When we reveal them to a closed Security Council meeting, and threaten to reveal them to the rest of the world—"

Archipenko smiled grimly. "Yes. Yes, that sounds very good. To show the Americans for what they are. And of course, once we know where the missiles are, we can expose them to the world anyway."

Sholopov relaxed slightly. At least he wasn't talking war. "And the study of the missiles? On the pack ice, there would be plenty of time."

"Why not?" Archipenko said. "Now, Admiral—"

"And the penetration of Lüta?"

Archipenko sighed in exasperation. "Very well, comrade. I will waste an agent for you. Now, Admiral Koltsov—"

Sholopov leaned back in his chair, barely following the details of the plan. If the Americans *were* behind the missiles, it would be good to use their own plot against them. But his instincts still said it was possible for someone else to be forced to the surface.

October 8
0925 hours

Samantha sat in D.L.'s study with the phone pressed to her ear. "Yes," she told the operator for the tenth time, "I'm holding."

Willy tramped in, clapping his arms across his chest. "Getting cold. I think maybe the snow comes early this year." He stopped in the middle of the room and looked at her quizzically. "Miss Keenan, this thing still seems strange. If Dr. Childe didn't tell me, I don't think I'd believe it."

"You and everybody else," she muttered. "Where is D.L., anyway?"

"At the Great Whale Social Club. The *Baie du Nord* came in. He and Captain Faschereau went for a drink."

She grimaced. As charming as she found the rest of Post-de-la-Baleine, the Great Whale Social Club was a blot. Formerly a Royal Canadian Air Force officer's club, it still had the same cracked, leather sofas that had done duty in the Second World War. The worn pool table and the dart board definitely looked old enough to date from then. And Pete, the bartender, had nearly had a stroke when D.L. brought her into its all-male precincts.

"Your call is through," the operator said suddenly. "Go ahead, please."

She took a deep breath. "Hello, Sal? Sal? Operator, you said my call was through."

"Samantha? Samantha, what's going on? What is this person-to-person stuff?"

She could picture him, hunched at his desk, chewing the cigar his doctor wouldn't let him light. "Sal, I have a story. The story of the century."

"A story! Samantha, have you been drinking? You called me on some damned story? You forgot how you're supposed to file?"

"Sal. Your ulcers, Sal. Quiet down and listen, will you? I said the story of the century."

"Well, it'd better be the Canadians selling Hudson Bay to the Russians. I can't think of anything less that'd justify this. You realize I've got the budget meeting in thirty minutes?"

She rolled her eyes at the ceiling. "I'll make it fast, Sal. The Chinese have put missile launchers on the bottom of Hudson Bay. They used a submarine to build the launchers on the bottom of Hardings Fjord last year. An Inuit hunter—"

"Inuit hunter!" he exploded. "I take it back about drinking. You've been smoking some kind of Canadian hash."

"This is straight, Sal. I saw the launchers myself. They're—"

"Samantha? Just do your story on the dam. All right? Chinese submarines."

She was sure she could hear the phone slam all the way from New York. She glared at the phone, and started to dial the operator again. Instead, she hung up. She might be able to convince him later, but not now. Not until he'd had a chance to cool off.

"Willy," she said, "would you get the Jeep out? I want to go to D.L."

Sal Campana pushed the file of budget figures into his brief case, then stopped to glare at the phone. He was a jowly man, and his close cut hair didn't hide the fact that he was going bald on top. He took out a cigar and began savagely to masticate the end.

Samantha's story had been crazy. There wasn't any other word for it. Still, he'd never known her to try filing rumors. What he needed was somebody to check with. Somebody who knew Canada and the military. Those poker games in Georgetown last year. There'd been a Canadian Air Force Colonel there, assigned to the Pentagon.

He pushed the intercom button. "Janic, get me Lieutenant Colonel Stephen Brooke, at the Pentagon. He's a Canadian Air Force officer on liaison duty."

"Right away, Sal."

Campana settled back, chewing the end of his cigar to

rags. The more he thought, the more he became convinced the story was too crazy to be real. She had to be
drunk.

"Sal, I have Colonel Brooke on the line."

He picked up the phone reluctantly. "Colonel
Brooke? This is Sal Campana. From the poker games at
Harry Mael's place in Georgetown?"

"Yes, Sal. I remember When are you coming back
down so I can win some more of your money?"

"Not for a while, yet. Look, I have a favor to ask.
We've gotten a rumor from one of our people in Canada, and I want to check it without going through six
miles of red tape."

"So long as it's not classified, I don't see why not.
What is it?"

He hesitated, then spat it out. "The rumor says there's
been a Chinese submarine operating in Hudson Bay."
It took a moment for him to realize the sound he heard
from the other end was laughter. His face flushed, and
he jerked out his chewed-up cigar and hurled it into the
trash basket.

"Certainly, Sal," Brooke laughed. "And we have
Martian blimps in Montreal. Chinese submarines." He
went off in another gale of laughter.

"You're sure?"

"Oh, I'm sure, Sal. Believe me, I'm sure. Listen, when
are you coming down again?"

"I don't know. Soon, maybe. Look, I have to go. A
meeting." He managed to truncate the goodbyes and
hang up. His face was still burning. Damn Samantha!

When Samantha and Willy walked into the Great
Whale Social Club, D.L. and Faschereau had their
heads together at a table in the corner. Except for the
bartender, and three Inuit laughing over their beers, the
Club was otherwise empty.

Samantha sighed. The faded green walls did nothing

for her mood. "I need a drink before I give him the bad news," she muttered. Willy trailed after her toward the bar.

As they passed the table where the Inuit were seated, one of the dark, stocky men deliberately spat on the floor. She couldn't help staring at him. One thing she had learned was that Inuit were almost never rude. The swarthy man looked away and scraped back his chair. Muttering gutturally among themselves, the others rose and followed him out, casting dark-eyed stares over their shoulders at Willy and her.

"What was *that* all about?" she asked.

Willy shrugged. "Me. Some people don't like living in today."

"What's that supposed to mean?"

He shrugged again. "A couple hundred years ago, Cree and Inuit fought all the time, raiding, killing. The Inuit got pushed north, some of them out to the islands. Some people, on both sides, they just don't want to forget about it."

Abruptly, she realized that the bartender was looking at her sourly. "Pete, bring a double scotch and a— What'll you have, Willy? Beer? A double scotch and a beer to Dr. Childe's table. And two more of what they're having. Come on, Willy."

D.L. and Faschereau were bent over, D.L. scribbling on a scrap of paper. She recognized the outline of Harding's Fjord. The X's must represent the launchers.

"How you know these things not already on the launchers?" Faschereau asked.

"I don't. Maybe I'd better fly—" He saw her, and half rose. "Samantha. Sit down. Good news?"

"No." She dropped into a chair across from him. "Maybe after Sal cools down, I can try again."

He shook his head sadly. "Thanks for trying, Samantha. I hope you're right, but—" His voice trailed off.

Faschereau was still frowning at the sketch. "D.L., how they unload those things, those missiles? Where that sub anchor?"

D.L. tapped the drawing with one finger. "In there. That's where Simon saw it, and it's the safest place. With good camouflage, even a plane flying overhead might not spot it."

"Right on top of them launchers."

"Yes," D.L. said slowly. "Yes, it is. If only there was some way to keep it in there."

Faschereau nodded. "Something across the mouth of the fjord. Some kind of net."

"The propeller," Willy said suddenly. "You tangle a net in your propeller, you don't go no place."

"I'd imagine," D.L. mused, "submarine propellers are too big to be stopped by a net. You'd need chain. Heavy chain."

"Plenty anchor chain on the *Baie du Nord*," Faschereau said.

Suddenly the two men were looking at one another, unblinking. Her breath caught in her throat.

"It's crazy," D.L. said quietly.

Faschereau nodded. "By damn, ain't it."

She looked from one man to the other, unable to believe what she was hearing. They were going to do it. They were going to try to capture the submarine. *"You're* crazy. Both of you." Their heads jerked around in surprise. D.L. started to speak, but she cut him off. "You've seen too many John Wayne movies. This is real life. People on submarines have real guns that shoot real holes in you. Damn it, don't you realize you just can't do things like this?"

They still stared at her as if she were talking in a foreign language. Suddenly, she couldn't sit there any longer. She jumped up and headed for the door. The bartender, bringing the drinks, dodged out of her way and shouted after her. She didn't hear. She just wanted to get outside and walk until she cooled down.

D.L. caught her before she reached the door. He grabbed her by the shoulders and swung her around. His gray eyes blazed. She had angry words ready, but he didn't let her get started.

"Damn it, Samantha, what do you think this is? Real, you say. It's real, all right. It's real that millions of people are going *die* unless something's done. But nobody's going to do anything. Nobody."

"But— "

"That leaves us, Samantha. Us. We're elected. Do you think Martial and I *want* to play hero? But what else can we do?"

"You could wait. By tomorrow Sal will have cooled down—" It wasn't his cool gaze that cut her off. She was kidding herself.

"Tomorrow?" he asked quietly. "Or next week? Or next month? We can't wait. It might be too late already."

She heaved a sigh. "I know. It's just - strange as it may seem, D.L., I don't want you to get any more holes in that hide of yours."

"I don't either." Something in his voice made her look up. He was studying her face intently. "But whatever happens, you'll be safe here. There's plenty of food in my cellar, and the emergency generator in the shed out back. If it does all go wrong, we're far enough north-."

"Hold it, D.L. What are you talking about?"

"About you. I just want you to know you'll be safe at my house."

"And what makes you think I'm staying at your house? I'm going out there, too." He opened his mouth, and she added quickly, "If you say it's no place for a woman, I'll break your neck."

His worried frown didn't slip an inch. "I'm not sure it's a place for anyone. Look, Samantha, you don't know one end of a rifle from the other, and I've tasted your cooking. There's nothing for you to do out there." He cupped her face gently. "It's holes in *your* hide I'm worried about."

"I can do my job," she said quietly. "I'm a reporter, remember? I'm going, D.L. You have no right to stop me."

He looked at her without speaking, his face drawn with worry. Taking her hand, he led her back to the table.

Faschereau looked up from close talk with Willy as they sat down. "D.L., we got to get us some more men. Submarine got - what? - hundred men?" He studied their faces a moment, then jerked his head at her. "She don't talk you out of this? Somebody got to do it if the government won't."

"She's going along," D.L. said flatly.

Willy merely nodded, but Faschereau raised an eyebrow. "D.L., you think—"

"She's going."

Faschereau stopped, frowning at D.L. With a sigh, he nodded. "Okay. She go. But the men?"

D.L. spared only a glance for her, but she read the smile in his eyes. "We may need to stay two or three weeks before the sub comes. October is all we know. The only men who can spend that much time are the Cree and Inuit."

"You can get plenty Cree," Willy said.

"Good, then. I have a Cree clinic at 9:00 tomorrow morning, and an Inuit one at 1:00 in the afternoon. We'll recruit then."

Samantha settled down to listen as they planned, talking over supplies and fuel and a hundred things. She felt buoyant, and it was with a sense of surprise that she realized why. D.L. projected an image of solid surety, despite his worry. He almost had her convinced they could do it. Almost.

XII

October 9
0820 hours

The work had begun as soon as the first light appeared over the ice-covered mountain spine of Novaya Zemlya. Sholopov watched from the shore, bundled in a heavy coat and fur hat, as an Mi-12 helicopter, its two huge rotors straining, rose vertically above the water. Dripping cables stretched from the helicopter's underside to the water, and below. Then, with a splash like a small whale surfacing, the missile broke the surface and hung, swinging. The helicopter turned and whopped out toward the freighter offshore, where the first missile already lay. A second Mi-12 hovered into place and lowered its cables to the frogmen below.

Sholopov shifted his attention to the small boat near where the missile had been lifted. Frogmen lifted something into the boat, and it headed directly for the shore where he stood. Some of the black-clad men jumped out to ground the boat. One splashed to the rocky beach and saluted.

"Comrade Sholopov? Lieutenant Fedorenko, sir. My orders are to deliver these to you personally." The other frogmen were carrying foot-long sections of structural members up the beach.

Sholopov motioned for his Army escort to take the samples to the helicopter waiting on a small level patch behind the beach. "Did you see anything, Fedorenko, that might indicate who put these launchers here?"

"Sir?" the lieutenant said blankly.

Sholopov sighed. It was difficult to demand unquestioning obedience and then expect independent thought. He tried a new tack. "There were explosive charges? To destroy the launch platforms in case of tampering?"

"Yes, sir. We disconnected them, but that was why we were not allowed to attempt defusing the warheads. There might also be such devices *in* the missiles, perhaps attached to trigger mechanisms."

"Yes, yes. But the explosives, the detonators. There was some indication of where they came from?"

"They are common, sir," the lieutenant said stolidly. "Readily available throughout western Europe, and manufactured in the United States of America."

Sholopov nodded, his face a careful blank. He could not believe the Americans would use explosives so easily identifiable as their own. But would Archipenko see clearly enough through his hatred for the Americans to agree? "Very well, lieutenant. Carry on."

The helicopter was waiting for him, scattered snow patches being blown away by the rotor's downblast. The ten samples, each in a small wooden crate, were already aboard. As soon as he was in his seat, the helicopter lifted off.

Buffeted by crosswinds and downdrafts, it crossed the mountainous island to the civil airport at Matochkin Shar. The airport had been cordoned off by Naval Landing Force troops, and a twin-engine TU-26 supersonic bomber that had been converted to a transport stood on the main runway. The plane's engines whined to life as the helicopter touched down.

Sholopov and the samples transferred to the jet. It

roared down the runway as soon as the hatches were closed. Even as it left the ground, the pilot cut in his afterburners. Through a specially cleared air corridor, he sped south at two and a half times the speed of sound, heedless of the sonic boom sweeping the ground below. When he reached Moscow, he was directed, not to Sheremet'yevo or one of the other civil airports, but to Shchelkovo Air Force Base, northeast of the city.

A black ZIL limousine pulled up as Sholopov climbed down through the belly hatch. He brushed himself off and watched the samples carried to a truck that had followed the car, before he moved to get in. Marshal Archipenko was in the back seat.

"Get in, Gregori. The wind is too chilly to keep the door open."

He got in slowly. The car started forward immediately. "I did not expect to see you here. There has been no change of plan?"

There was a smile on Archipenko's face that didn't seem to belong there, as if something might break from the unaccustomed strain. He waved a hand ahead at the delta-winged TU-144 supersonic transport, the starting units being pulled away from the engines. "Not at all, Gregori. Your staff went aboard as soon as your flight was picked up visually. If you had not insisted on going to Novaya Zemlya personally, you might even have been in the air a few minutes sooner."

As the Marshal became more ebullient, Sholopov grew more uneasy. "I told the Committee why I wanted to see the actual site, and—Marshal Archipenko, I have the feeling there is something you are not telling me."

"Not at all, Comrade. Not at all. I know for a fact that you have heard the same information that I have. The explosives, Comrade. Is it not good of the Americans to be so generous with proof?" He began to laugh, a deep, bass rumble.

"Too generous to be true," Sholopov said dryly. "Have you ordered that agent to penetrate the Navy Base at Lüta yet?"

Archipenko's laughter cut off with a snort. "Yes, for all the good it will do. It will be days before we hear anything, if then. Security at Chinese military bases is tight."

"Perhaps satellite photographs—"

"Satellite—? The next scheduled *Glaza* pass over Lüta does not come for almost two weeks. Or are you suggesting a special launch to investigate your—hunch?"

"Even for *my* hunch I do not propose to spend twenty million rubles. The next Eye pass will be soon enough. But I want to know. Are those submarines still incapable of putting to sea? That information is vital, despite your, ah, evidence."

"If you want it, Comrade, you will have it." The car drew to a halt beside the supersonic transport, sitting like a pterodactyl at the end of the runway. Sholopov started to get out, but Archipenko put a hand on his arm. The Marshal's smile was gone, and his voice was deadly serious. "If you wish to stop this short of war, Gregori Mikhailovitch, press the Americans. Press them hard."

Ten minutes later the transport roared aloft.

October 9
1420 hours

D.L. paused to study the seventy Inuit arrayed in a semicircle facing his front steps. Their dark-eyed faces were expressionless. Faschereau and Willy, down by the gate with a clipboard to take the names of volunteers, looked as worried as he was over the lack of enthusiasm. Samantha stood to one side, frowning and chewing her lip.

"So you can see," he went on, "why I asked you to stay after the clinic. If these men are allowed to go on, it means death. Not just for the people in the cities that will be bombed, but for you." The same blank faces watched him. "There'll be no more fuel for snowmobiles and outboards, no more ammunition for rifles. No more food. No more medicine. No more clothes. You'll have to try going back to your grandfathers' way of life. Hunger and suffering and early death. The old people will starve. The children will sicken. There's only one way to stop it." Not one face changed so much as a wrinkle. He'd lost them. Or rather, he'd never had them. And most frustrating of all, he didn't know why. "Those who are willing to volunteer, please leave your names with Captain Martial Faschereau on the way out. Thank you all for listening."

Slowly, muttering among themselves, the group broke up and began to stream through the gate. Some of them looked at Faschereau, some even paused before going on at a grunt from another, but no one stopped to leave his name.

As the last one left, Samantha shook her head. "What happened, D.L.? You were better this afternoon than you were this morning, and the Cree lined up eager to volunteer."

"I don't know. I don't understand it."

Faschereau and Willy walked back from the gate, the French-Canadian cursing under his breath.

"We got one by damn big problem, D.L. Twenty-two Cree this morning, six in my crew, you, me, Willy. I don't think we going to do it with thirty-one."

Willy shook his head. "I don't understand it. The best hunters were here. And they weren't afraid."

"You live too long among the white men," Simon Maktaq said to Willy as he stepped around the corner of the building. "You are *kabloona* yourself, now."

"Hello, Simon," D.L. said. "What brings you to Poste-de-la-Baleine?"

"I came to tell you the submarine has not come yet.

But it must come soon. I heard you talk. You think to fight these men on the submarine?"

"Hey," Willy said, "what you mean I'm white? What are you talking about?"

Simon smiled, flashing strong white teeth. "You do not know why the Inuit would not go with you. You have grown apart from your people."

"Wait a minute," D.L. said. "You know, Simon? Why wouldn't they volunteer?"

He shrugged. "Always there have been bad feelings between the Cree and the Inuit - and you asked the Cree first."

D.L. stared, dumbfounded. Faschereau was just as surprised, but Willy nodded slowly.

"Simon," D.L. said, "I've been on the Bay a lot of years, and I never knew the bad feeling ran *that* deep. Don't they realize what's at stake?"

"You *kabloona* always talk as if everything must come from a reason. A fox will chew off his foot if he is caught in a trap, but I have seen many white men chew off a foot when there is no trap. How then can you insist on reasons?"

Faschereau snorted. "Reasons, no reasons, it not important. What is important is, we have thirty-one men to do what we need a hundred for."

"I know," D.L. sighed. "Martial, do you know where we can get some explosives?"

"I have some commercial dynamite on the *Baie du Nord*, bound for a construction site. They will not miss it. You have an idea?"

He shook his head ruefully. "Not really. I'm just trying to figure how to even the odds. Damn, we need more men."

"There are men out on the Belchers," Simon said. "Not so many as here, but I, at least, will go with you."

D.L. gripped the Inuit's shoulder. "Thank you, Simon. We need everyone. Martial, how soon can we be ready to go?"

"The Cree, they want Sunday to be with their families, just in case. Say day after tomorrow. Monday afternoon."

D.L. grimaced. Everything was taking so bloody long. But he couldn't ask them to forego what might be their last time with their families. "All right. I'll fly over Harding's Fjord tomorrow, to see if the sub's come. If it hasn't, we sail for the Belchers Monday afternoon. If it has—Well, in that case, God knows."

Faschereau nodded grimly. "I think I go see if I can hurry those supplies a little. Willy, Simon, you come with me?"

The three men left, but D.L. was too deep in his own thoughts to notice. If he could use that dynamite to mine the fjord—

"D.L.," Samantha said, "how are you going to handle the animosity between the Cree and the Inuit? I mean, cramped together on the *Baie du Nord*, then at the fjord for God knows how long, there's bound to be friction."

"I don't know. I suppose it has to be handled somehow, but I don't know. Here we are, trying to keep a dispute between the Cree and the Inuit from allowing World War III to start, and the rest of the world doesn't know there's any danger. Funny, isn't it?"

"No," she said shortly.

"No," he said after a moment, "I suppose it isn't."

XIII

TOP SECRET
URGENT
UNITED NATIONS SECURITY COUNCIL

RESTRICTED
Ambassador Level Only
Hand Delivered

S/1892
9 October/2130 hours
English
Original: French

Sir:

As President of the Security the honor to convene a meeting of the Security Council to be held at United Nations Headquarters, New York, at 10:00 A.M. (EST), Sunday, 10 October. This meeting is to be attended by Ambassadorial level personnel only. The matter to be examined is a situation which presents the gravest threat to the peace and security of the world.

In view of the extreme gravity of the situation, I must urgently request that, in spite of the short notice and the unusual day of meeting, all member nations attend. Additionally, I urge that the greatest care be used both in disseminating information to mission staff and in all contacts with home governments concerning the meeting.

Accept, sir the assurances of my highest consideration,

(Signed)   Jean-Paul Delcour
                President of the Security Council

87-31467

DISTRIBUTION:

Mr. Jean-Paul Delcour	—Kingdom of Belgium (President of the Security Council)
Mr. Roberto Dantas	—Argentine Republic
Mr. Stefan Nedela	—Czechoslovak Socialist Republic
Mr. Hassan Abboud	—Democratic Republic of the Sudan
Mr. Louis Brun	—French Republic
Mr. Yoshida Nagra	—Japan
Mr. Tz'u Wei Huang	—People's Republic of China
Madame Tobanda Marceau	—Republic of Guinea
Mr. Arthur Charan	—Republic of Guyana
Mr. V.J. Singh	—Republic of India
Mr. Hector Rios	—Republic of Panama
Mr. Mahmoud Rashid	—Somali Democratic Republic
Mr. Fedor Baranov	—Union of Soviet Socialist Republics
Sir Julian Crowell-Collins	—United Kingdom of Great Britain and Northern Ireland

Mr. Lawrence Johnson   —United States of America
(cc) —distr: 15
       file: 1

URGENT
TOP SECRET

October 10
1950 hours

There was a frown on Lawrence Johnson's face as he pushed through the double doors, inlaid with silver Viking swords, into the Norwegian Room. He'd tried a little discreet inquiry about the reason behind a meeting held when most ambassadors would normally be heading for the country or partying, but he hadn't been able to find a whisper. In the UN, where a man's private words were being hawked in the halls five minutes after they were spoken, that was unheard of. It worried him.

The Conference Officers at the small table just inside the door made respectful half-bows as the tall, slender American entered, but for once he went past without acknowledging them. He'd seen Tobanda Marceau and Yoshida Nagra at the foot of the horseshoe-shaped conference table. The white-haired black woman seemed to be lecturing as she leaned on her ever-present ebony walking stick. Nagra, stiff at best, listened dourly.

Madame Marceau brightened when she saw Johnson. "Ah, Lawrence," she called in lightly accented English. "Come, you must help me. Ambassador Nagra is convinced this meeting is truly serious."

"President Delcour's letter-," Nagra began gutturally.

She snorted a laugh. "President Delcour is an old woman, though I suppose it is not diplomatic to say so. What happens to men at the United Nations? You ignore wars, and magnify shadows into lions. You turn your backs on suffering, but if someone sneezes, it is a grave threat to world peace and security."

"Perhaps, Tobanda," Johnson said, "there *is* something this time to the shadows. Is it coincidence that the Russians sent a supersonic transport here yesterday, on less than twelve hours notice? And that wasn't a request, just an announcement that the plane was coming. And who were the passengers? They were whisked away to the Soviet mission before anyone could find out."

"I, too, listen to the six o'clock news, Lawrence. I know what you know."

"Ambassador Johnson is correct," Nagra said suddenly. "I also believe the Russians are involved in this. I have received instructions from my government to register a strong protest before the Security Council over harassment of my country's fishing vessels and freighters in the northern Sea of Japan by Soviet ships and aircraft. In the past thirty-six hours there have been several dozen incidents."

Thoughtfully, Johnson looked around the large room. Abboud of Sudan and Brun of France had already taken their places at the conference table. Sir Julian Crowell-Collins, graying and distinguished-appearing, gave him a friendly nod from the door. The others stood in a knot by the President's chair, at the apex of the table, querying Delcour. The diminutive Belgian fended them off with monosyllables and waves of his hands. Only the Russian was missing. And they had a habit of arriving late when they had a bomb to drop.

"I think I'd better see what Delcour can tell me," he said. "If you'll excuse me, Tobanda, Ambassador Nagra."

He started around the table confidently. He and his wife played bridge frequently with Jean-Paul and Anne Delcour. It wasn't a close friendship, but now that the meeting was about to begin, he thought he could rely on it to gain him a jump on learning why there was a meeting at all.

Delcour saw him coming, and the Belgian's eyes

widened. He pulled out a handkerchief and, mopping his face, turned to begin talking nervously with Rashid, the Somali Ambassador.

Johnson stopped in his tracks. Tobanda's evaluation of Delcour was correct in many ways. He especially disliked being associated in the slightest with anyone who was being shown in a bad light. What that meant in this case, he wasn't certain, but he wished he had time to send another message to the State Department. Something more than just a copy of the convening letter, this time.

Except for the President, a position that rotated monthly, the other members of the Council were seated alphabetically. Johnson had started toward his chair, at one end of the U, when there was a slight disturbance at the door.

A short, round man in an ill-fitting suit that branded him a Russian, wanted to enter. The Conference Officers quietly began explaining that the meeting was for ambassadorial personnel only, and cut off as the Russian flashed his credentials. Johnson didn't need the Conference Officers' polite bows to know the man would be admitted. After four years at the embassy in Moscow, he had no trouble recognizing Deputy First Secretary Gregori Sholopov.

Delcour didn't seem to be surprised at Sholopov as the Soviet representative. He took his place before the discussion at the door was finished, and rapped his gavel as soon as the Russian took his seat, two down from Johnson. "Gentlemen, Madame, I call this meeting of the United Nations Security Council to order."

Some of the delegates hadn't made it to their chairs, and more than one turned to stare as the staff personnel filed out of the room and firmly closed the door. Only a single Conference Officer and two stenographers, one each in French and English, the official languages, were left at the small table in the center space of the conference table.

"Mr. President," Johnson said before anyone else

could speak, "I believe that the presence of Deputy First
Secretary Sholopov as the representative of the Soviet
Union indicates a seriousness to this meeting beyond
what many of us expected. For that reason, I suggest
that this meeting be adjourned until we all have a chance
to communicate with our home governments."

Delcour glanced at Sholopov. "The seriousness of the
situation was made quite clear in the convening letter."

Johnson briefly considered demanding the question
be put to a vote, but a single glance around the table
decided him against it. The make-up of the Council was
wrong. There were too many Third World countries
present that would vote no just to demonstrate they
wouldn't blindly follow the US lead. It was a small
thing, but losing the vote could shift psychological
momentum against the United States. And he was convinced he was going to need every edge he could find.

"Mr. President," Charan said, holding up his earpiece
in a dark hand, "there seems to be some problem. I am
not receiving the simultaneous translation."

"Nor I," Rashid barked, and a chorus of others
joined in.

Delcour tapped his gavel rapidly. "Please. Please. Order, please." Slowly, a muttering quiet came. He
stretched his neck and tugged at his coat. "I have ordered the translation lines disconnected to preserve security. As everyone present is fluent in English, I propose that the meeting be conducted in that language. Of
course, translations of the transcripts will be provided.
If-" he had to raise his voice as the muttering increased-
"if necessary, the simultaneous translation will be resumed. I remind you, however, of the extreme
seriousness—"

"Mr. President," Rashid broke in angrily. He was a
spare man, in a severe, almost military, suit. "We hear
much of the seriousness of the matter at hand. What *is*
the matter at hand? Why has no agenda been dis-

tributed? I am aware of no major crisis in the world. Why must we meet on a weekend? A weekend, Mr. President."

"*Smert'za vorotani ne zhdet*," Sholopov intoned.

Johnson felt his hackles rise. Death keeps no calendar, the Russian had said. "Mr. President, this could all be straightened out by allowing whomever has brought this, ah, matter to the Council's attention to explain it to the rest of us." He wondered if he was imagining things, or had Sholopov shot him a short, speculative look.

There was no mistaking Delcour's relief at being offered a way off the hot spot. "Yes. Yes, of course." He banged the gavel sharply. "For the purpose of presenting the agenda item to the Council, the chair yields temporarily to the representative of the Union of Soviet Socialist Republics." He dropped back into his seat, mopping his face vigorously.

Sholopov rose ponderously, but at first he just stared at the table in front of him. He shifted his pad, his pen, his water glass, while quiet fell.

"Less than forty-eight hours ago," he began without looking up, "my country discovered, in the waters of Novaya Zemlya, missile launchers. I say discovered. Those missile launchers were not ours." Suddenly, he looked up, straight at Johnson. "We have every reason to believe they were erected by the United States of America."

There was deathly silence in the room. The delegates were used to confrontations between the superpowers, but this had the chill of a conflict they wanted no part of. Sholopov's voice echoed in the quiet.

"This provocation, which is but little short of an outright act of war, requires immediate redress. The peace-loving peoples of the Union of Soviet Socialist Republics demand the immediate removal of all such launchers from their coastal waters, reparations for their having been emplaced, and a public apology from the imperialist government of the United States."

He sank back into his chair looking as if the stunned silence were applause. Johnson studied him, wondering what he was trying. If it was to create a crisis, he was well on the way to it. He'd reached every delegate except Tz'u. Every one of them looked either sick or afraid. No, *including* Tz'u. The bland-faced Chinese was turning a pencil over and over in his hand, pushing it through his fingers first one way then the other against the table. For him, that was agitation.

Delcour finally rapped his gavel. He wet his lips. "The Council— The Council is now open to discussion of the charges laid before it by the Soviet Union."

Johnson spoke before anyone else could. "Mr. President, this ridiculous and totally unsupported charge is a blatant attempt by the Soviet Union to create an artificial crisis. If Deputy First Secretary Sholopov's government put as much effort into its own human rights as it—"

"Blatant?" Sholopov shouted. "Unsupported? I will give you support." He upended his briefcase over the table, cascading a pile of folders in front of him. "You," he called to the lone Conference Officer, "distribute these to the ambassadors. Even to Ambassador Johnson, though I do not doubt he may well have seen the subjects before."

Johnson ripped open the folder the Conference Officer laid in front of him, and spilled out two dozen photographs, all of the same thing. There was no mistaking the missile launchers, the missiles, the frogmen working around them. He was aware of Sir Julian Crowell-Collins shifting beside him.

"I say, Johnson, not to be offensive, but these, ah, these *are* a trick, aren't they?"

"Yes," Johnson snapped. He made an effort to moderate his tone. "Yes, Sir Julian. Of course they are."

"Of course."

Sholopov wasn't finished. "They were really very careless. The demolition charges to prevent tampering were their own. American. My government is ready to provide immediate entry to a party from the Security Council to examine these launchers. Additionally, we will provide transportation to the point on the Polar ice cap where we have deposited the missiles. You see, we offer proof, proof for your own eyes."

Johnson studied the delegates. Some were staring at him openly, and even Tobanda had a quizzical frown. In another five minutes Sholopov would have the Council convinced.

"Mr. President," he called. The table came alert for his words.

"The chair," Delcour said, "recognizes the ambassador from the United States of America."

Johnson was still casting around in his mind for exactly what to say as he rose. The explosives. "The Deputy First Secretary has said the explosives found on the launch towers were American. Is it likely that any country would build a missile launcher in another country's waters, and mark its ownership by using explosives made in the building country? Why, American explosives are available all over the world, to anyone. Even the Soviet Union buys them." Thoughtful frowns appeared at that, and suddenly he knew the way to go. He took a deep breath and went on with renewed vigor. "That there is a missile launcher where the Deputy First Secretary says it is, I do not doubt. No. It will be there for our representatives to see, and the missiles on the Polar ice. But who put them there? Who built the launchers? I put it to you. Which is likelier? That the United States in some way constructed them, undetected, in heavily patrolled Russian waters? Or that the Russians themselves built them? That they have these photographs because they put the missiles on the launchers, and then moved them to the Polar ice. That they have done all this for the purpose I first cited, to create an artificial crisis for their own ends."

The thoughtful frowns had turned to nods of agreement, but Sholopov only laughed. "You demand more proof? So. I have with me five sections of structural members from the launchers. Analyze them. Test them. See where the steel was made. The Council will no doubt find it was made in Pennsylvania. You will only confirm what our own analysis will show within the next few hours."

"The United States will want one of those samples," Johnson said. "The Rantelle Laboratories have one of the world's most sophisticated computer analysis systems. In forty-eight hours I'll be able to tell you if that steel was made in Rostov or in Magnitogorsk."

"Gentlemen." The single word from Tz'u caught everyone's attention. They had begun to think of the meeting as an argument between Russia and the United States, and the Chinese intervention seemed an intrusion. Johnson noted with surprise that Tz'u was sweating, despite the air conditioning. "The problem," Tz'u said, "is not simplified. Moscow will announce that the metal was manufactured by whomever they wish to embarrass. Washington will do the same."

Sholopov snorted. "You have a solution, I trust? Comrade?"

"I do. It is that neither the Soviet Union nor the United States be entrusted with the analysis."

"The Soviet Union," Sholopov growled, "has already begun its analysis, and it will not be stopped for anyone."

"And the United States," Johnson said, "demands the right to analyze a segment so that we may answer the charges brought against us."

Tzu's pencil snapped between his fingers. "In that case, may I suggest that this Council vote not to accept either the American or the Russian analysis as official.

Rather, we should send the samples to a laboratory in a neutral country. Switzerland, shall we say? It may take a week or ten days to receive a report, in contrast to the computerized marvels of the Americans and the Russians, but we will be certain that it is untainted with political bias." Tz'u looked from Johnson to Sholopov. He appeared to have regained his composure. "I believe if either the United States or the Soviet Union exercises their veto power in this instance, it may be taken as a sign of who fears an independent analysis."

"A proposal," Delcour said, "has been placed before the Council. That the Council accept only an independent analysis of the metal samples submitted by the Soviet Union. I will call for a show of hands. All those in favor." One by one the hands went up - Tobanda Marceau's and Crowell-Collins' last - until only Johnson and Sholopov had their hands down. Delcour took a deep breath. "All those opposed."

"The United States," Johnson said, "abstains."

Sholopov grunted. "The Soviet Union abstains."

A sigh rushed out of Delcour. "The proposal is adopted. The Conference Officer will see to arranging an analysis in a Swiss laboratory of all samples except the one to be turned over to the representative of the United States." Tz'u made a move as to protest, then reconsidered. "I believe that we will all now wish to communicate with our home governments. If there is no objection-" he looked around the table, and seeing none, brought down the gavel- "I declare this meeting recessed until ten o'clock tomorrow morning. The first order of business when the meeting reconvenes will be sending investigative teams to Novaya Zemlya and the missiles on the Polar ice."

The delegates began rising to leave before Delcour finished, each already thinking of the message he had to send to his home government. Johnson hurried to catch Tobanda before she could get to the door.

"Tobanda. Tobanda, wait."

The old woman turned, but for once her face seemed more sad than amused. "Yes, Lawrence?"

"Tobanda, I saw the way you looked at me. You don't really *believe* the United States has anything to do with this?"

She sighed tiredly. "Lawrence, you and the Russians do things, and we barely comprehend how or why. Space satellites. Men to the moon. Atomic bombs so numerous you speak in terms of thousands of warheads without blinking an eye."

"But this is against everything the United States stands for, everything we've ever said or done."

"Lawrence, please. I do not know if your government put the launchers there, or the Russians did. I do not think it matters, now. I have often thought the world would end because you or the Russians made a mistake. Now, I must tell my government that mistake has very possibly been made, by whomever, but they must be quiet about it for fear of bringing the end a day sooner. I am an old woman, Lawrence, and today I feel every year. You will forgive me, please."

She made her way out, leaning heavily on her stick. He started to follow, but the Conference Officer intercepted him with the papers for the metal sample to be delivered to the American Mission. The room had been emptying all along, and when he was done with the papers, he found that only Sholopov was left.

The Russian waited, grim faced, until the Conference Officer had gone before he spoke. His voice was strangely intent. "You maintain this thing is not of your country's doing."

"You know it isn't. You've done it yourselves, for your own purposes."

Sholopov seemed almost not to hear. His voice became half-pleading, half-demanding. "If you can prove your country's innocence, do it quickly. If it cannot be done quickly—" he broke off abruptly, and stalked out of the room.

Frowning thoughtfully, Johnson followed.

October 10
1540 hours

Stephen Brooke pulled his Ford station wagon into his reserved space in the Pentagon parking lot, the area marked FOREIGN OFFICERS (ASSIGNED/ATTACHED), with a sense of relief at making it through the Sunday afternoon Washington tourist traffic. There was also a sense of frustration. In thirty minutes, after he found the papers he needed from his office, he'd be right back in it.

He was a short, whippet of a man, with brown eyes and close-cropped brown hair. There was a bounce and energy to him that overwhelmed most people and swept them along.

He fastened his ID to his shirt pocket, before he reached the entrance. Even in civilian clothes that was usually all that was required, but a sentry stopped him just inside the bullet-proof glass doors of the side entrance he'd chosen. The sentry, a bereted Army sergeant wearing a sidearm, took his name and ID number from the badge on his shirt and punched them into a computer terminal.

"Some kind of new security check, sergeant?" Brooke asked.

"Yes, sir," the sergeant said uninformatively. "Sir, you're not scheduled to be here today. May I ask your reason for coming, and how long you intend to stay?"

"To pick up some papers from my desk," he answered slowly. "About thirty minutes."

The sentry punched more data into the terminal, and watched a display screen that Brooke couldn't see. "Sir, you're cleared for entry. You are authorized to use this exit, but only this exit, for the next forty-five minutes. After that you will be required to be recleared."

"Sergeant, what's going on here?"

"I wouldn't know, sir."

The sergeant's face was professionally blank. Even if he did know, there was no way on earth to get him to tell, and there was always the chance he really didn't know. With a scowl Brooke turned away.

He noted more men than usual for a Sunday as he made his way to his office, and his civilian clothes definitely got more glances than they ordinarily would. Something was up, but the trouble was finding out what.

He dug the file he needed out of the bottom drawer of his desk, but it didn't seem as important any more. For a few minutes he sat staring at the wall. There was a polar projection of the northern hemisphere on one wall, and a map of Canada on the wall opposite. By the door were two Canadian travel posters, one touting skiiing in Quebec, the other fishing in Ontario, both featuring girls who seemed to have other things on their minds.

Picking up the phone, he dialed quickly. "This is Lieutenant Colonel Brooke, Room 1253. Send Sergeant Kincaid to my office immediately." Then he hung up.

In five minutes the door opened, and an American Air Force Sergeant with protruding ears and a pointed nose and chin stuck his head through. "You wanted to see me, sir?"

"Yes, Kincaid. Come in and shut the door."

Kincaid pushed the door shut behind him, and immediately cast a leering grin at the posters. "I ever caught anything like that fishing, sir, I wouldn't ever come back."

Brooke suppressed a grin, not at the comment, but at the inevitability of it. It had been the posters that made him think of Kincaid. The man never saw them without making some sort of remark. "Kincaid, you never fished for anything but a tip on the ponies in your life."

Kincaid grinned. "You got me wrong, sir. I don't spend all my time playing the horses."

"No, you spend some of it betting football. But I didn't call you here to talk about betting."

"No, sir. I didn't figure you did."

"There's something going on here today. What?"

The sergeant's smile faded. "Sir, I don't think anybody without stars on their shoulders knows about that."

"Bullshit," Brooke snorted. "Kincaid, if three people in this antheap know something, then you do too. What's going on?"

For a minute Kincaid stared at the floor. Then he shrugged. "Okay, sir. But it didn't come from me, right, sir?"

"I heard it in the hall from a couple of generals."

Kincaid flashed the grin again. "Yes, sir. Well, sir, it seems that what's happened is, the Russians have built some missile launch towers underwater off Novaya Zemlya. Then they went to the UN - there was a secret meeting this morning - and said we built them. Us. The United States." He laughed and hitched a shoulder. "Can you figure it, sir? Thinking they could pull something like that? They sure went to a lot of trouble, though. I understand they even put some missiles out on the ice pack. Claimed they'd moved them from some of the launchers. Can you figure it?"

Brooke walked to the polar projection map and studied the area around Novaya Zemlya. "It's pretty heavily traveled around there. Russian and Norwegian fishing fleets in the Barents Sea. Ore ships between Murmansk and Spitsbergen. Why, they'd have had to be built by submarine."

"Submarine? Sir, the Russians didn't need no submarine to build in their own waters. And who else could it be? The Chinese?"

Brooke felt like he'd been hit with a hammer. He whirled toward the map of Canada so quickly, that Kincaid started back.

"Sir," the sergeant said worriedly, "is something the matter? You don't look so good."

"I'm all right, Kincaid." He traced the perimeter of Hudson Bay. "You can go now. And thank you."

He didn't even hear the sergeant go. His mind was whirling. It had to be coincidence. Just a chance juxtaposition of two words. Chinese. Submarines. The Chinese *were* the only other alternative to the Americans and the Russians as builders of the launchers off Novaya Zemlya. And if in Russian waters, why not in American, or Canadian. But that story was just a rumor. He had to be sure.

He snatched up the phone. "Operator, get me an outside line for a long distance call. This is a personal call, so keep a record of time and charges. I am Lieutenant Colonel Stephen Brooke."

"Yes, sir," came a woman's voice. "It will be a minute, sir." It was almost five minutes before she came on again. "You have an outside line, sir. Do you wish to dial direct?"

"No, I don't have the number. I want to make a person to person call to Mr. Salvatore Campana, at *Newsworld* magazine, in New York city."

"One moment, sir."

Abruptly he could hear the empty hiss of long distance, with dimly heard, unintelligible conversations in the background. Vaguely, he could make out the operator talking to information in New York, and then to someone else. Then she was back on to him.

"Sir, the party you are calling is not there. Will you speak to someone else?"

"No." Campana was the only one he could be sure wouldn't take him for a madman. "No, thank you. I'll try later."

As he hung up, he noticed the clock on the wall. If he wanted to meet his allotted time, he had to leave then. He gathered up the folder—what had ever been important about it?—and hurried out.

He made it to the exit with time to spare, but there was a wait while the same sentry, who acted as if he'd never seen Brooke before, checked with the computer. Instead of motioning him through, the sentry said, "Sir, would you mind waiting a few minutes? It seems there's some difficulty."

"What difficulty?"

"I don't really know, sir. If you'd wait over there?"

With a grimace, Brooke took a place against the wall, where everyone who passed stared, but even two men who knew him didn't speak. He wondered what sort of glitch in the computer had caused the delay. Unless it wasn't a glitch. Suppose that, somehow, Security had found out about his pumping of Kincaid. If that information was classified, and it almost certainly was, he was technically guilty of espionage. That would be a hell of a thing. Arrested as a spy for getting gossip from Kincaid. His mouth twisted in a wry smile.

The smile faded as a major in the blue beret and armband of Pentagon Security stopped in front of him. "Lieutenant Colonel Brooke? I'm Major Hopkins, of Pentagon Security. Would you mind answering a few questions?"

Brooke straightened slowly. He still wasn't as tall as the major. "That depends on what they are."

"Nothing difficult. Did you just attempt to make a telephone call to one Salvatore Campana, who is the editor of *Newsworld* magazine?"

Brooke felt a touch of relief, and puzzlement. "I did. Are you monitoring phone calls now?"

"For the time being, all calls into or out of the Pentagon. What was your purpose in calling a magazine at this particular time?"

Briefly he considered telling Hopkins exactly why he *had* called, but he still had nothing but the wildest sort of suspicion. "I wasn't calling the magazine. I was calling Sal Campana. Whenever he's in Washington, he sits in on a poker game I play in. I wanted to ask him down. He's a pigeon." He grinned suddenly. "If you want to check on the game, some of the others are Brigadier General Tip Simon, from Andrews Air Force Base, and Representative Bill Oakes of California."

"General Simon and Representative Oakes," Hopkins said matter-of-factly. "Thank you, Colonel Brooke. If there are any further questions, Security will be in touch."

Brooke watched the major go with angry amusement. The man had no sense of humor at all. Still, it would be better to make the rest of his calls to Campana from home. A paranoid chill ran through him as he remembered the literal way Hopkins had taken his offer to check out the game. Not from home. From a phone booth picked at random. With a foolish feel of playing junior G-man, he hurried out to his car and set out to find a phone booth.

XIV

Yü studied the map of the operation spread on his desk, as he often did of late in the early morning hours, or at night after all except those who had duty were gone. It wasn't that he was anxious. He traced the movements of the vessels, and watched the plan unfold like a flower.

Cheng Fu had deposited its missiles and should be at that moment coming to rest on the ocean bottom beneath the ice north of Ellesmere Island. A small party put ashore would be listening for the radioed message that all was complete, that it would once more be safe for a submarine to move without being attacked as soon as detected.

Sheng Li was in the Labrador Sea, making toward the Hudson Strait. It was there the time was tightest. The Admiral snorted. To think the problem was aggravated because the captain of one patrol vessel chose to bend his government's directives as far as possible. Still, the missiles *would* be emplaced. The submarine would make its way out of the Bay, up the Davis Strait, and negotiate the difficult passages through the Queen Elizabeth

161

Islands. In his mind's eye it was all a precise, mathematical pattern.

But there were other things to be done. With a sigh he folded the map and returned it to the safe behind his desk. It was not ordinary, that safe. Built in Japan, to open it required that a seventeen digit combination be punched into the panel on its face, and attempts to circumvent the proper combination would bring certain special features into play. It was there he kept his most important papers, such as the map of the plan. And the recall signal.

Taken from a quotation of Wan Tz'u, an obscure military philosopher of the T'ang dynasty, the recall signal fit his feelings perfectly.

> Death is to be preferred
> to defeat; momentary
> retreat to surrender.

But it would never be used.

There was a tap at the door, and without waiting for a command to enter, Lieutenant Kou burst into the room. "Admiral," he said breathlessly, "the Russians have discovered the launchers at Novaya Zemlya."

Yü suddenly had a ball of ice in his stomach, but he gave no outward sign. "You are certain of this?"

"Yes, sir, Admiral. Our Ambassador at the United Nations has reported that the Russians have presented the matter to a secret meeting of the Security Council. They accused the Americans of building them."

"The Americans." The icy ball began to melt. "And what did the Americans reply?"

"They accused the Russians of building the launchers themselves to create a crisis."

A brief smile flashed across Yü's face. "Excellent. Excellent." The Americans and the Russians were focused on each other even more intently than before. When the missiles fell on American cities now, there was no chance of anything other than instant retaliation. The plan was as sound as ever.

But would the others see it so? Those timid civilians were searching for a way to back out. "Kou, prepare a message over my signature, calling a meeting of Implementation Group One. Subject of meeting: progress of the plan, and the effect on it of events in Russia. When your enemy believes you are weak, Kou, it is time to attack."

"Yes, sir," Kou said blankly.

The Admiral sighed. "You may go, Kou."

In the hall, the subservient air fell away from Kou, and his face settled into grimmer lines. One of Kan's aides had been sounding him out, very carefully. He had pretended that he didn't understand what was being asked of him. Now, he thought, it was time to stop pretending.

October 11
1500 hours

The Jeep skidded to a halt on the dock where the *Baie du Nord* was tied up, and D.L. climbed out. He glanced at the half-dozen Cree gathered at the end of the dock with their packs and bundles of gear. There were two women in the group. His mouth tightened as he stalked to the trawler.

"Martial! Martial!"

Faschereau appeared on deck. He vaulted over the rail to the dock. "The tanks all topped off, D.L., and the engine she purr like a woman."

"Martial, where are the Cree? They know we're scheduled to leave thirty minutes from now. And where's Willy? And Simon? Damn it, this isn't a game." His voice crackled with anger.

"Easy, D.L. Easy, my friend."

He took a deep breath and let it out. "I'm sorry,

Martial. Everything's taking longer than I thought. Don't they realize how important every minute is?"

"You should know the answer yourself. They do not have the white man's disease, slavery to the clock. Maybe they come little bit late, but they say they come, they come."

"I know that, Martial. It's just the time. Maybe I ought to send Willy up there."

Faschereau shook his head. "He's already gone. Maybe he bring them a little faster."

"And Simon?"

"On the *Baie*, keeping out of sight. He figure maybe the Cree don't want to go if they think an Inuit have too much to do with it. Maybe he is right."

D.L. grunted. The friction between the Cree and Inuit had been so much a part of the background for his years on the Bay that he hardly noticed it. It had always remained in the background, though. He hoped it wasn't going to cause problems now. "Are there any more problems I don't know about?"

"Maybe a few. Most of the Cree want to take their women along."

"And more power to them," Samantha said from the boat. She swung over the rail and walked over to put her arm around D.L. "I don't see any reason why the women shouldn't be involved in this."

"Nor I," D.L. said. "From their point of view, this is the same as a hunting or fishing trip. They'll want the women along to cook and clean fish and the like." He smiled when Samantha wrinkled her nose.

"But, D.L.," Faschereau insisted, "with the women along, they take the tents, everything. They say they want their boats so they can fish if we stay long. I got to tow them boats, I don't make more than seven knots."

That was a serious problem. Time was the worst enemy they had. He'd taken a quick flight over Harding's Fjord the day before and seen no sign that the sub had returned. But it could come at any time. It could be there now. In which case, it wouldn't matter if they made seven knots or seventy. And they couldn't afford to alienate the Cree. There would likely be trouble enough when the Inuit volunteers were added. If the Inuit volunteers were added.

"We'll have to take them, Martial. Just see that they're arranged to give you the best speed you can get. That's all we can do." Faschereau shrugged and turned back to the trawler. D.L. led Samantha back to the Jeep. "I have something for you."

"Oh? Does it eat?"

He took his cased rifle from the back and leaned it against the side of the Jeep, then dug into his duffel bag. He dug out his heavy service revolver and handed it to her. "It's loaded, so be careful. I doubt you'll need more than six. I hope you won't even need one."

She held the pistol as if it were something too long dead. "D.L, I don't want this. You said yourself I don't know one end of a gun from the other, and you're right. Take it back."

Instead, he closed the duffel bag, hefted it to his shoulder, and picked up his rifle. "Keep it," he said shortly. Abruptly he turned to her, a frown on his face. "Samantha, I won't have time to worry about you out there. I won't be able to afford to. You can help me, a little, by carrying that."

After a moment, she pushed it into her pocket, the butt sticking out awkwardly. "So call me Annie Oakley."

He wanted to say something then, something special, but before he could, Faschereau called from the boat. "D.L., up the hill. They all coming at once."

Down the hill above the dock trooped the rest of the Cree volunteers, Willy at their head. The wives followed in their own group, and a host of others, friends to help carry gear and see them off, the curious. A dozen dogs trotted at the fringes of the parade. The Cree crowded onto the dock and immediately began loading the boats tied up opposite the *Baie*. Willy trotted over to him.

"I brought them, Dr. Childe."

"That you did, Willy. Thanks." He looked at Samantha, but the time was past. She smiled faintly, and nodded as if she understood. "We're behind schedule, Willy. Keep at them. Martial! Let's get this show on the road."

Twenty minutes behind time, the *Baie du Nord* breasted the first gray-green roller of the Bay, the open Indian canoes strung out like beads behind it. D.L. watched to see how they rode under tow, then made his way forward to the pilothouse. Auguste was at the wheel, and Faschereau hunched over the chart table with dividers. Samantha sat huddled in the corner, her hands in the pockets of her parka.

"They're riding it all right," he said as he slid the door shut behind him. "How about our speed?"

"Like I say," Faschereau said, "seven knots. And damn lucky she do it. It is much harder to tow than to carry the same weight."

Simon stuck his head up from below. "Time grows short, Dr. Childe. The air feels of snow."

"That's what Willy said," Samantha said. "That the snow was coming early this year."

He bit back a curse. That was all they needed. "We can't get to the Belchers before dark, Martial. Will you take the *Baie* in in the dark?"

"I would advise against it. But you are *le général*."

Le général. He had run away from it as a lieutenant, but here he was again, giving orders that might cause men to die. And going to face the Chinese.

"We'll anchor outside and go in at first light," he said, and his voice was so grim that no one spoke. He turned away in the silence and stared toward the horizon, toward Harding's Fjord. He remained there until long after dark had fallen.

October 12
0720 hours

Full light was just reaching Churchill as the line handlers ashore cast off the heavy hawsers of the *Pai Te Yün*. Normally, one of the Grain Authority's small tugs would help the grainer away from the grain docks and out of the Churchill River into the Bay. The Chinese ship, however, had bow and stern thrusters, and her captain always refused the assistance. It was odd, but the men of the Churchill grain docks had come to take oddity as normal for the Chinese vessel.

Powerful jets of water pushed the ship away from the dock, and then her main engines took up the task of moving the deep-laden vessel. As she cleared the mouth of the river, Captain Lo picked up the phone to the radio room.

"This is the captain. Commence transmission."

TO: ADMIRAL COMMANDING
    CANADIAN COAST GUARD FORCES
    HUDSON BAY
    COMMONWEALTH OF CANADA

FROM: PAI TE YÜN
    CANTON
    PEOPLE'S REPUBLIC OF CHINA
    DEPARTING CHURCHILL GRAIN LOADING DOCKS. DUE TO EXPECTED ICE CONDITIONS IN PASSAGE BETWEEN COATS AND MANSEL ISLANDS AN ESCORT IS REQUESTED.
    ESTIMATED DATE OF ARRIVAL (COATS/MANSEL): 14 OCTOBER
    ESTIMATED TIME OF ARRIVAL (COATS/MANSEL): 0700 HOURS

And in Chinese:

THE UNITY OF OUR TWO NATIONS STANDS AS A BEACON ON THIS FELICITOUS DAY OF FATE.

                        WHITE CLOUD

In the cold waters of the Hudson Strait, the *Sheng Li,* message received, reeled in its antenna float from the surface and began to move toward the entrance to the Bay.

October 12
0745 hours

D.L. cupped the hot mug of coffee in his hands to warm them against the cold. The low-lying arms of Flaherty Island, guarding the entrance to the harbor, were sharp and clear in the crisp air.

Willy walked around the corner of the pilothouse. "The canoe's ready, Dr. Childe."

D.L. set down the mug and followed him to the stern. The Cree boats had all but one been drawn up on the side of the *Baie du Nord* away from the island. The women had their stoves going, brewing tea and cooking fish for breakfast. The remaining canoe was on the other side, with Samantha and Simon already in it. Willy climbed down to it, but as D.L. started over the rail, Faschereau caught his arm.

"D.L., I still think you should let me take the *Baie* in. They be more impressed than with you going in in a canoe. We get more volunteers."

"We can't carry too many," he laughed. "Besides, Willy says the Cree are nervous about going into an Inuit village. We don't want to scare any of them off." Or any of the Inuit, he added to himself. There was no guarantee they wouldn't refuse to volunteer once they found out the Cree had been asked first, the same as the mainland Inuit. Which was why he wasn't going to tell them. "I'll be back out as soon as I get the volunteers lined up." And he dropped into the boat.

Willy, at the outboard motor, took them away from the trawler toward the narrow harbor mouth. Simon sat in the bow, while Samantha huddled against D.L. for protection from the icy spray that came back over the boat. Mainly, she tried to protect her cassette recorder between them.

"D.L.," she said after a few minutes, "how are you going to handle telling the people here that you already have Cree volunteers? Aren't you afraid they might refuse to come?"

"I'm not going to say anything about the Cree." He caught her puzzled look. "I talked it over with Simon and Willy, and I think it's the best way to handle it. The only way."

"But when they get to the *Baie du Nord*—"

Simon looked over his shoulder. "Then I will point out to them that we ride on the white man's boat, while the Cree are towed behind like whales being towed to the factory."

"While I," Willy said, "will remind my people that we were asked first, and that the Inuit don't even have their own canoes, but are being carried around like cargo on the *Baie*."

She bristled. "You mean you're going to *use* the racial problem?"

D.L. nodded sharply. "That's right. I'll use that and anything else I have to. Anything."

Even as he said it, it brought him up short. He *would* use anything, do anything, to stop those missiles being launched. How many years had it been since he was the man who would do anything, who could do anything, to achieve what he'd set out to do? In the past few days, he'd done things he'd never have believed he could do. What *was* driving him toward Harding's Fjord? Was the need to stop the missiles really all that it was? Or was the hunger back? The need to get close to the men who had killed Helen, to get close to the Chinese with a weapon in his hands?

The canoe scraping ashore pulled him out of his study. He leaped out to help Simon beach it, then offered a hand to Samantha. A crowd of curious Inuit were already beginning to gather on the rock shelf above the beach.

"I think I'll stay with the canoe," Willy said. "They don't look too happy to see me."

"All right," D.L. said. In truth, they did look suspicious of Willy. Two men walked to a boat down the beach and sat to watch him as the others trudged from the beach to the village.

The crowd followed along behind them, murmuring curiously. Why had Dr. Childe come? It was not time again. Where was his plane? Had he crashed? The question spread through the village, drawing those who had not been at the beach, until every man, woman and child crowded around to watch Simon and D.L. mount the schoolhouse steps.

As Simon stepped forward, they became attentively quiet. "All of us know Dr. Childe. He is a good man. He is an honest man. The words he speaks to us today are important words. You must listen carefully. What you decide must be from your own heart, but you must listen." He stepped down, and a soft murmur ran through the gathering, dying as D.L. moved to the front of the wooden steps. Samantha raised crossed fingers and gave him an encouraging smile.

"Some of you," he began, "know much of the white man's world. The tower outside the village picks up television programs. Some of you have been to the ports on the south of the Bay, to work or to visit. Those have heard of the A-bomb." Some of the men straightened at that, and others leaned forward intently. "You know that the greatest fear of the white man's world is World War III, when the A-bombs will fall and destroy everything."

"But what has that to do with us?" someone called.

"In the Sleeper Islands, at Harding's Fjord, some men have built towers to launch those A-bombs and start that war. I ask you, the best hunters of you, to come with me to Harding's Fjord. Help me stop this thing before it happens."

A short, grizzled man with a gold tooth stepped forward. "We respect you, Dr. Childe. But this World War is a thing of the white men. Why does not the white man's government stop it?"

"They do not believe that the towers are there, and there is no time to convince them. As for it being a white man's problem, look around you. Look at the things you get from the white man's world. Look at the rifles for hunting, the motors for your canoes, the refrigerators and stoves and radios. The medicine I bring. Think of the jobs if the iron mine comes. Then tell me how much distance there is from the white man's world to yours."

The grizzled man looked around at the others as if reading their faces. Finally, he gave a short nod. "We will talk of it. Will you talk with us, Simon?"

As the crowd moved away, following Simon and the grizzled man, D.L. stepped down to join Samantha. "Well, it's out of my hands, now."

"You did a good job, D.L. They'll come."

He had to smile at her earnestness. "I'm sure they will. Let's go on back to the canoe to wait."

Willy was glad to see them. The two men were still just watching, but it had begun to get on his nerves. Still, none of them felt like talking. Willy stayed in the boat, while Samantha talked softly into her recorder. D.L. squatted on the rocky beach, skipping stones across the water. How much time was left? That was all he could think of. How much time was left?

A shout from Willy pulled him to his feet. "Dr. Childe! Look!"

Down from the village came Simon, and behind him, strung out in a line, twenty men and six women, rifles and bags of gear on their shoulders. Simon went directly to D.L., the grizzled man at his side.

"Dr. Childe, this is Thomas Ampaka. You do not know him, but he is a good hunter."

"I have never come to you," Ampaka said proudly. "I have never been sick."

"He and these other men," Simon said, "will come with you. We will stay until you say the danger is gone."

D.L. felt a surge of relief. With forty men, there was a chance. A small one, but a chance. "Thank you, Thomas. Thank all of you. Now let's start loading. We have a long way to go."

Ten minutes later the first boatload of Inuit started out for the *Baie du Nord*.

October 12
0930 hours

Stephen Brooke had managed to get over the feeling that Security was watching him, and he'd almost decided that his idea about Hudson Bay was completely insane. But he was still trying to get in touch with Sal Campana, and he still wouldn't make his calls from the office or home.

The Pentagon had become a beehive since the first UN meeting on the missiles of Novaya Zemlya, though no one was admitting they knew anything about a meeting, or about missiles. In the crowded corridors his uniform and the ID pinned to his lapel were a cloak of invisibility. No one paid any attention to one more mid-rank officer, even if the uniform was foreign. The female GS-5 clerk behind the counter in Central Clearing and Disbursing didn't even look up from her typewriter at him.

"Miss, I'd like to speak to Sergeant Kincaid, please."

She sighed and took one hand from the keyboard to pick up her phone and dial two digits. "Kincaid? There's an officer here to see you." She hung up and returned to her typing. "He'll be out in a minute."

"Thank you," he said, but she'd already forgotten his

existence. He stepped away from the counter to wait for Kincaid.

In a few minutes, the sergeant appeared out of the maze of partitions behind the counter. He paused when he saw Brooke, then came forward with a worried look over his shoulder. "Colonel Brooke. What can I do for you, sir?"

"The same thing as yesterday and the day before. Information."

Kincaid shot a quick look back at the rabbit warren he'd come out of. "Please, sir, could you keep your voice down. That's gotten real hot, sir. I can't talk about something that hot." He fidgeted under Brooke's gaze. "Sir, I don't know much of anything new, anyway."

"Whatever you know will be fine, Kincaid."

"All it is, is the Russians are trying to pull some kind of fancy trick."

"What kind of trick? What do you mean?"

"It's that steel sample, sir. They slipped us a hunk of Chinese steel."

"Chi-!" Kincaid winced, and he moderated his tone. "Chinese steel? You're sure?"

"I'm sure. Or at least, the Randelle Laboratory is. Made in Liaoning province, probably at Anshan or Shepyang. What do you think those Russians are trying?"

"Kincaid, has anyone in this pile of bricks considered the possibility that the steel is Chinese because the Chinese built the launchers?"

The sergeant laughed softly. "Sure, sir, they considered it. They thought about it, they laughed about it, and they forgot about it. Sir, the Chinese ain't got that kind of technology. You don't need no inside information to know that."

Brooke shook his head wearily. "Nobody ever has 'that kind of technology' until you read about it on the front pages. Listen, Kincaid, you keep an ear open for me. I'm not asking for anything that'll get you in trouble, but keep an ear open."

"Sure thing, sir. Sure thing."

Brooke didn't go back to his office. He made his way out of the Pentagon to his station wagon in the parking lot. He took the Memorial Parkway down past the Washington National Airport until he came to a service station, and pulled in. Taking out the bag of dimes and quarters he'd started carrying in his glove compartment, he walked to the phone booth at the edge of the lot.

He dialed his number direct. The operator came on and told him how much to deposit, and when the last coin had dinged into the machine, there was one ring and a pleasant female voice said, "*Newsworld* magazine. Good morning."

"I'm calling Mr. Salvatore Campana. He's expecting my call." He *hoped* Campana was expecting his call.

"One moment, sir. I'll connect you to his office."

"Mr. Campana's office," another woman said.

"This is Stephen Brooke." He'd thought it best not to advertise his connection with the Pentagon. "I'm calling Mr. Campana. I called yesterday."

"Yes, Mr. Brooke. I gave Mr. Campana your message, and he is interested in talking with you. I'm afraid he isn't in the office just now, though. May I have him call you?"

"No!" he said, and tried to take some of the sharpness out of his voice. "I'd rather he didn't call me, either at home or at the office. I'll call him. Tell him, with regard to Chinese submarines, I now agree with him. He'll know what I mean."

"Yes, sir," she said as if she took the same message every day. "With regard to Chinese submarines, you now agree with him."

October 12
1030 hours
Delcour's drone cut off as Johnson walked into the

Security Council chambers. "Ambassador Johnson, I regret that we were obliged to begin without you. The scheduled time was thirty minutes ago. At the same time, may I offer the thanks of the Council to your government for these photographs. They are most impressive." He gestured to the walls, lined with giant blowups of satellite pictures. Details could be made out of the men around the missiles on the ice and in the boats over the launchers. It was even possible to discern what tool a man was using.

"Impressive," Sholopov grunted. "That the Americans have such efficient spy satellites overflying my country could be called other things besides impressive."

Johnson took his seat next to Sir Julian, placing his attache case carefully on the table in front of him. "I regret being delayed, Mr. President. It was necessary for me to confirm certain - information." He touched the case, and everyone's eye went to it.

Those around the table had changed in the past few days, Johnson thought. Tobanda looked perpetually tired. Sir Julian still showed a veneer of unflappability, but he constantly drummed his fingers on the table. Sholopov went around with his head hunched down between his shoulders. And Tz'u sweated.

Delcour cleared his throat, breaking the fascination with Moore's case. "I had just read the reports of our delegations to examine the launchers and the missiles, Ambassador Johnson. For your benefit, I will touch on the high points once more." He glanced at the papers in front of him and pursed his lips. "The launch towers are, as the representative of the Soviet Union has stated, in place in the waters of Novaya Zemlya. Our experts, borrowed from the Air Forces of Argentina, Czechoslovakia, and India, agree that they are indeed missile launch towers."

"I would have been surprised," Johnson said, "if they

had been anything else."

The Council President frowned at the interruption. "As for the missiles themselves, the examination could not be as complete as with the launchers. They are spaced at five-mile intervals across the ice, and our delegation was allowed only the most cursory examination of the one missile on which Soviet technicians are working and an aerial view of the others."

"I have explained," Sholopov broke in, "that we are now certain that the missiles are booby-trapped. Getting into them without detonating the warheads will be most difficult. Allowing even this Council's delegation to interfere—"

"Yes, yes." It was a measure of Delcour's agitation that he would interrupt. "In any case, neither delegation has been able to ascertain the country of origin. All they can do is confirm what we already know—that the missiles and launchers are indeed there. Ambassador Sholopov, have you any report from your government on this?"

"I regret, none."

"Mr. President," Johnson said, "I have information. If the Conference Officer will distribute these." He took a stack of folders from his case but didn't wait for the Conference Officer to take them. "This report from the Randelle Laboratories was what I had to have confirmed before I came to today's meeting. You will see why in a moment. That report names the country of origin for the steel section we were given with a margin for error of less than .01 per cent. The country is China."

In the dead silence, the pencil in Tz'u's hand snapped like a pistol shot. "Mr. President," he said at last, "this is exactly what I said would happen if we allowed the United States or the Soviet Union, to present an analysis to the Council. For some reason, the United States wishes to embarrass China. Perhaps it is because, as the Ambassador from the Soviet Union, has charged, it is indeed the Americans who have built these launchers. In any case, the People's Republic of China resents the implications of the American Ambassador's statement, and wishes to register a strong protest."

"If the Ambassador will allow me to continue," Johnson said, "the United States does *not* believe that the launchers were built by China."

Sholopov rumbled a sardonic laugh, and Delcour looked flustered. "I do not understand," the Belgian said. "You claim the metal is of Chinese manufacture, then turn around and say you do not believe the launchers are Chinese. With respect, sir, what *are* you saying?"

"I am saying that my government does not feel that the People's Republic possesses the, ah, capabilities necessary to emplace these missiles. Remember, the steel was given to us by the Soviets. What guarantee do we have that that sample actually came from the launchers our delegation saw? Until we have a sample of that metal that is under our control from the moment it is cut, we must still consider this to be a Russian trick. Therefore—"

"Mr. President," Sholopov broke in. "I—"

"I have not yielded the floor," Johnson said.

"Mr. President!"

"I have not yielded the floor!"

Delcour banged his gavel futilely. Tz'u sat and sweated.

XV

Brooke was just getting ready to go to lunch when he received a call from the main entrance.

"We have a Mr. Salvatore Campana here, Colonel Brooke. He says he's here to see you."

He thought fast. "I'm expecting him. Tell him I'll be down in just a minute."

If only Campana had enough sense not to say he was the editor of *Newsworld*. That he'd come to Washington was a prop to Brooke's hunch. He must be beginning to believe, too. But if his name triggered the wrong relays during the security check—and it would if he'd told them he was a journalist—they might spend days trying to convince Pentagon Security and the FBI and the CIA and God knew who else that their suspicions were worth checking. They had to be gone before the computers made the wrong connection. Brooke ran.

He slowed to a walk as he rounded the last corner, and walked forward with a smile and an outstretched hand. "Sal! It's good to see you. I didn't think you'd get here for lunch." With one arm around Campana, pumping his hand with his free one, Brooke got him turned toward the doors. His voice dropped momentarily.

179

"Play along, and for God's sake don't mention the magazine. How long's it been, anyway?"

Campana jammed an unlit cigar into his mouth before replying. "Months, I guess. How've you been doing?"

"Fine. Just fine."

They kept up the inconsequential talk until they were out of the mammoth building, then Brooke started ahead at a fast trot. "Come on," he called grimly. "No time to explain now."

Campana followed in a heavy jog. He didn't say anything until the station wagon was on I-95. Then, all he said was, "I checked into a motel out toward Dulles."

Brooke made the turns to get headed in that direction. "I'm glad my message finally got through. I've been trying for days."

"It almost didn't. Lucy, my secretary, Miss Wallis, decided you were either a first-class nut or important. She tracked me down to let me decide which. Now, what makes you think all of a sudden those Chinese submarines are real?"

"I can't tell you." All Campana did was grunt. "You don't seem surprised."

Campana took out his cigar and studied the chewed end sourly. "You don't stop being a reporter when you get to be an editor. My contacts in the UN are worried as hell. Something's going on. The Security Council's sweating blood. But they can't get a hint of a thing, nothing out of the ordinary. Right in the middle of that, you call and say now you believe in Chinese submarines. Hell, before I got on the plane I figured this was classified so only God and the President could see it. So what *can* you tell me?"

"Not much. Just that something has happened—don't ask what—that makes me want to check out that story you heard. I'd like to talk to whoever told it to you."

"Okay. Maybe I can arrange that. Now some questions not about Chinese subs. Why did you hustle me out of the Pentagon? Why didn't you want me to mention I work for a magazine? And if this thing is so important, why aren't we back there right now, sitting in an office with somebody, telling him about it?"

"They're touchy about contacts with newspeople right now. Very touchy. And as soon as I tell them how I made the connection, alarm bells will go off. It took knowledge I'm not supposed to have. If this is all a load of bull, I don't want to spend the next few days, or weeks, being put through the wringer by every security and intelligence service in Washington. And if it isn't, there's no time. We don't have any proof, you realize. Even putting your rumor with what I know, all I have is a crazy hunch. I have to talk to whoever told you the story."

"That's one of my reporters," Campana said. "Samantha Keenan. She's in Canada now, in Quebec. Some place called Poste-de-la-Baleine. Pull in right here. This is where I'm staying."

Brooke turned into one of a national motel chain, parking beneath the sign that proclaimed it 'Your Home Away From Home,' and they made their way up the tiers of balconies to a third-floor, glass-fronted room. The curtains were drawn to cut off the view of the parking lot.

Campana tossed his coat on the bed and picked up the phone. "This is room 358. I want to place a long distance call, person-to-person, to Miss Samantha Keenan in Poste-de-la-Baleine, Quebec, Canada. That's right. Poste-de-la-Baleine. No, I don't know where she's staying, but I don't believe there can be more than one or two hotels there. All right. Thank you." He hung up and dropped on the bed. "She'll ring back when she finds Samantha. There's vodka in the top dresser drawer. Help yourself."

"No thanks. I understand Poste-de-la-Baleine is a small place, but that's still asking a lot to have the operator try every hotel and boarding house. Do they know you here?"

"Christ, no. I didn't have a reservation, so I grabbed the first vacant room I could find on the way in from the airport. I just make sure to tip the right people on the way in. It's the only way to ensure good service in a strange hotel."

Brooke breathed heavily and ran a hand through his hair. "I guess I'm still worried about Pentagon Security or the FBI showing up."

"Relax. I—" The phone rang, and Campana snatched it before the first ring was done. "Yes?" He listened for a minute, grunting softly at intervals, then said, "Hang on." He pressed the receiver against his chest. "One boarding house in the whole town, and she's not registered."

"She must be staying with somebody."

"Sure, but who?" He put the receiver back to his ear. "Put me through to anybody at the airport at Poste-de-la-Baleine." He drummed his fingers on the coverlet and muttered to himself. "She had to go through the airport. Wherever she went, she had—Yes? Who is this, please? Well, Mr. Hawkins, my name is Sal Campana. I'm trying to locate a woman who works for me. Samantha Keenan. Red hair, busty, about thir—Oh, you know her? Yes. Un-huh. Un-huh. Yes. Yes, I have that. Thank you, Mr. Hawkins. Thank you. Goodbye." He hung up and sat shaking his head.

"Well?" Brooke said finally. "What about her? Is she there? Can I talk to her, or not?"

"She left," Campana said wonderingly. "On a trawler, with some doctor named Childe and a couple of dozen Indians. This man Hawkins—he works for a charter service—said he couldn't tell whether it was a hunting party or a warparty. He thought that was a big joke."

"You think maybe they're hunting a Chinese submarine?"

"You mean playing John Wayne to the rescue? Samantha's too level-headed for that. Besides, we don't know yet if there really is a Chinese submarine. I don't have any idea what it is you won't tell me, but even if there was a sub, why does it have to be Chinese? I know that's what the story said, but, hell, Canada has subs, too."

"I never heard of us having any in Hudson Bay, though. Let me make a few calls, and maybe I can find out." Campana dialed, said a few words to the operator, and handed him the phone. "Operator, I'd like to call the Inter-Service Liaison Office, Ministry of Defence, Ottawa, Canada."

"One moment, please."

He listened to the interchange between operators as the call was put through, then a man said, "Inter-Service Liaison Office. Sergeant Roget speaking."

"Sergeant, this is Lieutenant Colonel Stephen Brooke. Let me speak to Captain Donald Beauprie."

"Yes, sir. One moment, sir."

"Steve!" came Beauprie's voice suddenly. "Do you have any idea how long it's been? Nearly two years, that's how long."

"Since they sent me down to Washington," Brooke agreed. "Listen, Don, I have a favor to ask. I need some information. Without the whole world knowing I asked."

"Sure, Steve. No problem."

"Then tell me this. Do we have any submarines in Hudson Bay?"

"Submarines." Beauprie's voice was suddenly strange. When he went on, he spoke very slowly. "No.

No, we don't. If you don't mind, Steve, exactly what is your interest in submarines in Hudson Bay?"

"Just something I'm checking out," he said carefully. "Why?"

"It's just that there was someone in here to see me last week who talked about submarines in Hudson Bay. Chinese submarines, no less. And missile launchers." He laughed shortly. "Crazy, isn't it?"

Brooke took a deep breath to take the excitement out of his voice. He was only partly successful. "It certainly is. What did you do? Kick him out?"

"I probably should have. But since he was who he was, I showed his pictures of so-called missile launchers around. Got my ears pinned back for it, too. Nobody likes crazy ideas. Especially crazy ideas that could embarrass us with China."

"Of course not. But who was he, anyway?"

"Daniel LeTellier Childe. You wouldn't know the name, but any paratrooper would. He's a legend in the Princess Pat's. Won the Victoria Cross in Korea. Too bad he had to get hold of this thing."

"Yes, I suppose it is. Well, thanks, Don. We'll have to get together sometime."

"Sure, Steve." Beauprie paused. "Look, there isn't anything to all of this, is there? I mean, missile launchers?"

Brooke thought of the miles of microwave relay between him and Beauprie, open for listening by anyone who had the equipment. "Not a thing," he said finally. "I just wanted to check on this other thing, about our submarines."

After he'd hung up, he stared at the floor for a long time. "What was the name of that doctor? The one you said your reporter went off with."

"Ah, Childe. D.L. Childe, Hawkins said."

"D.L. Childe." Brooke nodded. "Last week one Daniel LeTellier Childe walked into the Ministry of Defence with a tale of Chinese submarines and missile launchers."

"Missile launchers! Samantha said something about missile launchers."

Brooke looked at Campana sharply. "You didn't say anything about that."

"There's a lot you haven't said anything about, too. I take it there's something to this missile talk?"

He hesitated before nodding. "Maybe. I don't know yet. It's beginning to seem that way, though. Did this reporter say anything about where the launchers are? Anything at all?"

"Yes. But I don't remember-." He scowled around his cigar and frowned in thought. "Some fjord. That was it. And an old president. Which-? That's right. Harding's Fjord. You ever hear of it?"

Brooke shook his head. "But the name may be enough." He dialed a number in Canada, and gave his number to the long distance operator when she came on. Campana looked at him questioningly. "A friend of mine. If only he's—"

"218 Squadron, Fighter/Recon Sergeant Holmes speaking, sir."

"This is Colonel Brooke. Let me speak to Colonel Reeman."

"One moment, sir."

The line clicked as the call was switched, then a familiar bass rumbled, "Steve! What are you calling again so soon for? Those Yanks take all your money in a poker game?"

Brooke chuckled. "As a matter of fact, Paul, I've been winning lately. I called to ask a favor. Paul, I want you to divert one of your training flights for me."

There was a moment's silence on the other end. "That's a serious request," Reeman said slowly.

"I wouldn't ask if the reason wasn't equally serious. I can't explain now, Paul, but it could be life or death, and that's straight. No joke."

"Where do you want it diverted to?"

"Do you know where Harding's Fjord is?"

"One minute." Papers rustled over the wire, "It's listed. It's in the Sleeper Islands, just outside our normal training area. There'll be no problem diverting a flight there."

"Thank God," Brooke breathed.

"What are they looking for, Steve?"

He hesitated. "I can't tell you. If it's there, you'll know it from the photos, but I can't say over the phone."

"Like that," Reeman said flatly. "All right. We'll do the Sleepers for you from top to bottom. There's a three plane training flight scheduled for 0700 tomorrow morning. I'll take it myself. Good enough?"

"Good enough, Paul. And thanks." He hung up and dropped back on the bed with a sigh. "Tomorrow. They'll do a photo-recon of Harding's Fjord tomorrow."

"And what do we do in the meantime?" Campana said.

"Where did you say that vodka was?"

October 14
0640 hours

The *Baie du Nord* plowed into the dark gray waves, and they broke over her bow, sending icy cascades back along the deck, drenching the Inuit huddled behind the deckhouse as they waited their turns to join the women below. D.L. braced himself with a wide stance and both hands on the cargo boom to study the string of canoes behind the trawler. They tossed and twisted in a nautical crack-the-whip.

He made his way back to the wheelhouse, where Faschereau wrestled the wheel to keep the bow into the waves. "Martial, we have to do something. Those boats are going to start swamping soon. They can't bail forever in this."

"I cannot reduce speed any more, D.L. She barely keeps headway as it is."

"How about trying to take them aboard?"

"In this?" Faschereau said incredulously.

D.L. sighed and shook his head. "I know. I guess I'm getting desperate. If this lasts much longer—Have you been able to get a weather report yet?"

Faschereau curled his lip scornfully at the radio. "The man who made that, his mother never knew who his father was. We don't get nothing but static."

D.L. studied the dark sky and the endless series of crashing waves ahead, then turned to the canoes again. It had grown worse for them, even in those few short minutes. At any instant, half were out of sight behind towering waves.

Samantha stuck her head up from below, and he knelt beside the companionway. "Are you all right? I'm afraid it may get worse before it gets better."

She smiled. "I'll have you know you're talking to an old salt. I used to love sailing Long Island sound when it was rough."

"I think this might get a little rougher than Long Island sound. If it gets too rough, lash yourself to a bunk."

She snorted scornfully, and scrambled the rest of the way up the ladder. Anna Ampaka, Thomas' stout wife, followed with a steaming kettle and a half-dozen tin cups on a cord.

"We aren't cargo," Samantha said. "We made hot tea for the men on deck." He glanced at the waves, their tops whipped into white froth by the ever-rising wind, that pounded the deck, but before he could speak she cut him off. "It's needed, D.L. Something certainly is. Every shift that comes below is half frozen."

"All right," he said slowly. "But you use one hand to

hang on to something solid at all times, understand."

"Agreed." She took the string of cups from Anna, and slid open the door. Wind howled in, carrying spray. "Come on, Anna."

As they darted out, D.L. followed. He didn't know why except that he felt a need to keep an eye on them. The wind had risen enough to be a third thing to brace against, along with the pitching deck and the torrents of water. The women shuffled down the deck from hand-hold to handhold. Then, with a crack like a rifle shot, the boom lashing snapped.

"Down!" D.L. shouted, but the wind shredded his cry.

The boom scythed across the deck toward the women. The end of it brushed Samantha, knocking her to her knees against the railing, but it caught Anna full across the backs of her thighs. The Inuit woman's arms went wide, flinging the kettle, as the boom lifted her over the rail and threw her into the sea.

D.L. dashed aft, dropping to his knees to slide under the boom as it whipped back. He ducked, and it brushed the top of his head. Then he was on his feet again, ignoring the toss of the deck. Anna was fast being carried away from the trawler. He grabbed a life-ring and, in one motion, shook out the line and hurled it toward the struggling woman. It arced toward her, and curved away in the wind to fall far short. Desperately he grabbed another ring, but even as he hurried to the stern he knew it would never reach her. Thomas Ampaka appeared at his side as he threw the ring. The wind, perversely, carried it toward her this time. It dropped a yard from her frantically outstretched hand. And she was still being carried aft, away from the trawler and the canoes.

"Look!" Samantha screamed, pointing toward the boats.

In the lead canoe a Cree stood, two others holding his waist to brace him. He held a harpoon poised, tracking the woman being carried off. In one smooth motion he reared back and threw. The harpoon passed just over Anna's head, and the trailing line dropped across her shoulders. She tangled her arms in it, and the people in the boat began to pull her in.

"Good throw," Thomas grunted.

"My God," Samantha breathed. She still knelt huddled against the rail. "I've never been so scared in my life. What are they doing now?"

Anna had been hauled into the lead canoe, and everyone was huddled around her. Then the circle opened, and it became apparent they'd taken her clothes off. Naked, she was thrust into a sleeping bag. Two men, also naked, stuffed themselves into it after her, and the bag was zipped up.

"Body heat," D.L. explained. "Cold water sucks it out of you, and hypothermia can kill even after you're safe from drowning. That's the quickest way they have to warm her up."

"Good people," Ampaka said. He looked at D.L. and gave a short nod. "Good people."

As the short man walked away, Willy stuck his head out of the deck house. "What's going on, Dr. Childe?"

"We nearly lost-." Out of the corner of his eye, he saw that the distance to the boats seemed to have lengthened. Another wave crashed over them, and the gap widened still more. "God, the canoes are loose!"

Samantha started to her feet. "I'll go tell Martial to turn back."

He grabbed her arm as she turned away. "No use. If we try to turn in these seas, we'll capsize."

She stared at him, horrified. "We have to do something."

"Doc," Willy called. He had darted past D.L. at the first shout and begun hauling in the tow rope. Now he held up the end of it. "They cut free."

"Cut?" He grabbed the rope and fingered the

smoothly severed end. "Why?"

Willy shrugged. "Maybe they figure the seas getting too high to be towed." He took a quick look at the sky and the way the spray was being carried by the wind. "They'll run before the wind. It'll carry them toward the King George Islands. I'll bet after the storm we can pick them up there."

D.L. smothered a curse. After the storm. More time gone. A corner of his mind noted that that wasn't like him. Normally he'd have had thoughts only for the men and women struggling for their lives in those small boats. Now, though, for whatever reason, the drive to get to Harding's Fjord had become the most important thing in his life.

"If only nothing else goes wrong," he said.

Something colder even than the icy spray touched his cheek. He stared at the white flakes beginning to fall with ever increasing heaviness, and didn't bother to stifle his oath. The first snow had come early.

October 14
0740 hours

Captain Milne studied the Chinese grainer sourly as his icebreaker moved toward it just south of the passage between Coats and Mansel Islands. This routine playing at nursemaid wasn't his idea of the proper use of an icebreaker. Icing had been light so far. Certainly no danger to a vessel the size of the *Pai Te Yün*.

Lieutenant Armand, his Executive Officer, stepped onto the bridge with a clipboard in his hand. "Weather advisory, sir. A sudden storm in the south-eastern part of the Bay. Force ten winds, and climbing. Two ore ships reported in difficulty in heavy seas."

Milne nodded sharply. "Plot a course—" He cut off at the look on Armand's face. "There's more?"

"Yes, sir. There was a special signal to us accompanying the advisory. *McLean* is to continue on her present mission. Not until the grainer is safely into the Hudson Strait are we to proceed south."

Milne slammed his fist into his palm. "Damn. Very well, Mr. Armand. Assume station one half mile ahead of the grainer. And as soon as we hit water we can call the Strait, we're turning back." As Armand turned to relay the orders, Milne noticed through the open door to the sonar room that the sonarman was frowning and attempting to adjust the dials of his equipment. He leaned through the door. "Something wrong, son?"

"Not exactly, sir. It's that grainer. She's making enough noise for a fleet."

"They aren't notorious for good maintenance. Just do the best you can, son. We'll have more important work soon."

Through his binoculars, Captain Lo studied the ice-breaker taking station ahead. No one seemed to be taking any undue attention to his ship, but then, it wasn't *his* ship that was important now, nor visual sighting the problem to be worried about. "Condition One is in force throughout the ship?" he said.

"Yes, sir," Lieutenant Teng replied. "All engines are varying rpm independently. All generators and winches are running. All—"

"I know what Condition One is," Lo snapped. "I asked if it was in force." He put the binoculars back to his eyes. He knew without being told that Condition One was in force. The pressure was becoming too much. He wanted it to be over, to go home.

Commander Chu straightened from the periscope and snapped the handles up against its sides. "Down scope." The patrol vessel and the grainer were entering the passage. "Dive to one hundred feet and rig for silent running. Ahead dead slow."

There was a palpable tension in the control room as

the submarine started forward into the passage. The screw noises of the surface ships grew louder and louder, the high-pitched swish of the icebreaker, and overlaying it the cacophony from the grainer. It was to be hoped that mass of sound overlaid the prop noises of the *Cheng Fu* as well, a mask and a shield to guard her past the ears of the cutter.

The noise grew louder, and louder, seeming to fill the control room, until the instruments seemed to quiver with it. Chu noted that Ta's face was wet with sweat. He felt cool, himself, almost cold. And then the ships were past, the screw sounds fading behind the sub.

Chu nodded. "Plot a course to the pickup point. I will be in my cabin."

October 14
1000 hours

Sholopov shrugged into his overcoat as one of the mission staff entered the office he had taken over.

"Your car has been brought around, sir."

Sholopov didn't answer as he stalked past. He was in no mood for pleasantries. If he opened his mouth, fire and brimstone would come out.

Another member of the staff appeared as soon as he reached the front hall. "Sir, there's an answer to your call to Moscow. Communications says it is Marshal Archipenko himself."

Sholopov brushed past him, as close to a run as he had come in twenty years.

The communications room was manned by a dozen technicians, most of them monitoring local micro-wave and radio transmissions. None of them looked up from his work as Sholopov entered.

"Clear the room," he rumbled. "All of you, out! Now!" He grabbed the arm of the nearest man as he started to comply. "My call is scrambled?"

"Of course, sir."

"Then get out." He dropped into a chair before the powerful radio set, but waited until the door closed behind the last man before keying the microphone. "Archipenko?"

"One moment, sir," came a strange voice.

Sholopov cursed. Even now the man played power games.

Suddenly Archipenko's voice boomed at him from the speaker. "Listen carefully, Sholopov. This is important."

"Damn you, Archipenko! Damn you! You listen. You're right. This is important. How do you expect me to carry on here without information? I haven't been able to get a whisper out of Moscow in over twenty-four hours. What's going on?"

"Are you finished, Comrade? Then let *me* finish. A decision has been reached by the Praesidium, and approved by the First Secretary and the Prime Minister. You are to deliver the following ultimatum. The United States has three days to reveal to us the locations of their other launchers. Three days. To be exact, the deadline is midnight, Moscow time, October 17."

"*Bog*! And what is the alternative?"

"Leave that for them to imagine. It will weigh more heavily on them that way."

"I was certain Johnson told me the truth about that metal," Sholopov sighed. "Where *was* it manufactured?" There was silence on the other end. "Marshal, where was the metal manufactured?"

Archipenko's reply was reluctant. "China."

"Then—"

"Then nothing, Comrade. The consensus is that the Americans acquired Chinese steel to cover just this eventuality. There has been *some* consideration of a conspiracy between them."

"Why do you refuse to even consider the Chinese as culprits?"

"Because they could not have done it. They are at least five years from the technology to build underwater launched ballistic missiles."

Sholopov snorted. "I remember the same being said of the A-bomb, and the H-bomb, and—the submarines, Archipenko. You have the report on the Lüta base?"

"No. The agent was killed attempting to penetrate the base."

"That sounds like very heavy security. Perhaps they are hiding something."

"Who is fixated now, Sholopov? Security is always heavy at Chinese bases. Oh, very well. I will order another attempt to enter the base."

"And the ultimatum. Request a delay."

"Impossible."

"You must. The agent cannot possibly get the information needed in only three days."

"Damn it, Sholopov, remember whose country has those missiles pointed at it."

"In view of the analysis of the metal, you must request a delay. Or put me through to the First Secretary and I'll request it myself."

"There is not the slightest possibility," Archipenko grated. "They will not even consider it. Three days, Comrade. Three days."

Suddenly the speaker carried only the hiss of the carrier wave. It took him a moment to realize Archipenko had switched off. He slumped wearily in his chair. Whether the Praesidium actually would not consider a delay, or Archipenko would not allow the request to reach them, the effect was the same. The world was going to end in three days.

"I must protest," Lawrence Johnson said as he rose to his feet. His eyes flickered to the empty Chinese and Russian seats. Where were they? "The representative from the Sudan is attempting to make this a Third World issue. The United States is merely calling on the Soviet Union to fulfill its pledge to allow our technicians to remove a metal sample from the launchers off Novaya Zemlya and return with that sample in their continuous possession."

Hassan Abboud, a swarthy, hook-nosed man, leaned forward intently. "When there is a confrontation of the super-powers, it is always a Third World matter, for we are caught in the middle. Now we are caught up in an event which, by its very nature, increases world tensions. We must try to lessen those tensions, but the United States instead makes demands of the Soviet Union. It is necessary—"

Johnson stopped listening as Sholopov appeared at the door. The Russian was haggard, and his steps dragged. Halfway to his seat he stopped and looked at the empty Chinese delegation chair. When he finally dropped into his seat, he broke in on Abboud immediately.

"-American Imperialism-," Abboud was saying.

"With apologies to Ambassador Abboud," Sholopov said hoarsely, "I have a matter which must be presented to the Security Council without so much as a moment's delay." Dead silence fell. "First, the analysis of the metal has been completed. It is Chinese." Someone gasped. Sholopov stopped to glare at the vacant chair near the head of the table, then turned to face Johnson. Johnson felt the hair rising on the back of his neck. "In spite of that," the Russian intoned, "my government does not accept that China is responsible." He sighed heavily. "Not responsible. On instructions from my government, I deliver the following ultimatum. The United States has until midnight, Moscow time, on the seventeenth of October, to reveal to the Soviet Union the locations of all other launchers in Soviet waters."

If there had been silence before, now no one breathed. Even the stenographers had stopped to stare at the Russian.

"Will-," Delcour began faintly. He stopped to clear his throat. "Will the representative from the United States reply?"

Johnson got to his feet slowly, studying Sholopov. The Russian's eyes were sunken, and his hands on the table were clenched till the knuckles were white. Johnson didn't have any doubt what the alternative was. "No," he said simply. "I must communicate with my government."

He picked up his case and started for the door. His shoes whispered softly on the thick carpet in the stillness of the room. Eyes followed him, but no one moved until he reached the door. Then they broke from their seats, leaving Sholopov staring at the table.

October 14
1500 hours

The lights in the missile control room near Kurya began to flash red, and everyone froze. Colonel Vashkov was the first to move. He walked to his command seat and punched the confirmation request into the console. Almost immediately two lights went on on the panel, CONFIRMED and HOLD FOR LAUNCH SIGNAL.

"Missile check," Vashkov said.

Behind him, six men bent over their panels. One by one, six green lights on his console came on.

"Assume launch status," he ordered.

Each green light was replaced by an amber one. The six missiles under Vashkov's control were in Launch Condition Two.

"Sir," one of the technicians said, "targetting information is being received."

"Display," Vashkov said.

The screen in front of his console lit, and words were printed across it.

TARGET ONE: WASHINGTON, DISTRICT OF COLUMBIA, USA
TARGET TWO: CHICAGO, ILLINOIS, USA
TARGET THREE: MISSILE FIELD WEST OF ST. LOUIS, MIS-
SOURI, USA
TARGET FOUR: FUSHUN, PEOPLE'S REPUBLIC OF CHINA
TARGET FIVE: TSINGTAO, PEOPLE'S REPUBLIC OF CHINA
TARGET SIX: SHANGHAI, PEOPLE'S REPUBLIC OF CHINA
XXXXXXXXXXXXXXXXXXXXXXXXXXXXXXXXXXXXXXXXX
TARGET CO-ORDINATES PRE-FILED.
XXXXXXXXXXXXXXXXXXXXXXXXXXXXXXXXXXXXXXXXX
CONFIRM RECEIPT OF TARGETING DATA.
XXXXXXXXXXXXXXXXXXXXXXXXXXXXXXXXXXXXXXXXX
197/155/243

Vashkov permitted himself a small grunt. He had one day expected one or the other, but not both at once. "Transmit confirmation of receipt," he ordered. "Commence programming coordinates into onboard guidance systems."

One by one small stars flashed on the screen beside the targets, and as each star appeared, an amber light on his console flashed to red. The missiles were now in Launch Condition One.

Vashkov lit a cigarette and leaned back. There was nothing to do now except wait for the launch signal.

October 14
1520 hours
When the klaxon sounded in the ready rooms at Lowry Air Force Base outside Denver, the B-52 crews piled into waiting station wagons and roared out to the bombers waiting on the tarmac. In ten minutes the first plane taxied into takeoff position at the head of Runway One. Nineteen more waited in line behind.

Captain Sherman Paige, navigator of the first craft in line, the Delta Rose, hunched over sourly, checking the ASN-131 inertial navigation system and the AFSATCOM global satellite navigation-communication system. He generally enjoyed training flights, unannounced or not, but not when they began thirty minutes before he was due to go off duty.

With a rising whine from the eight engines, the bomber began to roll forward. At the same instant the radioteletype in Paige's cubicle began chattering. Someone else was anxious about getting off duty, he thought. They weren't supposed to receive this broadcast until they were airborne.

AIRCRAFT NUMBER ONE FIVE NINE NINE FOUR TWO
ZULU KING
CODE: AMBER FIVE/RED FIVE/GREEN SEVEN
   OCEAN/CLOUD/JADE

Paige frowned. He didn't recognize that one. It was a mission they'd never practiced before, whatever it was. He slid over in front to the keyboard.

CONFIRMATION: TWO ZULU KING
      OCEAN/CLOUD/JADE
PASSWORD: ARMAGEDDON
COUNTERSIGN: RAINBOW

Taking a key from his pocket, he opened the outer door of the Mission Safe, then worked the combination to the inner door. There was no hurry. The next transmission wouldn't come for another hour at least. He ruffled through the heavy, sealed envelopes inside the safe until he found the right one. Amber Five/Red Five/Green Seven, Ocean/Cloud/Jade. Before he finished closing the safe, the teletype began working again.

He turned slowly, the envelope in his hand, and stared at the words printed out.

PASSWORD: ARMAGEDDON

COUNTERSIGN: RAINBOW
PAROLE: GÖTTERDÄMMERUNG
EXECUTE TO RELEASE POINT
EXECUTE

There was a brassy taste in his mouth. Briefly he considered requesting a reconfirmation, claiming his reception had been garbled, but even as he thought of it, he knew there was no need. That message wasn't sent automatically. It had to be transmitted letter by letter, on purpose. There just wasn't any chance of error.

He switched on the intercom to the flight deck. "Ah, Pete, this is Sherm. You'd better get Charlie and get down here. It's the real thing, Pete."

Captain Pete McDonald, the pilot, and Lieutenant Charlie Dell, the weapons officer, slid down the ladder into his compartment in a matter of seconds. The three men looked nothing alike, but they were all cast in the same mold, tall and lean.

McDonald held out his hand without saying anything. Paige tore off the teletype page and handed it to him. He read it, grunted, and read it again. "You have the target assignment out yet, Sherm?"

Paige handed the envelope to him. McDonald tore it open, and whistled tunelessly while he read. When he was done, he handed it back without a word.

Sherm unfolded the heavy sheets and read. Primary target: Soviet Navy base at Vladivostok. Secondary target. "The Chinese Navy base at Lüta? Pete, what the hell's going on?"

"I don't know, but it must be bad or we wouldn't be targetting both. Better get the courses plotted. And make the third leg on the deck. We'll be hitting Peking if the primary strike there doesn't get through, and the air defenses around there are hell. Charlie, draw your fuses from the safe, and start fusing the devices as soon as we cross the coast."

Paige sank back into his seat as the other two started forward for the weapons safe. Fuse the devices. This *was* the real thing. He thought of the fighter sweeps out of Siberia, and the North China interceptor bases. Somehow, he didn't think they were going to make it to that third target. Grimly he began plotting the great circle route that would bring the Delta Rose sweeping down on Vladivostok.

XVI

October 15
0750 hours

By the dark hours of Friday morning the storm had blown itself out enough for the *Baie du Nord* to bring her bow out of the oncoming sea. Dawn found her in the King George Islands. The wind had dropped to merely brisk, but even in the shelter of the islands heavy swells were running.

Samantha braced herself against the front of the wheelhouse and watched D.L. He was in the bow, with binoculars clamped to his eyes. He had been grimmer than ever since the Cree had loosed their boats, but now it had to do with something else. Something more was troubling him. With a sigh, she raised her camera and snapped three quick shots of him. She couldn't help him, and there was still a story to be done.

Suddenly, without lowering the binoculars, he waved one hand toward a point of land. "Martial! It's them!"

On the point a man in an Indian parka waved back. And then they were far enough beyond the point to see the five boats drawn up on the shore, out of reach of the surf. The people ran down to the water's edge, waving and shouting at the trawler.

"They're all there," D.L. called over his shoulder.

"All safe." The trawler moved around the point, into its shelter, and Auguste ran forward to drop the anchor.

Samantha slipped her arm through D.L.'s. "You can relax now."

A smile flickered in her direction. "About that, anyway." He went back to studying the shore. The first boat was launching through the surf. "We should be at Harding's Fjord by now, in place."

"Even the mighty D.L. Childe can't control the weather," she smiled.

"If we leave the boats here, take the Cree on board, we can make up some time."

She sighed. He wasn't going to be drawn out of his mood. She unslung her camera and began snapping the first boat, the tall Cree who had saved Anna standing in the bow with a tow rope. Anna sat in the boat behind him.

"Come alongside," D.L. shouted. "We're taking you on board."

Faschereau, just stepping out of the wheelhouse, shot a look at him, then exchanged glances with her. "Maybe," he said. "Maybe."

Thomas Ampaka caught the rope from the boat and tied it off, flashing a quick grin to his wife. He leaned over the side to help her up. Once she was on deck, he enveloped her in a hug.

The tall Cree clambered over the rail behind Ampaka and his wife. Thomas turned to regard him soberly, and the Cree returned the gaze just as gravely. Thomas offered a hand. After a moment, the Cree took it. For a heartbeat the two men stood, then from somewhere chuckles bubbled up. They began to shake hands, instead of merely gripping them, and pat one another on the shoulder. The chuckles turned to laughter.

Samantha lowered her camera with a smile of her own. It was a moment she wanted to remember outside of any story.

"I don't never think I see something like that," Faschereau said.

Other boats had come alongside in the meantime, and other Cree were climbing over the rail. They and the Inuit looked at each other awkwardly, shifting from foot to foot, and only the two men shaking hands seemed to sustain them. Then an Inuit woman darted forward to offer a mug of tea, and after a startled look, a Cree woman took it. One of the Indian men held out his pouch of tobacco. Slowly the Inuit men brought out their pipes. Bit by bit, as more Cree climbed to the deck, the two groups flowed together.

D.L., who had been waiting impatiently, made his way to Ampaka and the Cree. "Thomas, we must keep moving." He looked around the group intently, and the chatter stopped as they listened. "We must keep moving. Simon, Willy, as soon as the rest are aboard, ferry the canoes ashore. We're leaving them all here except one. We can pick them up on the way back. Everybody get your gear stowed and lashed down. It's still rough enough to toss loose bundles around."

The gathering by the rail began to break up, men and women hunting for places to stow their belongings. Willy and Simon climbed down into the canoes to lash them together.

Samantha confronted D.L. as he started for the wheelhouse. "You've got damned big feet, D.L., and you just trampled on something fine. Don't you realize we may just have seen the beginning of the end for two hundred years of hate?"

He looked at her blankly for a minute, then glanced at the men and women clustered on deck. "I'm trying to get them another two hundred years." He gave her a look she couldn't read and ducked into the wheelhouse.

Troubled, she turned back to taking pictures of the Cree and Inuit, and the preparations for getting under way.

An hour later the *Baie du Nord* rounded the point again, heading out into the Bay.

October 15
1000 hours

"To recap the top story on the Morning Report," the man on the television said, "the armed forces of the United States are at this hour in the middle of a massive alert. Soldiers and sailors have been recalled to their bases, and many Navy ships have sailed from both coasts, including a number of nuclear submarines and two task forces formed around the nuclear aircraft carriers *Enterprise* and *Nimitz*. A spokesperson for the Pentagon stated that the unannounced alert has been planned for months as a test of the nation's defences, and denied that it has anything to do with a similar alert reported under way in the Soviet Union. In spite of this, there are persistent rumors in the capital, denied by the White House, that the President will address the nation tonight, subject unannounced. The Russian Embassy has refused comment on the situation. And now, here's Red Holt with the sports. Red, how about those Redskins?"

Brooke switched off the TV violently. "Russia," he snorted. "They don't even have an idea who's really to blame. Sal, you think the President's really going on TV?"

"No." Campana, sitting on the bed, lowered the phone long enough to rub his ear, then started dialing again. "Maybe I haven't picked up anything important from my local contacts, but I did get some bits and pieces. Three of the Joint Chiefs, including the Chairman, are supposed to attend one of Theodoria Waring's parties tomorrow night. The President's scheduled to be at the Navy–Air Force game. A few other things like that, and none of it cancelled."

"What's that have to do with TV tonight?"

"If they're keeping on with things like that while everything looks like it's going to hell, they're putting up a front. Normality. The situation's not really as bad as it seems. That doesn't square with a TV—" He held up one hand. "Tommy? Tommy, this is Sal. I'm glad I caught you. No, I'm not in New York. Listen, Tommy, what do you have for me?" He listened intently, with only an occasional grunt for punctuation. Finally he let out a long breath. "Son of a bitch. Yes, it's important. I think it's damned important. But sit on it, Tommy. Right. Not a word. Thanks. I owe you a big one." Hanging up, he jammed a cigar in his mouth and began chewing furiously. Brooke might have ceased to exist.

"Well? What did he say?"

Campana started, then tossed the cigar in the wastebasket. "That was Tommy Chou, one of my stringers in New York. He has his own reasons for being interested in Chinese diplomats. Anyway, he was out at Kennedy, and he recognized half a dozen of them, boarding the Pan Am flight to Peking. One was Tz'u, the UN Ambassador. Tommy dug around at the airport, and he says people from the Chinese mission have been taking that flight every day, four or five at a time."

Brooke whistled. "Pulling their people out."

"Right. He went to their mission, on West 66th Street. It's locked up tight. Nobody there, and no sign that anybody's expected back."

Brooke took the phone and dialed quickly. "I have a few contacts myself."

At the second ring, a man answered briskly, "US Customs. Passport Division."

"Let me speak to Michael Gavin, please," Brooke said.

The phone clicked with the sound of the call being switched.

"Gavin."

"Mike, this is Steve Brooke."

"Hey, Steve. Game still on for Sunday night?"

"I suppose. Look, Mike, I need a favor."

"Anything but money or women. What do you need?"

Brooke hesitated. "I want to know about some diplomatic personnel. To be exact, I want to know how many people from the Russian Embassy and how many from the Chinese Embassy are out of the country."

"Trying to steal a jump on the news?" Gavin laughed. "No matter. Just a minute." Brooke waited impatiently, but Gavin was as good as his word. "Here it comes. For the Russians: six. Including the Ambassador. He left yesterday for consultations. And for the Chinese—." There was a silence, then Gavin said softly, "Christ."

"What is it, Mike?"

"The dates are spread out, so maybe nobody noticed, but the computer has a list as long as my arm. There's the Ambassador, and the First Secretary, and— I don't know what their staff is, but, hell, they can't have more than two or three people left in Washington. Maybe none. Steve, I think I'd better report this on up the line."

"Fine. But first, check your New York office about their UN mission people."

There was a long quiet. "You expected this. You expected it before you—. I listen to the news. What the hell's going on?"

"After you call New York, Mike, call the Pentagon. The man you want is General Walt Singletary, on the Joint Chief's Planning Staff. Tell him."

"Steve, what—"

"I can't say any more. Believe me. Just call Singletary. Call him." He hung up and took a deep breath.

"So they pulled out the Embassy people," Campana said. "Well, we could have figured that. Who's Singletary."

"The only man I know at the Pentagon who'd be willing to look at evidence—even if it *is* oddball. And he has the clout to get others to look, too. He's the man I'll get Paul's pictures to, if they show anything."

"Speaking of which, when do you call him back?"

Brooke glanced at his watch. Takeoff had been scheduled for three hours earlier. "Now."

But the sergeant in Reeman's office said, "I'm sorry, sir. The Colonel isn't here. He's on a training—just a moment, Colonel Brooke. Colonel Reeman just walked in."

"Steve," Reeman broke in, "you didn't even give me a chance to get back on the ground good. I'm still in my flight suit."

"Screw the flight suit. What did you see? What's at Harding's Fjord?"

"Slow down. I didn't see anything. That island's bare rock, and rough enough for the backside of the moon."

"But the fjord itself?"

"I made one low pass the length of it, but I still didn't see anything. Water and rock, that's all. The film cartridges are over at photoanalysis now. If there's anything there, they'll find it. You ready to tell me what they're looking for, yet?"

Brooke hesitated. "Launchers."

"Launchers? What kind of launchers? What are you talking about?"

"That's as much as I can say, Paul. I'm sorry."

"Uh-huh. Well, how do I get in touch once I find out, one way or the other?"

Brooke gave him the phone number at the motel room. Time was getting too short to worry about discovery any longer. "As soon as you find something, right?"

"Sure, Steve. The minute. Now I'd better pass the word on to the photo-analysis people."

"All right, Paul. Let me hear something soon."

"Nothing?" Campana said as Brooke hung up. "What about the pictures?"

"In photo-analysis," he said absently. "Sal, what if we've blown it? I mean, what proof do we have that's the right place?"

Campana snorted. "It's a little late to worry about that. Everything we know points to it, but only the Chinese can be certain."

"Yes," Brooke echoed grimly. "Only the Chinese."

October 15
1200 hours

It took an effort for Chu not to pace the control room. He realized he was drumming his fingers on the large-scale chart, crosshatched with the lines of the *Cheng Fu*'s search pattern. Ta was chewing at his lip, and the man who listened for the transponder with the missiles had to be replaced every thirty minutes. In that time he would begin to try too hard, to hear things. They were eighteen hours behind schedule.

The run from Coats and Mansel Islands had been perfect, ten hours at maximum speed. The pickup point had been reached, the low level radio signal sent to make the transponder reply—and there had been silence. Chu had not been alarmed, then. The transponder didn't have much range. It wouldn't take a large error to put them out of its range. He'd ordered the search sweeps with the confidence that they would be loading the missiles within the hour.

He was worried now, though. With her streamlining broken by the humps of the missiles, the *Cheng Fu* would take forty-eight hours to reach Harding's Fjord. Launch hour was 1400 on the seventeenth. The submarine was supposed to be safely out of Hudson Bay by then. She wouldn't be. And now every additional minute the search lasted increased the danger of the unthinkable, that the missiles would not be in place at the appointed time. That could not be allowed, whatever the risk.

"Increase the signal strength," Chu ordered.

Liang hesitated, then stepped closer. "Sir— Sir, if I might suggest, increasing the signal strength again—"

"I know, Liang." The signal strength had been specified in the plan. And Liang would adhere to that plan even after it was in shreds. "Some risks must be taken."

Liang nodded reluctantly. Before he could speak, the sonar operator said, "Sir, I have a contact."

"Report," Chu said.

"Medium speed screws, bearing one three five. The range is closing, sir. No indication of sonar ranging by target vessel."

"Sound signature comparison."

"Running, sir." The sonarman paused to check the computer readout. "All probabilities below critical, sir. No identification possible."

Chu took a deep breath. Given their location, it was almost certainly a freighter. But it *could* be a destroyer, or a Coast Guard cutter, running slow, not using their sonar. They could be using passive listening devices.

"All stop," he ordered. "Silence in the boat."

The slight vibration of the deck plates ceased, and the ever-present background whir of the ventilation fans stopped. The air began to seem stuffy almost immediately.

The thrumming of the surface vessel's propellors grew closer, and louder. The control room crew, sweat rolling down their faces, turned to follow the sound as if they could see through the steel hull plates. The sound increased as the vessel passed close to starboard, no more than a hundred yards away. As the sound faded, Chu relaxed.

"Sir, I have a contact."

Chu whirled toward the sonarman, but it was the crewman who was listening for the transponder who had spoken.

"Where away?"

The man clamped his earphones more tightly against his ear and adjusted the knobs on his console. "Bearing: zero one five. Range—Sir, it's within a hundred yards."

A smile flickered across Chu's face. "Liang, have the diving parties prepare to disembark."

October 15
1250 hours

D.L. eased up the rocky ridge to peer over it down the length of Harding's Fjord. Empty gray water rolled along it to crash in spray below him. He examined it more closely through binoculars, but he couldn't see anything that might tell him if the Chinese had come and gone.

"So long as they don't come while we're down there," he muttered.

"What was that Doctor Childe?" Willy hissed.

He slid back down to where Willy and Simon waited with two men from each party. "Nothing, Willy. Just talking to myself."

"I thought maybe they were down there already."

"No. But we need to know when they do get here. Simon, you and Willy each tell off a man for lookouts." Willy touched a slender youth on the shoulder, and Simon nodded toward a grizzled old hunter. "Good. You," he said to the boy, "climb this ridge and watch the fjord. And you," he directed the hunter, "go down to the cliffs at the mouth of the fjord. If either of you sees anything unusual—anything—fire two shots in the air and get back to the boat. Right, then. Off with you."

As the two scrambled toward their positions, D.L. started back across the island. The others fell in behind.

The *Baie du Nord* had been anchored off the side of the island opposite the fjord. The single Cree boat they'd brought along had carried D.L. and his party ashore. He had left orders that everything was to remain on board till he returned, but when he reached the beach both the

Cree canoe and the trawler's launch were drawn up
above the lapping water. The Inuit and the Cree, all of
them, were busily sorting through their stacked supplies,
readying for the move up to the rim of the fjord.

Samantha, snapping pictures of the people working,
paused long enough to smile and wave from atop a
boulder, but D.L. jogged down to the beach in search of
Faschereau. The trawler captain was down by his
launch, talking with Auguste, his crewman.

"You handle it fine, I think. Ah, D.L. We got every
damn thing ashore, all ready to go up to the rim."

"I see that." He grabbed Faschereau's arm, and took
three steps away from the others. He kept his voice low.
"Martial, what are you doing here? I told you to keep
everybody aboard. What if the submarine had been
here? What if they'd had men ashore? With machine
guns, likely. Damn it, if you're not going to do what I
tell you-"

"I'm sorry, D.L." Faschereau shrugged. "I'm sorry. I
think maybe I was right, though. If they are there, or if
they ain't, we got to fight them sometime. Waiting on
the *Baie* don't seem to have no point. No?"

"No," D.L. said slowly. "It doesn't." Somewhere in
the back of his mind, where he hadn't even known it,
must have been the thought that, if the Chinese were
there already, if there wasn't anything they could do,
they could escape on the *Baie*. Escape what was coming.
"But it's too late. We're committed."

"What?"

"Nothing." He climbed up on a nearby boulder, and
raised his voice. "Everybody! Everybody listen." Slowly, the work stopped, and faces turned to him. Samantha
jumped down from her perch and trotted down the
beach to him, snapping pictures all the while. "The submarine isn't here. I hope it just hasn't gotten here yet.
Anyway, we're going to act as if that's the case until we
find out different. There are some good, big hollows

south of the fjord where you can set up tents and
cookstoves. I left two lookouts up there. The signal for
sighting the submarine is two shots. Remember that.
Two shots. Let's see. The radio. Martial, are you certain
that radio can reach the *Baie*? It looks even worse in the
daylight than it did on board."

Faschereau hefted the two knapsacks, one holding the
radio and the other the batteries. "She will reach. Barely, but she will reach."

"Fine. We'll keep it simple. Just 'Submarine!', 'Submarine!' over and over, until we get a response from
you. When you hear that, you start broadcasting. It
doesn't matter what. Tell the Coast Guard you're a
freighter sinking off the fjord. Tell them you stumbled
on drug smugglers. Just get somebody official out here,
fast."

"I remember what to do, but—" Faschereau shifted
uncomfortably. "Well, I thought maybe I stay here with
you. Maybe I can help a little bit. And Auguste can handle the *Baie*."

D.L. shook his head. "Since when have you ever let
anybody handle the *Baie* but you?"

Faschereau grinned. "That is why he needs the experi-
ence."

D.L. sniffed, and cleared his throat. "All right,
Martial. You can stay. Maybe I can keep you out of
trouble for once, ay?" He jumped down. "All right, let's
go. Martial, Willy, Simon, get the boat in the water, and
we'll get on around to the fjord. The rest of you, start
moving the supplies up to the rim. And be careful, all of
you. It's rough up there."

Everyone turned back to their work, and he went to
help push the Cree boat into a moderate surf. Samantha
took a place beside him, heaving with all her might. After one startled look at her, the others bent their shoulders to the freight canoe.

"Be careful," she panted. "Be careful, you say. How careful is it to dive alone? You tell me that. You know the most basic rule of diving safety is never dive alone. Never."

"Do you know explosives? Can you fuse dynamite?" He didn't wait for a reply, if she intended making one. "There's not one thing you can do down there except get me in trouble."

"Get you-. I can *save* you if you do get in trouble. I can do just what a diving partner is supposed to do."

He stopped, leaving the others to launch the canoe. She stopped to glare at him. Her chin was firmly fixed. He tried to brush some hair from her cheek, but she slapped his hand away.

"All right," he said quietly, "the truth. Working with explosives is tricky, even when all the conditions are perfect. And God knows nothing's perfect now. I'll need one hundred percent concentration. Everything I've got. If you're in the water with me, with the dynamite, I won't be able to help worrying about you. I don't care if you like it or not, but that's the way it is. With half my mind on you, I could make a mistake and kill both of us."

There was an expression on her face he couldn't read. "Damn you," she whispered. Suddenly, she grabbed his parka and kissed him, hard. He put his arms around her. Then, just as suddenly, she pushed free of him. She ran up the beach as fast as she could go, stumbling on the rocky ground but not slowing. He stared after her.

"D.L.," Faschereau called. "D.L., are you coming?"

He turned and splashed out to the canoe, scrambling over the side. Before he was properly in, Faschereau twisted the outboard throttle, and the boat leaped ahead. The two crates of dynamite were in the bottom of the boat, along with a blasting kit and seventy-five feet of anchor chain.

He shrugged out of his parka and bent to unlace his boots. "Willy, would you pull my wetsuit and tanks out from under that tarp?"

Simon sat in the bow, scanning the horizon. No one felt like talking.

D.L. laid a hand on the nearest crate. It had been a long time, but this was just commercial forty percent gelatin dynamite. Half the men on the Bay knew how to use it, though he knew a bit more than most. Each stick weighed a half-pound, and took a number six commercial blasting cap. It had a detonating velocity of seven thousand nine hundred feet per second, and was a little less than half as effective as the same amount of TNT, about one third as effective as the same weight of plastic explosive. But, important for them, it had a good resistance to water.

Willy, with the parts of his wetsuit, pulled him back to the present. He took them in silence. By the time they reached the mouth of the fjord, he was ready.

The rock walls seemed to tower higher than their fifty feet. The canoe, tossed on rollers running into the fjord, seemed dwarfed. The walls appeared to tilt inward, as if they might topple at any second.

Then the men began to appear along the rim, and the walls were just solid rock again.

One man appeared almost directly above them on the edge of the cliff. He waved at them, and immediately began lowering a rope over the edge. D.L. waved back, then motioned to the cliff face where the rope was coming down. "There, Martial. Bring us in as close as you can."

D.L. stood as Faschereau swung in closer to the rock wall. Willy and Simon stood ready with boathooks to fend off the rock if they were swept too close. Quickly D.L. grabbed the end of the line and bent it onto one end of the anchor chain.

"Take us across, Martial. But slow."

They paid out the chain behind the boat until they reached the far side of the fjord, where another rope had already been lowered. That was fastened to the other end of the chain, and the rest of it was dropped over the side.

"All right," D.L. shouted. He turned and waved back across the fjord. "All right."

Jerkily the ropes were lowered still more, until the slack in them told that the chain rested on the bottom.

"You place the charges now?" Faschereau said.

"Not yet," D.L. replied. He strapped on his air tanks, then slipped on his fins and climbed over the side. A little water in the mask guarded against fogging. "I'll be back in a minute." Gripping the mouthpiece between his teeth, he rolled backward and down.

The storm had kicked up the bottom, and it hadn't all had time to settle out yet. Sediment and mud hung in the water, swirling violently with the rollers near the surface, not stirring at all near the bottom. Then, through the murkiness, the first launcher was there.

He grabbed hold of a girder and hung there. The open framework was empty. He heaved a sigh of relief into his mouthpiece. He swam hurriedly down the line, stopping to touch each empty launcher. Eight launchers. There had only been eight? He hadn't miscounted the first time? He swam a few strokes beyond the last tower, then stopped with a curse. He was wasting time. They hadn't come yet. They wouldn't escape him. He turned for the surface.

When he grabbed the side of the boat, Faschereau leaned over to help him in. "Where did you go? I was beginning to think you found a mermaid."

D.L. began prying open the dynamite crates. "The launchers. I had to make sure they were empty."

Faschereau gave a short laugh. "I never even thought of that. I guess all this don't be no use if the missiles they already in place. Say, these launchers. We use this dynamite to blow them up, no?"

D.L. continued ripping the last boards off the second crate. "No. In the first place, we might damage the launchers, but we couldn't destroy all eight. They might be able to repair them, or use them anyway. And in the second place, we need the dynamite to hold the sub here. Without that, we've got nothing." He dug into the blasting kit and pulled out a ten-cap blasting machine, the type with a twist-handle. With a smile, he gave it a pat and handed it to Willy. "Hang onto that tight. We'll need it."

"Sure," Willy said. He stuffed the blasting machine into his parka pocket. "Why the grin, Doc?"

D.L. laughed. "I like to have the blasting machine where I can see it. As long as it's with us, I know nobody's trying to be helpful and hooking it up. Can cause unpleasant surprises, that."

Willy whistled softly and took a sick look at the two hundred pounds of dynamite in the bottom of the canoe.

"Unload one of the crates," D.L. said. "Wire the sticks together in bundles, five or six sticks to a bundle. I'm going down to find where to put them."

As the other three began gingerly lifting out the dynamite, he went back over the side. Starting near the mouth of the fjord, he swam along the rock wall searching for a crack or hollow. Fifty feet into the fjord, he turned back and went deeper. On his third pass, at fifteen feet, he found a ledge. It was just a tiny shelf, two feet wide by four long, and completely open and unprotected. He went deeper, flutter-kicking down through the murk. The side of the fjord remained unbroken. Fifty feet down he stopped. Too deep. It had to be the ledge.

When he pulled himself up on the side of the boat, Faschereau gestured to the neatly stacked bundles of dynamite. D.L. shook his head. "Not yet. I need this."

He lifted the empty wooden crate out of the boat and sank beneath the water.

The crate stirred up a small cloud of mud as he slid it onto the ledge. It fit perfectly. The mud hung, barely drifting. He waited till he was certain the canoe wouldn't drift, then swam back to the surface. Filling his arms with dynamite bundles, handed carefully over the side, he made the round-trip to the ledge until the box was almost full and there was only a single bundle left.

Faschereau started to hand it to him, but D.L. motioned him back. Pushing his mask up on his forehead, he levered himself up to hang on the gunwale. A scrap of rag did to dry his hands. Then he pulled the dynamite bundle and the blasting kit to him. Faschereau and the others unconsciously eased back.

The task was a simple one, and one he'd performed a hundred times. Years ago. Still, the brain remembered, and the hands quickly regained the feel of the old motions. The pointed handle of the crimping pliers put a hole in the side of one stick of dynamite. He opened the wooden cap-box and pulled out a number six electrical blasting cap. Removing the small disc of the shunt from the leads, he touched them to the poles of the kit's galvanometer. The needle twitched across the scale. The cap was good.

It slid neatly into the hole in the side of the stick. The leads he pulled back and tied around the wire holding the bundle together. From one of the reels of firing wire he pulled off about six feet, and used the crimpers to strip the wire ends. He spliced the leads in with quick movements, then wrapped the splice in black electrician's tape. When he looked at them again, Simon and Faschereau were looking at him as if he were odder than the dynamite. Willy was frowning worriedly.

"Everything's okay, ain't it, Doctor Childe?" he said.

"Everything's fine, Willy." D.L. settled the mask

back in place. "When I give three tugs on the wire, start across the fjord, letting it out slowly. And you can start bundling that other crate." A loop of wire in hand and the capped dynamite under one arm, he started back down.

He laid the wired bundle in the middle of the rest. Sympathetic detonation would take care of it. Bracing one foot against the ledge, he lifted one end of the crate and slid the firing wire under it. That would hold it in place against almost anything. He gave three sharp tugs at the wire and headed for the bottom, trailing it behind him. The boat's motor revved and the wire grew taut in his grip as it was let off the reel from above.

He swam across the fjord just above the bottom, pulling the wire hand over hand, letting it settle into near invisibility in the mud. Halfway across, he realized he was moving sluggishly. The cold was seeping through his wetsuit turning his muscles to jelly. He knew he should head for the surface. More than one diver had died in those waters because he ignored the warning symptoms. Grimly he pushed the thoughts out of his head and swam on. There was no time to waste.

He found the far wall of the fjord by swimming into it. Groggily he stared at it for a long minute before dropping the wire and starting for the surface. He felt his way up the rock face inch by inch. His eyes didn't seem to be functioning very well. He knew that was supposed to tell him something, but he couldn't remember what.

Suddenly, his fingers found an opening in the rock. It was a crack, running horizontally across the face of the wall, a foot wide and deeper than his arm could reach. How far it went in each direction, he couldn't see, but it would take the other crate of dynamite.

The swim to the surface was a struggle against arms and legs that seemed to have no strength. When he reached the boat, he could just hang on the side and pant.

Faschereau leaned over with the first bundles. "Here —D.L., you are shaking." He put down the dynamite and grabbed D.L.'s arm. "Holy Mother of God! He is ice. Help me get him into the boat."

D.L. jerked free. "Give me the dynamite. Have to place the charges."

"But, D.L.—"

"Give me the God-damned dynamite!"

After a moment, Faschereau picked up the bundles he'd set down. "Very well, D.L. Here."

He made the trips to the crevice in a fog, and each trip was slower than the one before. Twice he had to hunt for the crack. He grouped the bundles with fingers that had turned to wood. He didn't feel the cold any longer, but he felt the fiery pain in his joints.

There were two bundles left when he reached the boat. He pushed one aside and tried to fumble the blasting kit closer. Faschereau gently took the dynamite and the kit from his almost nerveless fingers. He grabbed the trawler captain's wrist weakly. "You - don't - know - what—"

"You will help me," Faschereau said: "I will do what you did, and you will shake your head if I do it wrong."

"Do - it - wrong," D.L. managed, "and - boom." But he didn't try to stop Faschereau again. He couldn't.

He watched as closely as he could while Faschereau went through the steps. The French-Canadian worked almost in slow motion, with frequent pauses to wipe the palms of his hands.

When the splice onto a second reel of firing wire was done, D.L. took the bundle. "Wait," he said. "Don't do - anything - till I get back."

"We will wait," Faschereau said. "And you take care."

D.L. nodded, and let himself sink.

The crack seemed to have shifted. He swam along the wall three times before he realized he was going past the

opening each time. Feeling his way along it, he found
the dynamite and pushed the capped bundle in. The
lethargy in his muscles was growing stronger. Dimly, he
knew there was something else he was supposed to do
now, but he couldn't think of what it could be. It was
simpler just to drift. Drift. He fumbled at his weight
belt, unfastened it and let it fall. Drift. Drift.

Hands grabbed him, and he realized he was being
pulled into the boat. "The wires," he said. "Last connections."

"All right," Faschereau said. "All right. Willy, you
and Simon go ahead and get him out of that suit and
into some clothes. And the blankets." He stood up and
cupped his hands around his mouth. "Tommy Ampaka," he bellowed up the cliff. "Let down the wire."

The grizzled Inuit appeared on the overhang above
them and waved. In moments a black line of firing wire
was snaking down. As Faschereau cut loose the other
wires from their reels and gathered in the one coming
down the cliff, D.L. twisted around to watch. Simon put
another blanket around his shoulders, and Willy put a
flask to his mouth. The warmth of brandy trailed down
his throat and exploded in his stomach.

He watched intently, though, as Faschereau made the
three-way splice, wrapped it, and tossed the wires over
the side. The single line down the cliff was barely visible,
even knowing it was there. "It's done," he said.

"It is done," Faschereau agreed.

"Then we can go back to Helen. I mean Samantha."
He pulled the blankets tighter around him and let his
eyes close. "Samantha."

Around the rim of the fjord pockets of snow left in the
hollows made even the sunlight seem bleak, but the men
and women seemed to get some enjoyment out of posing
for Samantha's camera. She could never get more than
one candid shot of a woman cooking or a man setting up

a tent before they stopped to pose.

The men along the rim grumbled about their work, lashing rocks to the ends of wires, then dropping them over the edge, until she drifted over with her camera. Then they made it a game. They laughed and shouted across the fjord, competing to see who could throw his rock the furthest, or make the biggest splash. Men whose rocks hung up on something short of the water became the butt of good-natured laughter, but the biggest laughter was reserved for those who made the mistake of dropping their rocks from an overhang. Even if the rock reached the water, the wire hung in plain sight, and Dr. Childe had said they had to lie flat against the cliff.

At the sight of D.L. climbing up from the beach, she left the rim. Leading the others, D.L., wearing a pair of blankets like a cloak, disappeared into the hollow where the cookstoves were set up. He took a steaming mug of tea from one of the pots, and turned at her step. There were circles under his eyes. He looked worn down.

"Are you all right, D.L.?"

"I'm fine." He dropped to the ground with a sigh and leaned back against the side of the hollow. "I'm just tired."

"I got some good shots of you and the others in the boat." She paused. "It looked like they had to lift you into the boat, there at the end."

"I just got cold, that's all."

She found a smile somewhere and put it on. "Well, we know the cure for that, don't we? Body heat." She flipped up the corner of his blanket and snuggled in next to him. She ran a hand into his parka, and almost swore. He wasn't cold. He was freezing. "D.L., what happened down there?"

"It doesn't matter. Sometimes, I wish— Hell, I don't know."

She frowned as he buried his nose in his mug. It

wasn't like him to let his doubts out. She tried to keep her tone light. "Probably you wish a certain reporter would stop poking into your private affairs."

It took him a minute to take up the banter, and when he did, his tone was forced. "Well, if she did that, life might get pretty dull, don't you think?"

He put his arm around her and hugged her closer. She laid her head on his chest, but twisted to watch his face. It was bleak, and his eyes were watching something far away.

XVII

October 16
0300 hours

The phone ringing woke Brooke. He straightened from his cramped position, curled on the seat of a motel chair, and tried to work the stiffness out of his neck. The television was on, showing snow and putting out static. The phone went on ringing.

Brooke got to his feet and staggered to the phone, on the way poking Campana, sprawled on the bed. "Wake up, Sal," he said. Campana snorted and opened his eyes as he picked up the receiver. "Yes? Who is it?"

"Steve? It's me, Paul."

Brooke was awake instantly. "Paul, the pictures?"

"They were there, Steve. God, when you said launchers, I just never thought-. I never even said anything about that to the photoanalysis people. One of the women picked them up. She even dug out some old pictures of early Polaris missile test stands for comparison."

"Paul? Paul! Paul, that's great! When can you get the pictures up the ladder?"

There was a silence at the other end. "I'm in Ottawa right now. Flew down right after I got the pictures back. I spent yesterday afternoon trying to get somebody to listen, and last night harassing people at home."

"And?"

"Well, I've ruined my career. I accomplished that much."

"I don't understand."

Reeman laughed bitterly. "One Deputy Minister of Defence told me it looked like mining apparatus to him. Another looked me straight in the face and said he didn't see a damned thing. General Bradford wouldn't even look at them. Dressed me up one side and down the other for bothering him with, I believe his exact words were, damned fool nonsense. He said the whole idea was insane, and the only excuse for the photoanalyst was that she was probably having her period, but there was no excuse for me. Hell, he was politer than some."

Brooke was stunned. "Damn it, they can't all be blind."

"Not blind. Just scared. You can smell it, Steve. Everybody knows World War III is about to begin, no matter what Washington and Moscow say. They're afraid of being caught in the middle, hoping there's still something left of Canada when it's all over. I suppose they're afraid if they even admit those things are on the bottom of Harding's Fjord, they're going to get pulled in deeper."

"I can't believe that, Paul."

"Would *you* invite H-bombs on Ottawa and Montreal, when you knew all you could do would be sit there and take it?"

Brooke sighed heavily. "Maybe not. I don't know. Look, can you come—."

"This is the long distance operator," a nasal voice broke in. "Please deposit ninety cents for the next three minutes."

Brooke listened incredulously as chimes sounded the receipt of the coins. "Paul, are you calling from a phone booth?"

"I am. I'm at the airport. If I fly to Washington, can you get me and the pictures to somebody who'll look at them?"

"I have just the man in mind."

"Good, because I am about to break nine different laws, that I know of, concerning national security and official secrets. The next direct flight to Washington leaves for Dulles at nine o'clock. I'll be on it."

Brooke was laughing softly as he hung up. Campana looked at him questioningly.

"Our proof is on the way," Brooke said. "Our God-damned salvation is on the way."

October 16
1130 hours

Yü shuffled through the latest intelligence reports as he walked to the wall map. Colored pins, coded for nationality and weapons type, showed the known deployments of American and Russian forces. He didn't stop to look at the pins. He liked to do that, to visualize the forces represented, to contemplate them being used to destroy each other, but this time he had more pins to add. And they were most disturbing.

Eight yellow pins - Soviet squadrons of TU-26 bombers, the one the Americans called the Backfire - had to be placed in Siberia. There were other yellow pins in Siberia, each accompanied by the green pin of a tanker squadron, but these eight pins were unaccompanied. And they were far from America. They were also very close to the Chinese border.

In the Philippines he placed four amber pins - American B-52 squadrons. Briefly he wondered what strings had been pulled or pressures brought to bear to allow them to stage there. Whatever the cause, though, they would never fly against the Soviet Union from there.

He looked at the map without seeing it. The conclusions were inescapable. The United States and Russia were going to attack each other, but they were also going to attack China.

It must be that analysis of the metal from the Novaya Zemlya launcher. As so often, events of great moment turned on a happenstance. But they were not convinced, not completely. Not enough to abandon their attacks on each other. And that meant the plan could still go forward. Someone had once told Chairman Mao that, in a nuclear attack, six hundred million Chinese would die. That, the Chairman had replied, would leave two hundred million. And there were more Chinese now than there had been then. It would be necessary, however, to convince the Implementation Group.

He switched on the intercom. "Kou, prepare a memo—Kou?"

Silence answered him. Disbelieving, he pushed open the door to his aide's office. Kou was always there when he called. It was his function. The office was empty.

Angrily he swept up the phone - and stopped. Kou *wouldn't* simply absent himself. He laid the phone back on the hook. Something was not as it should be. Straightening his tunic. he left the office and walked to the elevator at the end of the hall. He pushed the button for two levels higher. Lien's office was there.

When the door opened, Yü immediately pushed the CLOSE button. One glance had been enough. The hall had been full of troops in full battle gear, troops wearing the badge of the Special Political Action Cadre. They were the ones called in to deal with high-ranking officials who became politically unreliable. Two of them had been pulling General Lien down the hall, his feet dragging on the floor, blood running down his face. Kou had been there, too. And he hadn't looked like a prisoner.

When the first elevator door opened on the level with Admiral Yü's office, the square-bodied General Shih was the first one out, his submachine gun thrust ahead of him. Others followed, and more soldiers poured out of the other elevators, fanning out, ordering everyone in the halls to the wall for an immediate check of identification papers. Shih strode down the hall without looking right or left. Behind him trailed a small knot of guards. And Lieutenant Kou.

At the Admiral's office, he kicked open the door without slowing. Yü sat rigidly behind his desk, cold eyes fixed on Shih.

"In the name of the Central Planning Committee," Shih began flatly, "I arrest—" With an oath, he strode forward and grabbed Yü's shoulder. Slowly the Admiral toppled forward onto the desk, his eyes cold as ever. A small bottle rolled away from his hand. There seemed to be a hint of a smile on his lips.

Shih raised his gaze slowly to the door. Kou flinched. "He knew we were coming," the General said softly.

Kou swallowed violently. "It was none of my doing. None of my doing. You must believe me. Why would I cooperate and then—"

"The safe," Shih said. He put one foot against the chair and pushed. The chair rolled a few feet, then fell on its side, spilling the Admiral's body. "Open it, Kou."

Kou stared at Yü as if he expected him to get up off the floor. His eyes came slowly up to Shih's, and he licked his lips. "Of course. Of course." He slid open the panel in front of the safe and knelt before it. He babbled nervously, as if trying to convince them how useful he had been. "He kept this combination to himself, of course, but he was sometimes careless in opening it in my presence. I did not count, you see. I was never one of his followers, never one of his political—You see, I punch the combination in, so, then punch this large button." He laid one finger on a small plastic panel. "In a second this will light, and the safe will be open." The panel remained dark. "In a second." It stayed damningly dark.

Shih's words were very quiet. "Open it."

Kou closed his eyes and swallowed. "I must have made an error in the sequence." He ran through the numbers again. "It has to open." The panel stayed dark. "It has to. I-."

Shih pushed him roughly aside. "Obviously, at some point, you betrayed yourself, and he changed the combination." Kou's mouth worked soundlessly, and he shook his head, but the General was no longer looking at him. "Hsi, how long to open the safe?"

A wizened man in a uniform without insignia came forward and knelt before the safe. He pulled a multimeter from under his coat and began checking various parts of the safe control panel. At last he knelt back on his heels. "It will take forty-eight hours, Comrade General. At a minimum."

"Forty-eight hours." Shih worked the bolt of his submachine gun, ejecting a round onto the carpet, to make certain there was a round in the chamber. With great care he pressed the muzzle against the left eye of the still-kneeling Kou. "Is there any other set of the recall signals outside this safe?"

Kou opened his mouth, but no sound came out. He shook his head jerkily.

"And how long," the General asked quietly, "until launch hour?"

Kou worked his mouth to get moisture enough to speak. "Tw-twenty-two hours." He was trying to say "no" when Shih pulled the trigger.

October 16
1220 hours

The crowds hurrying through the airport lounge seemed to ignore the large TV screens, suspended overhead, where arrivals and departures were constantly being flashed. Brooke sat hunched in a chair and stared at them. Digging out his cigarettes, he fished out the next to last one and lit it. It tasted like the bottom of a shoe. After two packs, he wasn't surprised. He ground it out in a sand-box ashtray and looked up just as the flight he was waiting for flashed on the screen.

Air Canada: Flight 127: From Ottawa: Now Arriving Gate 19:

Brooke bounced to his feet and stopped only long enough to check the signs for directions before breaking into a trot. He dodged around people as if they were standing still, occasionally flinging an apology over his shoulder. When he reached the gate, Reeman was just coming through the Customs check.

Reeman was in the short, wiry fighter-pilot mold, like Brooke, a man whose every motion spoke of energy under control. As he picked up his bag and stepped away from the counter, Brooke grabbed his arm and hustled him toward the main entrance.

"Christ, Paul, I thought you'd never get here."

"Don't blame me," Reeman said wearily. "We were stacked up three hours in a holding pattern, waiting to get in. God, I'm beat. I haven't had any sleep since night before last. Never could—."

"Do you have them, Paul? The pictures?"

Reeman hefted his bag. "In here. Just like I said."

Brooke heaved a sigh of relief. "So far it's seemed as if every new opening on this thing has turned out to be a dead end."

"These aren't a dead end. If the people down here will look at them."

"They'll look." Brooke wished he was as confident as he sounded.

The automatic doors hissed open in front of them, and they ran across the access road to the parking lot. In twenty minutes Brooke's station wagon had merged into the weekend traffic.

Cars were thick on the exit road, and it was worse once they hit I-66 and the Memorial Parkway. The

roads that led to the Pentagon were the same roads that
led to the Lincoln Memorial, Arlington National Ceme-
tery, and the Washington Monument. Weekends
brought tourists by the thousands, clogging the high-
ways bumper to bumper. The twenty miles took an
hour, Brooke grimly gripping the wheel, Reeman drumming his fingers on his knee.

When they got out of the car, in Brooke's parking
place, Reeman started to pull out the suitcase. Brooke
stopped him. "Bring two sets of pictures, and leave the
rest here."

"Why?"

"A suitcase, or even that aerial film cartridge, would
have to be searched. With just a couple of folders, we
might make it to General Singletary's office without
drawing Security's attention."

Reeman shrugged, but extracted two folders. Brooke
locked the car, and they walked to the entrance.

The extra guards were still there, as well as the computer terminal Brooke suddenly wondered what that
computer had recorded about his contact with Sal Campana.

"Your ID's, sirs," the sergeant behind the terminal
said.

Brooke unclipped his card from his lapel and handed
it over. Reeman dug his out of his wallet.

"I'm Colonel Brooke, Canadian Liaison. This is
Colonel Reeman. We're here to see General Singletary,
of the Joint Chief's Planning Staff."

"Yes, sir," the sergeant said. He went right on feeding
the ID information into the terminal. After a moment he
read something off the display screen and handed them
back. To Reeman's he added a clip-on badge with a
green-and-red stripe. "Sir, this will authorize your presence on level four, section seven, where General
Singletary's office is located. You must be in the escort
of a cleared officer at all times. Colonel Brooke has been

registered as your escort."

Reeman clipped the badge to his lapel. "Thank you, sergeant."

Brooke hurried him toward the elevators.

"Tight security," Reeman said.

"Not so tight, thank God. They didn't ask where I've been for the last three days, or why I left in the company of the editor of *Newsworld* magazine. Let's get this over with. Quick."

They stepped into a waiting elevator; Brooke pushed the button marked 4.

On the door a brass plate read WALTER G. SINGLETARY III, GENERAL, USA. Inside was a secretary with middle-age spread and a pleasant smile. "Can I help you, gentlemen?"

Brooke took the folders from Reeman. "We're here to deliver these to General Singletary."

"I'll see that the General gets them." She held out her hand.

"We need to give them directly to the General," Brooke said. "There are some points we have to explain."

"I'm afraid that won't be possible, sir. General Singletary left for Colorado this morning."

"Damn," Reeman said. "When will he be back?"

"I really couldn't say, sir."

Brooke realized she was studying them. It *was* odd to have two strange officers, and foreigners at that, burst in unannounced to see a member of the Planning Staff. He laid the folders on her desk with what he hoped was a disarming grin.

"I'm certain we can leave these with you. They aren't really that urgent. I'll leave a note."

Her face relaxed slightly, and she pushed a pad across the desk to him. He scribbled "here are the pictures you wanted" and signed the name of the Canadian Defence Minister. She only glanced at the note before clipping it to the folders, but he was sure she had read it. Her smile was back in place.

"I'll see that he gets it first thing, sir."

Reeman's face was a study in puzzlement, but Brooke managed to get him into the hall before he opened his mouth.

"Steve, what the hell was all that at the last? Leaving a note. Leaving the pictures."

Brooke pushed the DOWN button impatiently. "We have more copies. And she was getting suspicious. In another ten seconds she'd have been calling security."

"Well, what the hell?" Reeman was irritated. "At least we'd have gotten the pictures to somebody."

"You don't know Pentagon Security. It would take them days to decide this wasn't a Russian plant. Until then, neither the pictures nor we would go anywhere."

They had the elevator down to themselves. It seemed to crawl. When the doors opened, Brooke headed straight for the exit without even glancing at the checkpoint. As the big glass door swung shut behind him, he thought he heard his name. He quickened his pace, pulling Reeman along.

On the walkway to the parking lot, he knew it hadn't been his imagination. From behind them someone called, "Colonel Brooke? One moment, sir?"

"Run," Brooke said, and took off as fast as he could.

"What the hell?" Reeman said. Then he was pounding after Brooke.

From behind came a startled shout. "Colonel Brooke! Halt!"

Running, Brooke fished out his car keys; at the station wagon, he dove into the driver's seat, threw open the other door, and revved up as Reeman leapt inside. The wheels squealed as he backed out of his parking place, slammed the transmission into drive, and floored it. In the rearview mirror he could see two men in blue

Pentagon Security berets; they turned and ran back toward the Pentagon.

"For Christ's sake, Steve," Reeman said. He held up his temporary badge. "We were just supposed to turn this in."

Brooke shook his head. "They called me by name. I refuse to believe that sergeant at the checkpoint just remembered me. Something clicked in that God-damned computer. They know about my contact with *Newsworld*."

"Hell, I didn't plan on running from the United States Army!"

"That reminds me. We have to get rid of this car. They may give the license number to the police."

"Oh, shit!" Reeman sagged in his seat. "The Army *and* the police. Jesus Christ! So what do we do now?"

Without answering, Brooke cut across a lane of traffic and pulled into a service station. He stopped by the phone booth in the corner of the lot. "I'll just be a minute."

Campana answered on the first ring. "Yes?"

"Sal, this is Steve. Remember that party in Georgetown, the one the Joint Chiefs are going to?"

"Sure. Theodoria Waring's. What about it?"

"How do I get there?"

Campana whistled. "You're serious? She only talks to ambassadors, cabinet members, a few favored senators, and a *very* few admirals and generals. You'll never get past the door."

"Let me worry about that. Now, what's the address?"

Campana sighed and gave it to him. "But listen," he went on, "the only way you're going to get to the Chiefs is if they're already there. No way Theodoria Waring will let you wait around for them. Now, I understand Kneightson likes to arrive late, about ten o'clock. Hardiman—."

"That's okay. Kneightson's the one I want."

"You shoot for the top, don't you?"

"It's the only way, Sal. Wish me luck."

"Hell, I wish us all luck. But it's riding with you."

When Brooke got back in the car, Reeman just said, "Well?"

"We're taking the pictures to Admiral Kneightson."

" 'Hardtack' Harley Kneightson? The Chairman of the Joint Chiefs?" Reeman whistled between his teeth. "I hear he eats Vice Admirals for lunch and doesn't even spit out the braid. What do you think he's going to do to a couple of mid-rank Canadian Air Force types?"

"Whatever. He's our man." He started the car and pulled out into traffic. "At ten o'clock. Now to get rid of this car."

Brooke drove the rental car slowly past, while Reeman studied the house. It was well lit, and people could be seen at the curtained windows. A car pulled up in front of the house, and a man in a red coat ran down to take the keys and drive off as the driver went in with a woman on his arm.

"Valet parking," Brooke said. "Fancy." He turned the corner.

"What are we waiting for?" Reeman asked. "It's quarter to eleven, now. Damn it, if Kneightson is going to be there, he's there. Maybe we missed seeing him go in. Maybe he got here early. Maybe I'll like civilian life." He sobered. "If I have any life left to like."

Brooke nodded grimly. He pulled up in front of the house and got out, clutching the attaché case. Reeman followed.

One of the redcoats appeared. "Your keys, sir?"

Brooke tossed them to him without slowing. He trotted up the stairs and pushed the bell. Soft chimes sounded.

The butler who opened the door took in their low

rank with a raised eyebrow; his voice was professionally polite. "Yes, sir?"

"Couriers to see Admiral Kneightson." Brooke lifted the attaché case slightly. The butler's eyes widened.

A handsome woman in black silk evening pajamas appeared behind the butler. Her smile became questioning when she saw Brooke and Reeman. "What is it, Jepson?"

"Couriers, ma'am," the butler said. "To see Admiral Kneightson."

She put a hand to her throat, but her voice remained level. "Thank you, Jepson." The butler bowed and disappeared. "I'm Theodoria Waring, gentlemen."

"Lieutenant Colonel Brooke, ma'am, and this is Lieutenant Colonel Reeman. It *is* urgent that we see the Admiral."

"Of course. If you'll wait here." It wasn't a request.

A babble of conversation escaped before she closed the door behind her. Reeman looked at Brooke questioningly.

"I guess they don't let peons in with the guests," Brooke said.

Reeman grunted sourly.

Five minutes later she appeared again. "Come with me, gentlemen." She led them through a side door, by way of halls where the only sign of the party was the scurry of waiters and maids, to a broad oak door. She pushed it open. "Here they are, Harley."

"Thank you, Theodoria," came a gravelly bass. "Let me see them alone, please."

She slipped out as Brooke and Reeman entered, pulling the door to behind her.

Admiral Harley Kneightson was standing in front of the fireplace. His craggy face, with brown eyes that commanded attention, was familiar from magazine covers and the TV news. Naval aviator wings topped the rows of ribbons on his chest, and the blue ribbon of the Congressional Medal of Honor.

Brooke and Reeman stiffened to attention. "Sir," Brooke began.

"You'd better have a good explanation for this," Kneightson said in a tone that made anyone with less than four stars sweat. "The Pentagon doesn't use the Canadian Air Force for couriers, and the Canadian government uses civilians. So who the hell are you?"

"I'm Lieutenant Colonel Stephen Brooke, sir, attached to Canadian Liaison at the Pentagon. This is Lieutenant Colonel Reeman, commanding officer of 218 Squadron, Fighter/Reconnaissance. And we do have something that you must see, sir." He opened the attaché case on the desk. Quickly he shuffled the clearest shot of the launchers to the top and held it out to the Admiral. "These are not from Novaya Zemlya, sir."

Kneightson's hand stopped short of the picture, then he took it slowly. "I'll ask later how you know about that." He frowned at the photo. "If not Novaya Zemlya, then where?"

"Hudson Bay, sir," Brooke said. Kneightson looked up with a startled exclamation. "I—. I have reason to believe, sir, that those launchers were built by the crew of a Chinese submarine."

The Admiral raised an eyebrow, and held out his hand for the rest of the photographs. "And those reasons are?"

Brooke took a deep breath. At last! "It began, sir, when I got a call from Sal Campana—."

Kneightson went through the folder of pictures, never looking up, while Brooke recounted his story. From time to time he grunted. Finally he nodded and closed the folder. "You flew the mission to take these?" he said to Reeman.

"Yes, sir. I led it."

Kneightson picked up the phone on the desk. "This is Admiral Kneightson. Have my car sent around to the front." He hung up and started for the door, the folder under his arm. "You two come with me."

"Begging the Admiral's pardon," Brooke said, "but where are we going?"

"The White House," Kneightson said, and disappeared through the door.

Brooke and Reeman hurried after him.

The guard at the White House gate checked the ID's the Admiral's driver passed him, and waved the car on. All were silent as they rolled through the grounds, as they had been since Georgetown.

The car stopped in front of the south portico; the driver hopped out and ran around to get the Admiral's door, but Kneightson was out before he could get there. He sourly held the door for Brooke and Reeman instead.

Kneightson was already talking quietly to the doorkeeper when they got inside. The doorkeeper hurried away without even a glance in their direction, but two athletic young men appeared on the instant. One stood watching them while the other spoke to the Admiral. After a moment the man talking to the Admiral straightened and nodded. He said something to the other young man and started down the hall. Kneightson followed, waving to Brooke and Reeman to come along.

"I guess we go," Brooke said.

"It's too late to stop now," Reeman murmured.

The second young man fell in behind them.

Brooke was so conscious of the man following, and the cool gaze of the other man, who held the door, that it took him a minute to realize exactly what they were entering. The Oval Office. For a minute he gaped like a tourist. Then William Hughes, the President of the United States, came through the door.

Hughes was in his bedroom slippers, and still belting a robe over his pajamas, as he crossed the room to his

desk. He'd aged since his election, but the former sena-
tor from Wyoming still had what the newspapers called
the look of the prairie.

"I apologize, Mr. President," Kneightson said, "for
waking you."

Hughes waved it away as he sat behind the desk.
"Sleep? Not much of that, the past few days. You
wouldn't have come if it wasn't important, Harley.
What do you have for me?"

Kneightson laid the folder on the desk in front of him
and opened it. "These were taken in Hudson Bay, Mr.
President. This is Colonel Brooke, and Colonel Reeman, of the Canadian Air Force. They will explain it,
sir. Exactly as you told it to me, Brooke."

Brooke cleared his throat. He began slowly, while the
President leafed through the folder. Five minutes into
the story, Hughes looked up and leaned back in his
chair. He studied Brooke unblinkingly, hands clasped
across his middle, thumbs tapping together. When
Brooke finished, he leaned forward to look at the pictures again.

"Gentlemen," he said finally, looking from Brooke to
Reeman, "would you mind waiting outside in the hall
for a few minutes? If you'd like something to drink, just
ask one of the Secret Service men."

"Of course, Mr. President," Brooke replied. He gathered Reeman up by eye, and they left.

In the hall, the two athletic young men—Secret Service, Brooke supposed—were sitting across from the
door. Immediately beside the door was a grim-faced
Army Warrant Officer with a locked black case on his
lap. It was handcuffed to his wrist.

"What do you think? Reeman asked.

Brooke sighed. "How the hell do I know? It's the last
chance, anyway. I guess we hope."

President Hughes waited until the door closed, then
swiveled to face Kneightson. "You obviously believe

this is straight, Harley, or you wouldn't have brought it to me. How reliable would you rate it?"

"By the book, Mr. President, no better than grade two. But my gut tells me it's better than that, and there's no time to check it."

Hughes nodded and pulled open the drawer that housed the red, hot-line phone to Moscow. He lifted it just far enough to hear the hiss of static and dropped it back. "Our people say it's definitely on their end. Trying to put the pressure on, I suppose." He picked up one of the desk phones instead. "Wilson? Try to get me a satellite connection to Moscow. Through the embassy, if you have to. And get me a line to the Canadian Prime Minister. Urgent." He dropped the phone back on the hook and pushed himself up out of his chair. "This Chinese angle, Harley. You think there's anything to that?"

Kneightson shook his head slowly. "All we have now, more than we had before, is a third-hand story from that reporter and the Canadian doctor. We don't have any idea how reliable they are."

"They were right about the launchers."

"Yes, sir. But whoever built the launchers, Mr. President, you can bet the Russians will take full advantage once the ball starts rolling. If they're going to get roughed up, they're going to take everybody with them."

Hughes rubbed at his eyes, and peered out the window. The light from the office windows didn't spill very far into the garden, but he could make out shapes moving among the shrubs. "Harley, do you really think those Marines are necessary?"

"I'll remove them if you order it, Mr. President, but—."

"Yes, yes, I know. I read the report. 'Given the present set of circumstances a high order of probability exists that a well-organized team of assassins—' Damn."

"The regular guards, and the Secret Service, are capable of dealing with the lone crackpot, Mr. President. But a team?'' Kneightson shrugged.

"I know, Harley. It's a hell of a thing, isn't it." The phone on the desk rang. Hughes took two long strides and had it up halfway through the second ring. "Yes?"

"This is Wilson, Mr. President. I have Prime Minister Montrechet on the line, sir. No luck yet on the call to Moscow."

"Put him on, Wilson." The line clicked. "Pierre? This is Will Hughes."

"Yes, Will," Montrechet said in his accented English. "I was told this call was urgent, and I can quite believe it at this time of night. Of course, I am aware of the problems you are having at present with the Russians, but—."

"Pierre, I hate to break in on you, but every minute *could* be vital. Some pictures of a part of Hudson Bay have come into my possession."

"Come into your possession? May I ask how? I was not aware your surveillance satellites were aimed at Canada."

"These pictures were taken by one of your recon squadrons, Pierre. The 218th. You can check back down the line, or I can send you copies."

"Now I would very much like to know how these photographs, as you say, came into your possession."

"They were taken," Hughes went on, "at a place called Harding's Fjord, in the Sleeper Islands. And they show missile launchers on the bottom of the fjord."

"Missile—. That is absurd. Canada does not have any missile launchers. We leave that to you and the Russians."

"Well, I didn't think *you* put them there, Pierre. You see, that trouble you spoke of—with the Russians?— started when they found some missile launchers just like these off Novaya Zemlya. At least, they say they found them. Now, these launchers at Harding's Fjord don't have missiles on them. Yet. But—."

"No Missiles?" Montrechet sounded relieved. "Are you even certain they *are* missile launchers? It could be anything. An old shipwreck, or—."

"They're launchers, Pierre. Missile launchers. And given the present state of affairs, I want to make sure they don't get any missiles put on them."

There was a moment of silence. "How do you propose to do that?"

"Well, you could send some Navy demolition people out there."

"To a sunken ship?"

Hughes voice hardened. "To missile launchers, Pierre. If you don't want to use your own men, I can loan you part of the 82nd Airborne."

"American paratroopers, on Canadian soil? I would be voted out of office, and deservedly so."

"Pierre, this is considerably more important than politics."

"It is my duty to preserve Canada, not to involve it in the problems of the superpowers. I am sorry."

"Pierre—." Abruptly there was only the hiss of an empty line "Damn!" Hughes roared. "That fat bastard!" Visibly he collected himself. "The deadline is midnight tomorrow, Moscow time. Eight o'clock here. Harley, how soon can you move the 82nd from North Carolina to the Canadian border?"

"I can have two battalions in staging areas in six hours, Mr. President."

"Good. I can stop at least eight missiles from striking this country, and I intend to. If the Canadians don't move first, I want those two battalions on that island before dark tomorrow." He sighed bleakly. "Now run those two officers back in here. Let's see what else they know."

October 17
1210 hours

Chu peered through the periscope, studying the approach to Harding's Fjord. Finally he straightened. "All seems as it was. Signal the diving parties to commence moving the missiles into the fjord, Liang. Then we will surface and go in."

"Sir," Liang said seriously, "standard operating procedure calls for us to remain outside the fjord until a landing party has been put ashore and reported back that—."

"Enough, Liang." Chu clenched his jaw to fight off the sudden wave of rage that swept over him. Could the man never see when plans *must* be altered? He made an effort to keep his tone moderate. "We were originally scheduled to arrive yesterday, just at dark. Remaining on the surface long enough to put a landing party over the side would have presented much less hazzard then than it does at noon. But most importantly, a complete sweep of the island will take at least two hours, and we have *less* than two hours to launch. Which do you think is more important?"

"The launch, of course, sir. I just—."

"Pass the orders," Chu said disgustedly. "I will put the landing party ashore once I am in the fjord. Now, stand by to surface."

The warning klaxon sounded, and the submarine rose toward the surface.

XVIII

In the hollow, D.L. had just finished attaching the fuse to the last of the dynamite, when a shot sounded at the mouth of the fjord. He froze with the stick in his hand. A second shot came. Carefully, he set the dynamite beside the other sticks. The men, clutching tea mugs and plates of stew, looked at him expectantly.

"It's time," he said. He was glad he sounded calm. It might help the others. "Go to your places, now. You remember what we planned. Wait for my signal."

The men picked up their rifles and filed out silently. D.L. unzipped the case containing his own rifle. He'd had it ever since coming to the Bay. It had taken mountain sheep, caribou, a bear that was trying to kill some fishermen. It had never taken a man. It wasn't meant for that, not like the guns he'd carried in Korea. He gripped the stock; his finger curled around the trigger. With an oath he shoved it back in the case and rezipped it. Korea was long in the past. Whatever happened, he wasn't going back to it. He wasn't.

Samantha slid down into the hollow and stopped to change her telephoto lens for a zoom. "That boat's a monster, D.L. I got some terrific shots. There might be a cover in one of the ones framed by the mouth of the fjord. D.L., are you all right?"

"I'm fine." He managed a smile. "Listen, now. You take care out there. Take your pictures from cover."

"From under the covers, if I could." She frowned suddenly. It *will* work, won't it, D.L.?"

"It'll work." He touched her cheek. What was he doing, worrying about the men on the submarine? It was *she* who might get hurt, she and the rest who'd followed him. "Samantha—Well, you just take care." He scrambled up out of the hollow before she could speak.

He ran, half crouched so he couldn't be seen from the Bay, and flopped to the ground short of the rim. Heedless of the snow, he worked his way closer. Faschereau was hunched over the old radio, the earphones clamped to his head and the mike in his fist. Willy and Simon crouched nearby clutching their rifles. D.L. ran a quick eye over the others, scattered around the rim. Across from him a Cree had crept close to the edge. His rifle barrel stuck over the side of the fjord.

"Get that rifle back," D.L. shouted. The offender, and half a dozen others, pulled back from the rim.

D.L. crawled closer to the edge himself, then, and fished out his binoculars. Carefully, cupping his hands to shield against glare off the lens, he raised up enough to study the approaching sub.

The torpedo shape knifed through the water toward the fjord, its sleek conning tower giving it the appearance of a gigantic killer whale. The men in quilted parkas, balancing on the rounded deck with submachine guns in their hands, were deadlier than any orca, though. Behind the sail two large rubber boats were being inflated. On the small bridge in the top of the sail were two men, watching the island through binoculars. One must be the captain, he thought. He moved back before they spotted him.

Willy gave him a confident grin, and Simon nodded.

Faschereau gave the thumbs up. They seemed to think it would all go according to plan. He tried to remember a military operation that had gone according to plan, but couldn't. They never did.

He dug the blasting machine out of his parka pocket and carefully fastened the wires to the poles. Gripping the machine tightly, he eased back to the rim.

The submarine was closer. In another minute it would be entering the fjord. He could make out the men on deck plainly, without the binoculars. Then he saw the skindivers.

There were a pair of them, being pulled along by sea-sleds, ahead of the sub, pilot fish riding ahead of a shark. They must be meant to guide the sub into the narrow confines of the fjord. But if they spotted the wires the sub might never come in. If that happened—He inserted the handle in the blasting machine. The bow of the sub was almost to the mouth of the fjord. If the divers gave a warning, he'd set off the explosives and hope to damage the sub enough to prevent its escape. After that, they'd have to play it by ear. His breath rasped in his throat. Rifle stocks clicked on rock as men shifted nervously.

The divers were past the mouth of the fjord, past the explosives. The sub nosed in after them, its length sliding precisely down the center of the gash in the island's rock. Water thrashed at the stern, and it floated in place. Immediately, smoothly, the rubber boats went over its side, ten men descending into each.

"Now, Martial," D.L. said quietly.

Faschereau keyed his mike. "Submarine, Auguste. The submarine is here. Do you hear me? Submarine. Submarine."

D.L. took a deep breath and twisted the handle. With a roar like a volcano erupting, two gouts of water rose at the fjord's mouth, as high as the rock walls. On the side where the dynamite had been placed in the crack, a huge slab separated from the wall, tons of rock toppling into the water. The crashes echoed down the length of the fjord. The wave that swept down it flipped the rubber boats like toys. Men weighted with gear struggled to hold on to the capsized boats. Near them a diver floated to the surface, spreadeagled. The men on the sub stared incredulously at the scene.

Before they could recover, with the sound of the explosions still hanging in the air, D.L. stood and moved to the edge. "T'ou hsiang!" he shouted. "Surrender!" The men on the sub whipped around, freezing at the sight of the lone man facing them in a wide stance from the rocks above. While they stared, he went on in Chinese. "Look at the walls of the fjord. Observe the wires. If you do not surrender, the rest of the explosives will be detonated. Your vessel will be destroyed. I will give you-."

Suddenly the man D.L. took to be the captain snatched up a microphone and began shouting. The men on deck broke from their paralysis. They began spraying the rim of the fjord with submachine gun fire. And the sub began backing out of the fjord.

D.L. dropped to the ground in a spray of rock chips. "The chain!" he shouted. "Raise the chain!"

Dripping, the ropes jerked up the cliffs. The weight of the chain pulled them out from the faces, but the chain came up until its ends were out of the water and it hung in a glistening wet are directly behind the sub.

The crewman on the afterdeck stared disbelievingly, then directed their fire at the points where the ropes came over the cliffs. They shouted at the conning tower. Their bullets had no effect, and there was no time to halt the sub. The propellor struck the chain.

With a tremendous crack the ropes parted. The sea behind the sub was flailed to froth by the chain caught up in the propellor. One man on the stern was suddenly gone as the heavy links whipped around. And then it was still. The propellor was jammed tight. The incoming tide carried the sub deeper into the fjord.

Throughout it all the sailors had continued their fusilade. Now the men on the rim decided it was time to join in. With the skill of markmanship born of long hours hunting, they began to fire back.

A Chinese sailor abruptly threw his hands to his face with a scream and fell over the side. Another crumpled to the deck clutching a suddenly bloody leg, and a third shouted, dropped his gun, and slid slowly into the water. But the volume of fire put out by the submachine guns was taking its toll.

Next to D.L. a man grunted and slumped, the snow turning red beneath his head. Across the fjord an Inuit raised up too high to take aim, and a burst flung him back like a doll. Another man toppled soundlessly from the rim. Somewhere down the cliff a man screamed, "Doctor! Doctor!" over and over. And on the sub men were righting one of the rubber boats that had drifted alongside. If they got men ashore-.

Without even thinking D.L. was on his feet and running. He passed Samantha, holding her camera at arm's length to shoot over the edge, and then he was sliding down into the hollow where the supplies and cookstoves were. He pushed aside his cased rifle and snatched up a dynamite stick in each hand. When he turned, Samantha was standing above the hollow, shading her eyes with one hand.

"What are you doing?" she asked. "Oh, my God!"

He flipped open the firebox door on one stove and delicately touched the fuses to the flame. They hissed into life. He pivoted and scrambled up the side of the hollow.

Six seconds, he thought. No time to take care. No time to waste. No time to—He skidded to a halt at the rim and hurled the dynamite down toward the sub in the same instant. The two sticks exploded ten feet above the deck.

The concussion knocked him off his feet. Groggy and

shaken, he forced himself up. Willy and Simon tried to help him, but he pushed them away. He made it to the edge and looked down.

On the deck of the submarine, one moaning man tried to rise and failed. Otherwise there were only still bodies. The bridge was empty. One man lay halfway through the forward escape hatch. The sub had drifted closer to the wall of the fjord below him. The conning tower was directly under an overhang.

"Rope," he said. He turned and broke into a run toward the overhang. "Bring rope." He took a step onto the overhang and peered down. It would be a straight drop to the bridge.

Willy, Simon, and Faschereau pounded up behind him. The French-Canadian had a coil of rope over his shoulder. "Rope, D.L.?" he said. "What we do with rope?"

D.L. took the coil and threw a loop around a boulder. "I'm going down." He tied it off with a bowline and secured it with two half-hitches. As he tossed the free end over the side, Samantha appeared.

"This is insane," she said. Her green eyes glinted angrily, but her forehead was creased with worry. "You go down there, and you're going to get yourself killed."

"And if I don't? They could set frogmen to cut the chain, get away. They could put men ashore. They could-. Oh, hell, Samantha. I *have* to do this." He noticed that Faschereau and the other two were checking the loads in their rifles, and waiting expectantly. "You three stay up here. If I don't get back, you'll have to take over."

Faschereau closed his rifle bolt with a crisp snap. "No problem, D.L. There are no heroes here." Willy and Simon merely watched him impassively.

Samantha suddenly reached into her pocket. "Some John Wayne," she said. "You don't even have a six-gun." She pulled out the pistol he'd given her and shoved it into his belt.

He took a last look around at them, but he couldn't think of anything to say. Instead he grabbed the rope and went over the rim.

He went down hand over hand until his feet hit the deckplates of the bridge. It was empty, but he pulled the pistol free anyway. There was a hatch in the deck, closed. He tugged, but it wouldn't budge. That left the one he knew was open. The forward escape hatch.

He swung a leg over the edge of the sail, stuffing the pistol back into his belt, and lovered himself to arm's length. Then he let go. He landed with knees bent, arms clutching the sail. Perfect, he thought, but a clatter and splash brought an oath. He put a hand to his belt, but he knew already. The pistol was gone.

The grate of a shoe sole on the bridgeplates made him press tighter against the conning tower. He looked around for a weapon, but the closest submachine gun was twenty feet down the deck. Suddenly Faschereau's head appeared over the edge of the conning tower.

"D.L., this hatch up here, she bolted tight."

Willy popped up next to him. "Simon be down in one minute, Doct—Hey!" He pointed toward the bow excitedly.

D.L. whirled. The man laying in the forward escape hatch was jerking. Then it hit him. It was the men inside. They were pulling the body in. With the hatch shut, they could submerge.

He ran forward, balancing awkwardly on the rounded hull, and dropped to his knees beside the hatch. He was just able to grab the body's quilted coat before it went through the opening completely. Down past the man's legs he could see a Chinese sailor. The sailor's eyes widened when he saw D.L. He shouted, and more men appeared to help him pull.

D.L. braced his foot against the upright hatch cover, but he could feel the body slipping inside the coat.

Vaguely he heard Faschereau call to him to hang on.
There was no time. He couldn't hold against all of them.
Something swaying and bobbing at the dead sailor's
waist caught his eye. A grenade, just like the ones the
Chinese had used in Korea. A potato masher, they'd
called it, for its shape and for other reasons.

He bent to grab it. It swung just out of his reach. The
sailors below jerked at the body rhythmically, and at
each tug the grenade bounced almost high enough. It
brushed his hand. Again. He twisted lower. And he had
it.

In the same instant the men below succeeded in pulling their comrade's body out of his grasp. He maintained his grip on the grenade, ripping it free, but the
body slid below. He rolled back out of the way as a burst
of automatic fire ricocheted off the edge of the hatch.
With a fervent prayer that the grenade armed the same
way as those he's seen in Korea, he rapped it sharply on
the deck, and dropped it through the hatch. There was
a scream, and an explosion that set the deckplates
quivering. Then silence.

Instincts long dormant told him he had to move
before they recovered. He rolled back to the hatch and
dropped through feet first.

The interior was dark, lit only in spots by dim battle
lanterns. A klaxon sounded an incessant alarm. Still
shapes, a few moaning weakly, littered the compartment. It was so much like that radar station. So much.

He bent slowly to pick up a submachine gun lying by
the ladder. Triggered by the similarities, information
he'd thought long gone came flooding back. Chinese
Type 50 submachine gun. A copy of the Soviet PPsh.
Thirty-five round box magazine. Cyclic rate-.

A crewman ran into the compartment and froze in
confusion. Before the man could move, D.L. dropped
him with a butt-stroke to the temple. One of the bodies
had another grenade at its belt. D.L. tucked it behind his

own belt, in the back. Clicking off the safety, he started toward the control room.

A scrape of boots on the ladder stopped him. Legs appeared, and Faschereau called, "Be with you in one minute, D.L."

Blank-faced, D.L. turned back towards the control room. He moved in a half-crouch, soft-footed, close to the wall, the submachine gun thrust out in front of him. Where his unblinking gaze went, the muzzle of the gun pointed.

He slowed as he heard voices ahead. Carefully, he edged forward. It was the control room.

Men sat at radar panels, and at controls like an airplane's, but it wasn't them he watched. A dozen men with submachine guns were clustered in the center of the room, before a platform where the periscopes were. The man he'd picked as the captain spoke from that platform, addressing a stiff-backed officer.

"Liang," he was saying, "even to you it must be clear that if there were other explosives, we would have been destroyed by now. As it is, your delay with questions of surrender has no doubt allowed them to get men into the forward crew quarters. Leave two men here to guard the passage forward, and redeem yourself by taking the rest through the battery room and torpedo storage to—"

D.L. tapped the potato masher on a stanchion, tossed it around the corner, and threw himself back down the passage, hands covering his ears. Even so, in the confined space, the explosion sounded like an ammunition train going up. He grabbed the submachine gun and went around the corner with it at the ready.

At first glance only one man seemed in shape to move. The officer called Liang staggered to his feet with one of the guns in his hands.

"Redeem myself," he screamed, and triggered a wild burst.

D.L. tapped the trigger, and five rounds spun the officer around. He fell against the railing around the periscope platform and hung there, staring behind a console at something D.L. couldn't see. "You," he choked, and fell.

D.L. moved cautiously into the compartment. He could hear the sounds of Willy and Faschereau and Simon coming up the passage, but they didn't really register. What was behind the console? He took a quick sidestep so that he could see.

In the narrow space the ship's captain was pushing himself shakily up off the deck. Blood streamed down his face. He looked around at D.L.'s muzzle, and froze. Slowly he turned to support his back against the bulkhead and pushed himself erect. His eyes never left D.L.'s.

It was so much like the radar station, D.L. thought. Exactly like it. The Chinese officer. The gun in his hand. All he had to do was pull the trigger, and the body would be dancing under the impacts again. All he had to do—he could feel his finger curling, caressing the trigger. All he had to do-. Oh, God, Helen!

A shuddering breath poured out of him. With an effort he moved his finger away from the trigger. His hand felt as if it were cramping. The captain let out a long breath as well, and slumped against the bulkhead.

Faschereau and the rest poured into the room; D.L. raised a hand, and they stopped. He kept his eyes on the captain.

"My name," he said in Chinese. "My name is Daniel LeTellier Childe. What is yours?"

"Chu Fa-tzu. Captain of the *Chen Fu*."

D.L. nodded slowly. "I am afraid, Captain, that your *Conquest* has itself been conquered. Will you surrender, now? Or must this useless killing go on?"

Chu broke away from D.L.'s gaze long enough to look at the other men pointing guns at him, but it was

D.L. who seemed to hold him. "I—I will surrender." He stretched out a hand and unhooked a microphone.

D.L. stopped him with a gesture. "Speak the words with care, Chu."

Chu hesitated, then nodded. He keyed the mike. "This is the captain. I order you all to lay down your weapons immediately. You will go on deck by means of the nearest hatch, and you will surrender to those you find there. This is the order of your captain." He let the microphone drop. "The words were satisfactory?"

"Satisfactory," D.L. said. "Let's go topside and see what's happening. Martial, will you lead the way?"

Fashereau took the lead up the ladder to the bridge, undogging the hatch and climbing out. D.L. prodded Chu up next, then followed with Willy and Simon on his heels.

A small number of Cree and Inuit were on the sub's deck, covering the crewmen who were climbing up from below. Each sailor, as he reached the deck, put his hands on top of his head. They were being herded into two groups, fore and aft. Other men were covering them from the cliffs.

With a sudden crack of sonic boom, three jets in tight formation streaked the length of the fjord, fifty feet above the cliffs. D.L. stared, wondering what was happening. A second trio, moving as fast and as low as the first, roared past in the other direction. This time he recognized the planes. Royal Canadian Air Force F-5's, with bombs slung under their wings.

"Let's get ashore, Martial," he said. As soon as Faschereau started up the rope, he motioned Chu to follow. He went up right behind Chu.

On top of the cliff, everyone was staring south, their mouths hanging open. D.L. scrambled up over the edge, and then he felt like gaping, too.

Across the Bay, at almost wavetop level, came two

dozen transport planes. C-130's, he recognized, and suddenly he knew what they were going to do. He felt a lump in his throat. It had been a long time for this, too.

As the planes began to approach the island, they pulled sharply into a climb. They roared across the island at eight hundred feet, filling the sky with hundreds of blossoming parachutes.

"By damn," Faschereau said. "They send the paratroopers."

With what he knew must be a lunatic grin on his face, D.L. ran to meet the nearest group as they hit the ground. They had slapped the quick releases on their harness and rolled to their feet before he reached them. He found himself looking into the muzzles of five Sterlings.

"Easy, friend," a paratrooper with corporal's stripes said. "Just set that toy you're carrying down careful."

With a start D.L. realized he still had the submachine gun slung on his shoulder. Very carefully, he eased it off, using two fingers, and laid it by his feet. Then he took a slow sidestep away from it. "I'd like to see your commanding officer, if that's possible."

"I'm the commanding officer," said a gray-haired colonel, striding into the group. "Colonel William Dean, 21st Light Infantry. The Princess Pat's. And you are?"

"Dr. D.L.-."

"Childe," the Colonel finished. "Daniel LeTellier Childe. The wires have been humming about you in the past twelve hours. I should have known."

D.L. spread his hands helplessly. "I don't understand. We tried so hard to get somebody to listen, and no one would. Now this, How?"

"I'll explain later, Dr. Childe. For now, I'd like you to get your people back from the fjord. We know about the Chinese submarine that came here. The Navy's hunting for that, now. It's our job to stop the missiles from launching. Harry! Harry, where's my radio man? Get the demolition teams to the fjord on the double."

"Colonel-." D.L. stopped and turned to where Faschereau and the others were standing with Chu. "Colonel, may I introduce Chu Fa-tzu, captain of the submarine *Cheng Fu*. He and his crew and vessel are the prisoners of the *Baie du Nord* Expeditionary Force."

Dean stared at Chu disbelievingly. "The hell you say." He strode to the edge of the fjord and stared down at the sub and the men with their hands raised. He turned back shaking his head. "The hell you say."

"I do say, Colonel," D.L. said. "Now, maybe you'll tell me how this came about." He waved a hand at the paratroopers, converging on the fjord from all over the island.

The Colonel rubbed at his ear and peered at the ground between his boots. "Well, the story's being broadcast all over the world by television right now. I can't see that there's any harm in telling you what I know."

"Not the whole story, Colonel," Samantha said. She ignored D.L., beaming a smile at Colonel Dean. "I'm Samantha Keenan, of *Newsworld*. I have the entire story, from the first discovery of the launchers to the capture of the submarine, and every step in between. I realize that you don't have full facilities for the working press, but if you could help me get a radio patch through to the nearest Telex station, that would be just wonderful."

Dean's mouth was hanging open by the time she finished. "Ah, yes, Miss, ah, Keenan. I'm certain that— Ah, Harry, help this lady with whatever she wants."

Samantha smiled at him, then flashed a grin at D.L. "Going to make you famous, D.L." She disappeared with the officer Dean had summoned before D.L. could reply.

Dean stared after her, bemused. "Is she always like that?"

"Always," D.L. smiled. "Now, Colonel, you were going to tell me how somebody finally came to believe in all this."

"Well, one way and another, you managed to get your suspicions to a lot of people, and they got them to others, including the President of the United States. But I'm afraid it wasn't any of that that sent us here. Prime Minister Montrechet was one of several world leaders to receive a call this morning. From the Prime Minister of China. It seems, or so they say, that dissident elements in the Chinese military had planned to start World War III between the United States and Russia. Luckily, they were discovered, and their plans, in remarkable detail, were transmitted to the governments involved."

D.L. gave him a sideways glance. "I take it you don't believe in these dissidents?"

"I do not," the Colonel replied sharply. "There was *too* much detail in the plans they sent us for them to have just been ferretted out. And those so-called dissidents have already been executed. Saves the unpredictability of even a show trial."

"We were not dissidents," Chu said. It took D.L. a minute to realize he'd spoken in English. "We followed a plan approved at the highest level," Chu went on. "But if they say that we are dissidents, there will be no mercy for us when we return to China, nor for the crew of the *Sheng Li*."

"The *Sheng Li*?" D.L. said.

"There were supposed to be two submarines," Dean put in.

"Yes," Chu said. "There were two of us. In return for safety, I will tell your government where the second submarine is, and how to get it to abort its launch and also surrender. I will tell all I know of the plan, and of those who approved it, and betrayed us. All this in return for safety." He took a shuddering breath, as if a great weight had been lifted from him. "But we must hurry. There is little time."

"Well, I'll be damned," Dean said. "The other launch was aborted even before the message from China, but I'm sure my government will be only too happy to grant you asylum, Captain Chu."

D.L. shook his head sadly, thinking of the men he'd brought there to be shot, some of them to die. "So it was the message from China that stopped it after all. We did this for nothing. Your paratroopers could probably have handled it much more easily, and with fewer people hurt."

"Don't believe it," Colonel Dean said crisply. "We were a desperation chance, because with this terrain nothing except blowing up the launchers would guarantee the missiles wouldn't launch. But as of this moment-" he glanced at his watch, "-we would have nineteen minutes to launch. Frankly, I don't think we'd have made it. I'm afraid you stopped World War III, Dr. Childe, whether you want to believe it or not. Now, if you'll excuse me, I must see to arrangements for Captain Chu." He paused, and sketched a salute. "Dr. Childe."

D.L. half returned the Colonel's salute, and stood for a minute watching him lead Chu away. He dreaded having to face the others. When he turned around, the Cree and Inuit were waiting, Willy and Simon at their head.

He took a deep breath. "How many?"

They understood what he meant. "Three," Simon said. "Two from my village, one from Willy's."

"I'm sorry, Simon. Willy, I'm sorry."

Simon shook his head. "Men go to hunt, and die. Men go to fish, and die. This was more important, was it not, Willy?"

Willy nodded. "More important, Dr. Childe."

"Well," D.L. said, "at least they say we saved the world. Their world."

"Our world, Dr. Childe," Simon said. He held out his hand.

D.L. clasped it firmly, and Willy stepped forward to add his hand. For a minute they stood, looking one another in the eye. D.L. felt more a part of something than he had since Helen died. And he realized that for the first time in years he could think of her death without agony. The ghost of her death, at last, had been laid to rest.

The click of a camera pulled them out of it. "I'm sorry," Samantha said, "but I had to get that. That's the cover, not that thing with the submarine. If I have to break heads, that's the cover."

Willy and Simon moved back as if by agreement. D.L. didn't even notice them. "You got to your Telex?"

"Oh, yes. The soldiers were very helpful." She smiled suddenly. "I'll give them a good mention even if they did get here too late. It was D.L. Childe who was the hero."

"Don't say that, Samantha, not even—"

She stepped closer and put her fingers over his mouth. She spoke clearly, and softly. "D.L. Childe is a hero. He's a stubborn, bull-headed, rock of a man, who should have been born a hundred years ago. And maybe that's *why* he could do something like this, because he's a man like they don't make any more. I'm going to make you famous, D.L. You might as well shut up and enjoy it."

He smiled and shook his head. "As soon as Martial manages to contact the *Baie*, we can start moving down to the beach. Then it's back to Poste-de-la-Baleine, and you and I aren't going to get out of bed for—"

"Oh, no, D.L.," she said briskly. "I should have told you. Sal's sending a fast helicopter for me. It should be here any minute. And there'll be a chartered jet at Poste-de-la-Baleine. I'm sorry."

"I'm sorry, too," he said after a minute. "I knew you had to go back to New York sooner or later, but somehow I'd stopped thinking it could ever get to be later."

"D.L.," she laughed, "you *are* a rock. Between the ears. I'm coming back. As soon as this story's gone to press, I'll take some vacation. I'm long overdue. And then you are going to fly me up where the nights are six months long." She threw her arms around his neck, and he felt himself submerged in her kiss. When they came up for air, she leaned against him weakly. "I have the feeling I'm going to be spending a lot of vacations up here."

"Free guide service is our pleasure, ma'am," he said.

She pushed herself up. "I have to get my things together. I don't have long before that helicopter gets here." She turned away, then paused to grin over her shoulder. "Just don't give it all to that widow from Moosonee while I'm gone."

He threw back his head and laughed while she dashed away.

"Hey, D.L.," Faschereau called. He poked his head out of a nearby hollow. "I finally got Auguste on the radio. Finally. What you want me to tell him?"

"Tell him to come in to the beach. We'll start moving down now."

"I don't know, D.L. I think them Army types, they want us to stay around to answer questions."

D.L. looked away from the soldiers, out to the rolling gray waters of the Bay. It was calming, after the storm. And he realized that the storm inside himself had calmed as well. He wasn't running any longer, from Korea or anything else. He'd found a place to stop. "We'll be at home," he said.

THE SAINT
Follow Simon Templar in his struggle of right against might!

☐ ALIAS THE SAINT	01350-3	$1.95
☐ THE AVENGING SAINT	03655-4	$1.95
☐ CATCH THE SAINT	09247-0	$1.95
☐ ENTER THE SAINT	20727-8	$1.95
☐ FEATURING THE SAINT	23155-1	$1.95
☐ THE SAINT AND THE HAPSBURG NECKLACE	74898-8	$1.95
☐ SAINT'S GETAWAY	74905-4	$1.95
☐ THE SAINT STEPS IN	74902-X	$1.95
☐ THE SAINT TO THE RESCUE	74903-8	$1.95
☐ VENDETTA FOR THE SAINT	86105-9	$1.95

Available wherever paperbacks are sold or use this coupon.

ACE CHARTER BOOKS
P.O. Box 400, Kirkwood, N.Y. 13795

Please send me the titles checked above. I enclose _____.
Include 75¢ for postage and handling if one book is ordered; 50¢ per book for two to five. If six or more are ordered, postage is free. California, Illinois, New York and Tennessee residents please add sales tax.

NAME_____

ADDRESS_____

CITY_____STATE_____ZIP_____

Pc

CHARTER BOOKS
Suspense to Keep You
On the Edge of Your Seat

DECEIT AND DEADLY LIES
by Franklin Bandy   06517-1   **$2.25**
MacInnes and his Psychological Stress Evaluator could tell when anyone was lying, but could he discover the lies he was telling to himself?

VITAL STATISTICS by Thomas Chastain 86530-5 **$1.95**
A missing body, several murders and a fortune in diamonds lead J. T. Spanner through a mystery in which New York itself may be one of the suspects. By the author of *Pandora's Box* and *9-1-1*.

THE KREMLIN CONSPIRACY
by Sean Flannery   45500-X   **$2.25**
Detente espionage set in Moscow as two top agents find themselves as pawns in a game being played against the backdrop of a Presidential visit to the Kremlin.

THE BLACKSTOCK AFFAIR
by Franklin Bandy   06650   **$2.50**
A small town, a deadly medical mystery, and the corruption of power provide the dangerous mix in this new KEVIN MACINNES thriller.

SIGMET ACTIVE by Thomas Page 76330-8 **$2.25**
The author of the bestselling HESPHAESTUS PLAGUE presents another thriller proving it isn't nice to fool Mother Nature.

Available wherever paperbacks are sold or use this coupon

C **ACE CHARTER BOOKS**
P.O. Box 400, Kirkwood, N.Y. 13795

Please send me the titles checked above. I enclose _____.
Include 75¢ for postage and handling if one book is ordered; 50¢ per book for two to five. If six or more are ordered, postage is free. California, Illinois, New York and Tennessee residents please add sales tax.

NAME_____

ADDRESS_____

CITY_____STATE_____ZIP_____

Xa

CHARTER BOOKS
Excitement, Adventure
and Information
in these latest Bestsellers

☐ **THE PROPOSAL   68342-8 $2.50**
A novel of erotic obsession by Henry Sutton, author of
THE VOYEUR and THE EXHIBITIONIST.

☐ **CHESAPEAKE CAVALIER   10345-6 $2.50**
A passionate novel of early Colonial days, by Don Tracy.

☐ **BOOK OF SHADOWS   07075-2 $2.50**
A New York policeman, a beautiful actress, a coven of
witches, and a Druid priest come together in this spine-
tingling tale of horror.

☐ **THE ADVERSARY   00430-X $2.25**
Out of the ashes of history a battle is brewing—a novel of
occult power.

☐ **FIRE ON THE ICE   23876-9 $2.25**
Alaska is the setting for an explosive novel about the
passions flying in our largest state.

Available wherever paperbacks are sold or use this
coupon.

C **ACE CHARTER BOOKS**
P.O. Box 400, Kirkwood, N.Y. 13795

Please send me the titles checked above. I enclose _____.
Include 75¢ for postage and handling if one book is ordered; 50¢ per
book for two to five. If six or more are ordered, postage is free. California, Illinois, New York and Tennessee residents please add sales tax.

NAME_____

ADDRESS_____

CITY_____STATE_____ZIP_____

Ka

🎝 CHARTER BOOKS 🔊

Edgar Award Winner Donald E. Westlake
King of the Caper

WHO STOLE SASSI MANOON?   88592-6   **$1.95**
Poor Sassi's been kidnapped at the film festival — and it's the most fun she's had in years.

THE FUGITIVE PIGEON   25800-X   **$1.95**
Charlie Poole had it made — until his Uncle's mob associates decided Charlie was a stool pigeon. See Charlie fly!

GOD SAVE THE MARK   29515-0   **$1.95**
Fred Fitch has just inherited a fortune—and attracted the attention of every con man in the city.

THE SPY IN THE OINTMENT   77860-7   **$1.95**
A comedy spy novel that will have you on the edge of your seat—and rolling in the aisles!

KILLING TIME   44390-7   **$1.95**
A small New York town: corruption, investigators, and Tim Smith, private investigator.

The Mitch Tobin Mysteries
by Tucker Coe

THE WAX APPLE   87397-9   **$1.95**
A JADE IN ARIES   38075-1   **$1.95**
DON'T LIE TO ME   15835-8   **$1.95**

━━━━━━━━━━━━━━━━━━━━━━━━━━━━━━━━

Available wherever paperbacks are sold or use this coupon

ⓒ ACE CHARTER BOOKS
P.O. Box 400, Kirkwood, N.Y. 13795

Please send me the titles checked above. I enclose _____.
Include 75¢ for postage and handling if one book is ordered; 50¢ per book for two to five. If six or more are ordered, postage is free. California, Illinois, New York and Tennessee residents please add sales tax.

NAME_____

ADDRESS_____

CITY_____STATE_____ZIP_____

Ja

CHARTER BOOKS—The best in mystery and suspense!
JOHN CREASEY

"Consistently the most satisfying of mystery novelists."
—The New York Post

☐ **A SPLINTER OF GLASS** 77800-3 $1.50
A tiny clue was all Superintendent West had to solve a huge gold theft — and a murder.

☐ **THEFT OF MAGNA CARTA** 80554-X $1.50
Scotland Yard searches for international thieves before a priceless treasure vanishes.

CHARTER BOOKS—The best in guides for healthier living!

☐ **INSTANT HEALTH THE NATURE WAY**
37079-9 $1.50
Put natural foods to work to fortify your body against disease. **Carlson Wade**

☐ **RUN TO HEALTH** 73700 $2.50
The complete running guide by a foremost runner and expert on heart disease, **Peter D. Wood.**

☐ **THE NEW HUNZA HEALTH PLAN**
57151-9 $1.95
The astonishing secrets that have created the world's healthiest people.

Available wherever paperbacks are sold or use this coupon.

ⓒ ACE CHARTER BOOKS
P.O. Box 400, Kirkwood, N.Y. 13795

Please send me the titles checked above. I enclose _____.
Include 75¢ for postage and handling if one book is ordered; 50¢ per book for two to five. If six or more are ordered, postage is free. California, Illinois, New York and Tennessee residents please add sales tax.

NAME_____

ADDRESS_____

CITY_____STATE_____ZIP_____

Cc

NICK CARTER

"Nick Carter out-Bonds James Bond."

—Buffalo Evening News

Exciting, international espionage adventure with Nick Carter, Killmaster N3 of AXE, the super-secret agency!

☐ **TRIPLE CROSS** 82407-2 $1.95
It all began as a favor—a routine hit that explodes in Nick's face!

☐ **THE SATAN TRAP** 75035-4 $1.95
Nick infiltrates a religious cult whose victims are the most powerful men in Europe.

☐ **THE REDOLMO AFFAIR** 71133-2 $1.95
Nick must find and kill Redolmo—the mastermind behind a drug ring that is crippling the West!

☐ **THE GREEN WOLF CONNECTION**
30328-5 $1.50
Middle-eastern oil is the name of the game, and the sheiks were masters of terror.

Available wherever paperbacks are sold or use this coupon.

C ACE CHARTER BOOKS '
P.O. Box 400, Kirkwood, N.Y. 13795

Please send me the titles checked above. I enclose _____.
Include 75¢ for postage and handling if one book is ordered; 50¢ per book for two to five. If six or more are ordered, postage is free. California, Illinois, New York and Tennessee residents please add sales tax.

NAME_____

ADDRESS_____

CITY_____STATE_____ZIP_____
Dc

CHARTER BOOKS
—the best in mystery and suspense!

VICTOR CANNING

"One of the world's six best thriller writers."
— Reader's Digest

☐ THE PYTHON PROJECT   69250-8 $1.95
A Rex Carver mystery. British and Russian agents have Rex on their open contract lists, but he's the only one who can untangle a scheme gone wrong.

☐ THE DOOMSDAY CARRIER   15865-X $1.95
Rimster didn't have much time in which to find Charlie, a friendly chimp carrying a deadly plague bacillus. The problem was, he couldn't let anyone know he was looking!

☐ THE KINGSFORD MARK   44600-0 $1.95
A novel of murder and betrayal "in the best Canning manner," with a fortune as the prize.

☐ THE LIMBO LINE   48354-2 $1.95
The Russians are kidnapping Soviet defectors and brainwashing them.

☐ THE WHIP HAND   88400-8 $2.25
A stunning espionage novel whose twists and turns end at Hitler's corpse.

☐ DOUBLED IN DIAMONDS   16024-1 $2.25
Rex Carver returns in this brilliant novel of espionage and adventure.

☐ THE RAINBIRD PATTERN   70393-3 $1.95
Someone had already staged two kidnappings and the victims could remember nothing. The third target is the Archbishop of Canterbury!

Available wherever paperbacks are sold or use this coupon

ⓒ ACE CHARTER BOOKS
P.O. Box 400, Kirkwood, N.Y. 13795

Please send me the titles checked above. I enclose _____.
Include 75¢ for postage and handling if one book is ordered; 50¢ per book for two to five. If six or more are ordered, postage is free. California, Illinois, New York and Tennessee residents please add sales tax.

NAME_____

ADDRESS_____

CITY_____STATE_____ZIP_____
Gc